# STEPHANIE FLYNN

## A TIME TRAVEL ROMANCE

# HOURS

## *to Arrive*

stephanie@stephanieflynn.net

or

Small Fish Publishing
801 11th St #1251
Menominee, MI 49858-1110

First edition
Cover design by Stephanie Flynn
ISBN ebook:               978-1-952372-03-2
ISBN paperback:           978-1-952372-04-9
ISBN large print paperback:  978-1-952372-11-7

Time travel is real.

For a few short hours, you will be transported to 1853 and back again.

Enjoy the ride.

To Will:

Without your constant support, this would've never happened.


To my editor Jo:

Thank you for all your hours of work to whip this story into its best form.

# Chapter One

Green Bay, Wisconsin
Present Day

"SCALPEL," MATHEW McCall said, voice muffled by the paper mask. His eyes fixed on the shaved patch beneath his fingers, a temporary blemish. In a few short weeks, all traces would be covered with a new tuft of fur. But for Mathew? It'd take nothing short of a magic wand to fix his mess.

Mathew's trusty assistant, Becca Wagner, passed him the stainless steel implement, and he made the abdominal incision.

"Suction."

The electric motor hummed to life, and Becca moved the device along the opening. Mathew passed the scalpel back to his assistant and stuffed his fingers inside, retrieving a loop of intestine. Snoopy had eaten a sock, and as the x-ray showed, it was lodged right between his fingers. The ropy organ had a bulbous obstruction, as if a snake had swallowed a plump mouse. Man, it looked painful. But the pup was going to be okay because the owner brought him in quick enough—the tissue had a healthy coloration. Mathew blew out a breath, puffing his mask.

"How did this little guy eat something so big?" He chuckled.

"Determination is a powerful force."

He supposed she was right. But in practice, determination didn't guarantee results. Mathew was full of one and still lacking in the other.

"Becca?"

"Yes, doc?"

"Play something, would you?"

Becca crossed the sterile room with bright fluorescent tubes beaming on them like stage lights. In surgery, he sometimes felt like he was directing a show, only instead of a flurry of energy from the crew and audience, his was a quiet crew of one and the audience non-existent.

His assistant pressed a gloved fingertip to an old iPod and notes came through the budget-friendly portable speakers.

Mathew had considered his problems to be simply things floating around his head, never something he could grasp, a slight inconvenience when they buzzed too close. Rather than solve them, he'd focused on helping people and pets, and making kids smile. He'd always wished the problems didn't exist, of course, but the determination hadn't been there.

On the outside he had envious things—a late model SUV, a clinic, an education, but those were just things. The truth was he financed the SUV, mortgaged the clinic, and the shiny plaque on his office wall obscured the student loan debt. He had no hope of being able to upgrade from his dingy apartment—good thing he never had visitors.

Then his prime assistant, his sister, had gone missing. She was his ace, the Robin to his Batman, his only remaining family. Without anyone in his life, he realized he'd become a husk.

Determination had finally kicked him in the ass.

What Mathew wanted most—someone to go home to. A partner, a best friend, an equal. But what woman would tolerate debt far beyond his eyeballs? He couldn't even afford to pay for a date, for god's sake. Finding a woman who could see past all that was impossible, so until a magic wand cleaned up his life or his determination somehow lit the path, Mathew exhaled a deep breath and allowed the rhythm to flush away his self-pity. He smiled at Becca's choice and bobbed his head.

"Ah, old school Springsteen. Nice."

"Just promise me you won't start singing."

"Are you offended by my voice?"

"I like working for you, boss, so I can't answer that." She laughed, and Mathew was thrilled to finally hear it. She'd had a rough couple of weeks herself.

"Scalpel."

With a rustle of a paper gown, Becca passed a clean one to him. Mathew never felt anything for her beyond platonic respect, even before she'd gotten married.

"How's Brad handling things?"

The scalpel transected the swollen tissue—of which he steadied himself for. Mathew genuinely cared about how she and Brad were doing after their loss. Her rusty red curls were bunched under a bright-patterned hairnet and a paper mask covered her mouth and nose, leaving only her almond shaped eyes squinting at him in frustration.

"I wouldn't know."

Mathew picked up a tinge of sadness in her tone, and he felt terrible for her. Becca had lost her baby a couple weeks ago, and

he knew she was hanging by a thread. But now she and Brad were having problems too? He wanted to give her a hug…and a beer.

"Oh. Are you okay? If you need time off, just say the word."

She kept her eyes on the procedure while her paper mask bounced over her words. "Thanks for your concern, doc, but I'd rather work."

"Forceps." He held out his palm. She handed him the scissor-shaped tool, and he removed the dingy brown sock. The pungent fabric wad dangled in the air.

"It's half his size. Snoopy, dude, just no." He dropped the unfortunate chew toy onto the tray, and Becca switched off the suction.

"I'm not a therapist"—Mathew inspected the opening for abrasions and other obstructions—"but I can't see how that's possible."

"Good thing you aren't my therapist. She's helpful." Becca kept her tone light, but Mathew could tell she was annoyed.

Mathew chuckled. "I suppose I'm in the right line of work then."

"You are a good vet, doc."

He stitched up the layers of the hole in the intestine with absorbable suture thread and stuffed the tissue back inside the cavity. "But, I think you should take some time off. In fact"— his voice got louder as if a brilliant idea just struck him—"I don't have a release form signed by your doctor."

The woman needed to grieve. Why did she fight it so hard? Mathew threaded a sterile needed with more suture thread. Becca pressed the edges of the skin together.

"I'll get one on my lunch break." Then she mumbled, "Now I know what April always grumbled about."

"Excuse me?"

"Nothing. Sorry I said anything." Her voice was thick, and she sniffled.

Oh, damn. What did he say wrong? Mathew slowly released a deep breath and inserted the needle, while she still held the skin closed.

"I'm only trying to help."

She snorted to clear her sinuses. "I don't want help. I just want to work. Can't you understand that?"

He let April's initial missing status slide for a while knowing she was in the process of moving—after all, he told her to get a life, but the radio silence since then had made him nervous. Working helped keep his mind level, so he wouldn't dwell on it all day. It just kept popping into his head about every hour.

"Yeah, I can."

The police were no help, giving him a line about not enough time passing at first, and on later visits, her voluntarily leaving. Every day he talked himself out of returning to the police department. He didn't need to get himself arrested by causing a scene. That would only worsen his problems.

Mathew closed the pup's skin in a neat row. "Can you take Snoopy to recovery? I'll finish up in here." He tried to imagine the little furball Havanese swallowing that size sock and couldn't do it. With surgeries completed for the day, Becca cleaned up while Mathew spent the next couple minutes choosing procedures and supplies for the pup's bill, and Mathew dreaded that postsurgical update call. Mr. Van Gruden was not going to

be happy.

"Becca, when you're done. Take lunch."

His assistant nodded, ungowned, and left, the door clicking shut behind her. The deafening silence was only broken by the autoclave humming behind him, the final warrior on the battlefield.

Since Mathew was a realist, a magical wand wasn't going to appear under his pillow. He needed his determination to tell him what the hell to do before his financial mess sunk him too far. Then he would finally be worthy of a woman's hand. He couldn't imagine what it would be like to have a family of his own.

Until then, where was his little meatball, April? Mathew left the suite to make the dreaded call.

# Chapter Two

Astor, Wisconsin
1853

BLAND OVERCAST SKIES and ordinary green fields were as depressing as the reminder that yet another day passed while Verity Arris wasted away in her prison. Workers marched in and out of the cornfields with pails full and then empty of water. Others fed the pigs and cleaned their watering trough. Her brothers Jonathan and Graham were already out this morning, giving orders, managing the crew, or watering also. Since the farmhands didn't enter the house, she was alone.

Verity had already cleaned up after breakfast, and after finishing her morning household chores, she set about planning lunch. The basket on the kitchen counter was empty.

"How strange," Verity said. She crossed to the front window and checked for the late arrival of Mrs. Cottlewood. Dirt roads, cornfields, and patches of woods were all she could see. Ever since her mother had passed, Mrs. Cottlewood had been hired to run household errands, because men had more important things to do, her parents had always told her. Since Verity was the only remaining woman in the household and she wasn't allowed off the property, they depended on Mrs. Cottlewood.

For over a year, the reliable old lady had never missed a day, until today.

Well, those fruits and vegetables wouldn't hitch a ride to her house, and the likelihood of the farmer's market moving next door was nil. It had been a year and a half since that incident followed her home, and a year since Jonathan had allowed her off the family farm. No matter how many times she escaped, her brothers always brought her back. Well, today they were busy, and she had a legitimate reason for leaving.

Verity collected coins and linen sacks and tied a bonnet over her long nest of cocoa-colored hair. For a flash, she pictured herself packing a suitcase and turning tail across the country. Someday she would make her fortune in California, far away from the blistering Wisconsin winters, far away from the man who wanted her dead, and far away from her brothers who kept her prisoner. In her best interest—ha! She picked a horse from the stables and mounted up with her sacks. Verity walked the horse from the back yard to the front without anyone saying a peep. Before she realized, she was moving down the dirt road alone, and she didn't care.

Songbirds whistled, and a chorus of grasshoppers sounded like a symphony. Verity flipped her head back and smiled with her face greeting the warm gray skies. Her horse's hooves clomped in a beautiful rhythm, and Verity swayed with the music until that rhythm changed with the addition of more hooves.

A farmer with four draft horses pulling a Conestoga wagon approached. What if he recognized her? Perhaps trotting off the property unattended had been a poor decision. She tilted her face down, hiding her features behind the lacy trim of her

bonnet. The clomps became louder with each passing moment. The rhythm of her chest matched the erratic beats of their feet. Verity's horse nickered and she stroked its mane in comfort.

"Good day, miss," an unfamiliar masculine voice said.

She cleared her throat. "Good day to you as well." Verity kept her face hidden. The trailer squeaked as the horses pulled it by, and she blew out a breath of relief. What was wrong with her? After so long, no one would remember what she'd done. Jonathan and Graham were wrong. She didn't need to hide any longer.

Her boot kicked the horse into a trot, and the breeze tussled her bonnet. Freedom pulled her lips into a grin. She stopped next to the farmer's market, where several neighboring farms were selling their extra produce. Later in the season, her brothers would be delivering loads of corn for sale—the pigs and chickens can't eat all of it. She filled her sacks with the freshest apples, grapes, beans, potatoes, and onions. When she paid, she met the farmer eye to eye, and he made no sign of recognition.

Verity's heart sang.

She hefted her sacks up onto the horse and took the scenic route home. Jonathan wouldn't notice her missing for at least another hour or two. She bit into a plump red apple and admired the view. Fields speckled the landscape among the woods. The clouds allowed the sun to peek through, sending columns of light highlighting the flickering gold of the wheat.

She tossed aside the third apple core when she turned down her own road, and another traveler headed toward her—a man she didn't recognize on a single horse. He was lanky with a crooked nose and hard black eyes—just another hard-working

filthy man on his way to wherever he earned his tough living. His gaze met hers in a disinterested flash. But his head craned for a second glance, and his black eyes widened.

"Howdy, miss."

"Good day," she answered.

"Say, do I know you?" The lanky rider swung his horse in front of hers, blocking her way. Verity pulled her mount to a stop.

"I can't say that you do." She smiled, ready to deny the identity of his guess, and her cheeks heated under his calculating scrutiny. She brushed him off, "Now if you don't mind, I best be getting home. Lunch doesn't prepare itself." She patted the sacks hanging off her horse as if to prove her story true.

There weren't many farms out this way, and the rider craned his neck as if to pick out which must be hers. "Well then..." He smirked. Verity shivered at the unsettling change in his tone. He continued, "I suppose you're right. Any man would miss a beauty like you. Can ya spare a bite?"

How could she deny a thin rider a snack? After all, she'd just eaten three. She stuck her hand inside the sack and offered the rider an apple.

He shook his head. "Onion?"

Verity's nose scrunched at the unsavory request. "Are you sure?"

"Very much."

She shrugged and handed him a sweet onion. He smiled wide at the kind offering and took a healthful bite as if it were an apple. Verity suppressed a gag.

"What's your name?" he asked through his mouthful.

"My name?" Verity started in surprise. "Why?"

A mischievous grin split his face. "Well, you can call me Butch. I'm only asking 'cause I want to name the beauty headlining my story for the fellas tonight at Stanton's Spirits."

Verity was familiar with Lloyd's bar across the river in Bridgeport. Everyone was harmless there, and as far as she was aware, no one knew her. The thin rider was nothing more than a town drunk, she supposed. Verity smiled politely. "Miss Arris. Make sure the story is splendid."

He tipped his hat. "Will do, Miss Arris. Travel safe now."

She nodded and nudged the horse into a walk. *See*, she told herself, *everything would be fine.*

# Chapter Three

## Green Bay, Wisconsin
## Present Day

MATHEW PREFERRED TO call the customers directly after surgery completed to reassure them of the outcome, but Mr. Van Gruden called first and demanded to hold until Mathew was ready for him. Becca had left for lunch, as he instructed her. So, behind the reception computers was Kiko Takai, his sister's roommate, who volunteered to cover for April a couple weeks ago. Mathew held her landline phone to his ear, while he leaned over the tall desk.

"Yes, Snoopy did great during the procedure. He should be awake soon and ready to go home tomorrow...How much?" Mathew covered the mouthpiece of Kiko's multiline phone.

"How much was the estimate?" he asked her. Mathew only remembered the amount of the codes he billed for.

She clicked the mouse a couple times and said, "Twelve hundred even."

Mathew inhaled the eclectic mix of antiseptic and cedar to prepare him for the incoming rant. His clinic was a mix of old and new. Built in 1841 and changed many times over the decades, Mathew bought it at a bargain price and only remodeled

the bare minimum to suit his needs. He added the surgical suite and parking lot, and he changed the flooring to a new hardwood—engineered hardwood if he remembered right. The furniture was basic, plain and padded, but it was sufficient. Now he wondered if he'd still done too much.

Mathew cleared his throat. He didn't expect Mr. Van Grunden to pay that big of a difference, and it was Mathew's fault for not accurately estimating. He relayed the price and shouting came back into his ear. Kiko must've heard the gravelly voice of the cranky customer, because the corner of her lips lifted. Glad someone was amused, Mathew thought with sarcasm. When the owner finished his rant, Mathew said, "I understand your hesitation, Mr. Van Grunden. We here at Animal Care of Wisconsin pride ourselves in our fantastic care and best practices. We understand Snoopy's dilemma, so I'd like to extend a ten percent discount. How does that sound?"

More grumbling.

"The best I can do is twenty." A returning customer and some income were preferable to none of either.

"What's the new total then?" The raspy voice returned to his ear.

Mathew covered the mouthpiece and stared pointedly at Kiko. Mental math did not compute. She mouthed to him and Mathew relayed the new total.

"Absolutely not. That's no discount! What a rip off. It was only a five dollar sock!"

The line went dead in Mathew's hands. He sighed. *You're welcome for saving the poor thing's life.* He passed the handset to Kiko, whose eyes followed his pacing steps across the floors of the

empty reception and waiting area. He refilled his half-empty cup of coffee at the guest refreshment counter—third or fourth today? He lost count.

The door jingled and Becca returned from her lunch break with a smug smile. She handed him a folded piece of paper.

"What's this?"

His eyes skimmed the text while Becca said, "Doctor's note."

Her OB/GYN had signed off, allowing Becca to work against his better judgment. Considering he needed two assistants to run the clinic, he appreciated her stubbornness. Becca dropped her bagged lunch and purse next to Kiko and flopped into her squeaky rolling chair.

Mathew checked his cell phone screen for messages. "Have you heard anything lately?" he asked Kiko.

"Not since the last time you asked. I'm sure she's fine."

"How can you be so sure?" Mathew gulped his coffee until his heart thumped from the caffeine jolt. Was April in trouble or was she mad at him? Unknown answers pressed on him like a lead weight. Kiko clicked away at her keyboard, unconcerned. He darkened his cell phone screen, and with shaky hands, slipped the phone back into his lab coat pocket.

So many messages.

So many calls.

And still zero responses.

He couldn't take it anymore. "Enough waiting. I'm going to file a missing person's report tonight. They can't tell me no again, and I won't take no for an answer. To protect and to serve, my ass. They haven't lifted a finger. Sure, I told her to go, but I thought she'd tell me where she went and if she was doing okay."

He tapped his black dress shoe on the floor and finished his coffee. Mathew silently pleaded with his two employees for reassurance, even though he knew dragging them down with his troubles was unprofessional.

Mathew had failed to protect his sister when they were little. After enough liquor, Father beat her with his belt, and Mom turned her cheek. Mathew interfered twice, which ended with him in the hospital, and April made him promise never to try again. To him, she was still that scared girl wailing in the night, while he cried, squeezing the staircase spindles. He felt like he was failing her all over again. Mathew forced a long sigh to calm himself.

"I'm sure she's fine," Becca said. "She's probably getting her bearings in a new place, apartment hunting, job hunting, fielding calls. It can be all-consuming." She was trying to make him feel better, but there was no conviction in her words. He wondered how much of that was her life. Mathew overheard that she was planning to move away for a fresh start, but since that was privileged information, he thought best to ignore it until she came to him.

"I agree. Do not worry about her," Kiko said with calm authority. Easier said than done, but he saw why April liked her so much. Something about her just made him trust her words, but he couldn't put his finger on it.

"Two weeks isn't much time," Becca said.

"It is when we texted or called almost daily."

Mathew turned his back to the women and poured another cup from the new coffee pot. Turned out employees and customers appreciated a free cup of joe. Another jolt of caffeine

would help him focus, even if his shaky hands got worse. Being more productive during the afternoon lulls allowed him to finish the bookwork before the banks closed, rather than just before bar close. He checked the time on the wall clock.

"Buzz me when Mrs. Silvers arrives."

"Sure thing, doc," Becca said.

Mathew closed the door to his small office and fell into his seat, careful not to splash coffee on his keyboard. He opened Quickbooks and downloaded the data from reception. It was grim. Every month the revenues stayed the same, but expenses increased. So, he'd have to cut his salary withdrawals again, therefore his student loan balance would budge even less. At this rate, his epitaph was going to read: Mathew McCall, Lover of animals, who missed out on life but learned the limit of lending. The only Christmas card he received each year was from the mortgage company. He rested his elbows in front of the keyboard and plopped his head into his hands.

He believed that going to college, pursuing his dreams, and graduating with high honors would guarantee him happiness as an adult, since he hadn't had any as a child. Instead, each passing year kept getting worse. He'd be thirty years old in a couple weeks. As a child he'd been a burden to his parents, but as an adult he refused to burden a future wife. Six figures in student loans, six figures in business mortgage, and customers asked for ten bucks off their pet's vaccines. He honored their requests because happy customers were returning customers.

But at what cost?

It was staring him in the face.

If he had any hope of keeping the clinic open and any hope

of having a family of his own, he had to do something now. *Good of you to light the path, determination.* He cracked his knuckles. Mathew's finger traced the spreadsheet line on the screen. "Senior discounted services, gone." His eyes skimmed to the next extraneous expense line. "Charitable surgeries, gone. They can use CareCredit." As a last resort, he'd stop offering neuters and spays for free to the humane society. It would destroy everything he stood for, but if he didn't take a stand to stop this madness, he'd fall further into a hole—to where he couldn't climb out. Images of his gravestone flashed before his eyes.

"I need a beer." He checked the clock on the corner of his screen. "Settle for coffee."

The jingle of the front door's overhead bell alerted him to Mrs. Silvers's arrival. Mathew smiled with determination riding on his shoulder, and he turned off his monitor.

# Chapter Four

Astor, Wisconsin
1853

THE OLD FARMHOUSE sweltered from the afternoon sun braising the west windows, but Verity Arris didn't care. She dragged a freshly baked loaf of bread out of the fiery wood stove.

"It's mighty hot to be stoking a fire in the kitchen, Verity!" Jonathan complained from the bedroom. He had just come inside and was cleaning up after tending the cornfield and pigs all day. She didn't envy the back-breaking work, but she appreciated him leaving the pig stench behind.

"I don't hear you complaining at the dinner table!" she shouted back. Sweat glistened across her forehead and soaked through the chemise under her corset. The dampened fabrics kept her from fainting as long as she kept herself moving. She dumped the loaf free of the cast iron pan and left it to cool, and then drained the boiling water from the chicken and shook generous amounts of thyme and garlic over the glistening skin. Verity licked her fingers and murmured approval of her ratio.

Jonathan padded toward her, clean from a fresh sponge bathing, wearing only a pair of low hanging trousers. Tanned from hard labor, broad-shouldered, and built like a horse, he was

rather dashing. And to the local girls' delight, his contract to marry Sarah Hartley had fallen through last year, and in good time. The cash from the contract termination clause helped them float the last year in an ease they hadn't experienced before. They'd even hired farmhands, which was luck after being shorthanded when their parents had passed. Besides, Verity didn't want to share her kitchen with another woman. Eventually he would get married though, so in the meantime, she enjoyed her rule of the roost.

"I snorted another bucket of dust today. Some rain would be appreciated." Jonathan plopped on a kitchen chair and browsed the newspaper Verity had set out for him.

"And when it rains, you'll complain about the extra weight for the horses and the mud on your boots. There's no winning with you." She perched her hands on her hips to drive the point home. With a lift of his lips, she knew she'd won.

Verity set a plate full of steaming food next to his newspaper, and he folded it to feast. Then she set a plate in front of her seat and Graham's. Her little brother rarely joined them for lunch, preferring to grab and run after she and Jonathan finished. The brothers didn't see eye to eye, but as the elder, Jonathan's rules were followed...mostly.

Verity chuckled at the irony of cooking meals and tending house for the last year. It was exactly what Mother had raised her to do, and exactly what she'd fought against her whole life. Verity wasn't the housewife-type, preferring adventure and making her own fortune. Both parents brushed aside her ideas as childlike dreams, but after they'd passed away, she'd fled for the second time. The first attempt was after a humiliating

rejection by a potential suitor and she hadn't been old enough to truly make her way. It hadn't been grief that propelled her second attempt, it had been freedom. The irony was after one painful incident on her journey, she was forced to return to the farm and do exactly as Mother had taught her. She could hear Mother's tutting now.

Verity thought she'd hate every minute of being a housewife. Turned out, it wasn't torture as she'd expected, but it still wasn't for her. The moment freedom showed its hand, she would grasp it and never let go. Attempt number three—good luck lies in odd numbers, right? Verity returned to the kitchen to slice the bread when a knock on the door stilled the knife in her hand.

Verity and Jonathan exchanged knowing glances. She set the knife down, and with sweaty hands, she fisted her linen skirts and dashed across the kitchen, through the living room, and into her brother's bedroom. She left the bedroom door open so it wouldn't appear suspicious. Plus, she wanted to hear everything. Verity swung open the tiny hidden door and crawled inside, shuffling on her knees into the nook Jonathan had built for her. She sat with her legs folded underneath her bottom, back rigid from the corset, and tried to regain control of her breathing to calm the turbulence of her temples. She listened.

"Good evening, what I can assist you with?" Jonathan's voice was guarded. So it was someone he didn't know or didn't trust.

"I'm Joe Pool and this's my colleague Rob Bertrand. Last year Gabriel Grignon's operations were cut short due ta his untimely demise. We work for his predecessor. Ya may have heard of him, Jaime Perez. He has expanded operations beyond Bridgeport, so we're here ta discuss the business matters at hand."

Verity clamped a hand over her gasp. If Jaime Perez found her, she'd only hope for a merciful death. This scenario was the reason she had a personal safe cubbyhole. She never thought she'd need it.

Two sets of boots thumped across the hardwood. They stopped somewhere in the kitchen. Verity's jagged breathing caught in her throat.

"We didn't mean to interrupt your dinner," a raspy man's voice said.

"Sit," her brother replied. "And let us conclude this business. I am a busy man."

Chairs dragged across the floors and creaked under their weight. "We'll get right to it then," the raspy voice said. "Bandits are a problem. They steal livestock and harvest in transport and even rob travelers. For the safety of our towns, of our people and children, and to ensure commerce can continue successfully, Jaime Perez is offering his services to keep Bridgeport and Astor free from miscreants. These services are a danger to his people, to us"—he paused for emphasis—"and in exchange, we require compensation."

Jonathan's angry tone broke a short silence. "You want me to pay this Jaime fellow to prevent me from being robbed. Is that it?"

A deep chuckle came from the other visitor. "I wouldn't word it so crassly myself, but in the simplest terms, that's correct."

"It sounds like Perez is the one doing the robbing. If I refuse?"

"Refusal is greatly discouraged."

"That isn't an answer."

"Jaime will convince you," the raspy voice said with sharp warning.

Verity didn't recognize either of their voices or names, so they wouldn't recognize her. She crawled out from her hiding place and entered the kitchen. If Jonathan refused to agree right now, it was safe to assume Jaime would come along next for the convincing. She didn't want any death—merciful or not.

"We will pay."

Three heads craned toward her. She met Jonathan's shocked expression with calmness. But her stoic strength fumbled when the visiting men exchanged glances with brows popped. She didn't know them. How could they know her? She concluded they were simply surprised by her inappropriate outburst. Verity swallowed a lump in her throat and held her chin high.

"We will not," Jonathan declared over her. "We will not be giving in to these ridiculous demands, sister. I won't allow it, and as the man of the house, my word is final."

Verity's head swam, and she struggled to stay on her feet. The two men stood. One was short and lean with a long narrow face and menace in his eyes. The tall one sported a soft jawline and a sinister smirk. They were both trouble. Their gazes held hers for too long, but she refused to show weakness. Her brother led them to the door and the tall chubby man with the sinister smirk said, "That is not a wise decision."

Jonathan closed the door and spun on Verity with snarling rage.

# Chapter Five

Green Bay, Wisconsin
Present Day

SINCE IT WAS THE last appointment of the day, Mathew escorted Mrs. Silvers from the patient room to the reception desk. Her tiny Pomeranian had digestive issues, and after lengthy questioning, Mathew discovered his client couldn't resist the cute tiny doggy face begging for food, so she gave him treats. Now the dog was obese with recurring constipation.

"Thank you so much, dear," she said to Mathew. "You always offer the best service. And your prices are good."

"Thirty-five today, Mrs. Silvers," Kiko said.

"—for a woman on social security," Mrs. Silvers added.

Was she manipulating him or in honest distress? He had to give her the benefit of the doubt. "Kiko, give our loyal customer here five percent off."

Mrs. Silvers beamed with a broad smile. "Bless you, child. You're too kind."

"You're welcome. Come back again when Twinkies needs anything." Mathew held the glass door open for her and the tiny cotton ball of a dog.

"Sure thing."

While she and her dog stepped through the doorway, Mrs. Silvers said to it, "Does Twinkies need a treat? You look half-starved." The dog ignored her until she rustled in her pocket and tossed something on the ground. He sucked it up in a flash.

Mathew pressed his lips together in frustration and closed the door. He flipped the deadbolt and shut off the waiting room lights. He needed to grow a backbone, but if he stood up to his customers, bad reviews and word-of-mouth could sink him. But if he did nothing, he'd sink anyway. Mathew's resolve returned.

Kiko clicked away at the computer, face bathed in a glow from her screen.

"Hey, scram. The day's over. What are you still working on?" Mathew's eyes roamed the young woman's high cheekbones, angular eyes, and smooth lips. She had a unique beauty and an intimidating brain, but Mathew had no interest even though he'd known her for a year. He couldn't read her expression any better than braille.

"I'm working on a project for my master's degree. Would you give me a hand? It would only take a night."

Mathew kicked up an eyebrow. What kind of night did a school project require? "Tonight? I'm headed down to the police station to file the report. Or try to—again." Mathew hooked a thumb toward the SUV in the parking lot like a dummy.

She switched off the monitor and slowly stood. Was she delaying him?

"Do you need anything?" he asked, to hurry her along.

"I need your help."

Kiko stepped around the desk and stopped close enough that her floral scent reached his nose. Mathew's feet fastened to the

floor as if cemented. She had a commanding presence despite her short stature.

"It's due in two days. I just need to you sleep and report what happens in your dream."

"Can't it wait until after I return from the station?"

"I'd feel more comfortable doing the study this afternoon, rather than overnight. And I need a day to fill out my report. The deadline is the difference between graduating or not."

He understood Kiko wasn't comfortable conducting an overnight study with him, and he felt terrible that she relied on him to graduate. He wasn't heartless, but Mathew pictured himself laying on a clinical bed with electrodes all over his head and chest, beeping computers, and dental lights blinding him. *Nope, nope, nope.*

"I don't think so. I have to go." He motioned to exit, but not wanting to leave her in the building alone, he stopped at the door with his fist covering the handle. He needed to make that report and make the police cooperate. He needed help.

"Please?" she insisted. "Tomorrow I'll go with you to the station. I'll be your backup if things get hot. I promise we won't leave until it's filed, even if we both end up getting booked."

Her hand embraced his forearm. Having support at the police station would mean a lot to him. Besides, she could talk him down from doing something stupid. He couldn't afford to get himself arrested. "Okay, but no electrodes involved, right?"

She scrunched her nose at him and laughed. "No, I promise. Take us to your place."

Mathew and Kiko left the darkened clinic, and he steered them west across the bridge and south down Oneida Street to

the two-story, brick apartment building. It had been built in the 1960s, and it hadn't been updated much since. He parked in the surface lot just under his balcony. He chose the less-convenient second floor since he wasn't home much anyway, and the rent was less.

They stepped out of the SUV, and Kiko craned her neck toward his patio and then scanned the area. "I expected a nicer place."

He shrugged. Mathew had picked the best apartment based on a location-to-price ratio. Location being the closest to the clinic and price being the cheapest. It was sketchy, but so far, no one had been shot in the complex, and since he was so far removed from impressing a woman, there was no point in dwelling on it.

He unlocked the community door, and she followed him across the crushed carpet, the pairs of coin-op laundry units, and up the stairs. It smelled like stale piss and cigarettes. Hopefully Kiko didn't judge him too much. He unlocked his apartment door and waited for her to enter before locking up behind them.

"Mind the mess. I wasn't expecting visitors." Mathew's face burned hot while he scrambled to collect dirty dishes and toss them into the sink and wad up dirty laundry and shoot it toward the hamper. Satisfied, he drummed his fingers against his thighs and waited for her to take the lead. His throat felt like a scorching desert.

"Drink?" Mathew crossed to the refrigerator and stuck his head inside. "I have a beer we can split, bottles of water, and..." He trailed off and opened an orange juice carton. He sniffed and tossed it into the sink. "And that's it. I'm not home much."

"I am not judging. Have a seat." Kiko sat on his old recliner, a used lay-z-boy in mauve with a matching couch. Replacing his hand-me-downs was on the list of things to improve in his life. One step closer to finding his family. Mathew plopped on the couch, and his knee bounced. His eyes darted to her hands, searching for electrodes.

"So, what do I do?"

Kiko smiled, but it didn't help. She assessed his clothing and frowned. "Can you remove your lab coat?"

Mathew did, forgetting to leave the coat at the clinic, and transferred his phone to the coffee table. He placed a toe at his heel to kick off his dress shoes when she interrupted him. "No, leave your shoes on."

Mathew chuckled. "The smell in here can't get any worse, I promise."

"Leave them on," she repeated with a soft chuckle. He didn't know what to think of her sometimes. "Trust me on this. Everything will be okay. Lie down."

"Am I taking a nap here, Kiko, or running a race?" Mathew obliged and watched the petite woman loom over him. She showed him a small metal trinket.

"I'm putting this in your pocket. Don't lose it for any reason. You can use it to come back." It was a small round steel trinket, like those buzzing gag gifts from the 1980s.

"What do you mean, *come back*?"

"You can press the button to awake. That's all."

Mathew frowned. This study was going to be so traumatizing that he'd move in his sleep? "No electrodes though, you promised."

"No electrodes. Here's the last thing you need to know. It's part of the project, you see. Find a woman named Verity Arris. She's in trouble. You need to prevent her from being captured or she will be murdered."

"What?" he asked in disbelief. "What does this have to do with me dreaming?"

"It's a quantitative measurement for my research."

Mathew remembered stats from undergrad. That didn't make sense, but whatever, he was fine crashing on the couch for a night. He wasn't sure he'd sleep anyway. But tomorrow Kiko promised to help him at the police station, so this weird project was just a minor inconvenience.

"Anything else I should be aware of?"

"Be careful. Things are not as they seem. Now, close your eyes. Any queasiness is a normal part of the process."

With blackness under his eyelids and dusty cushions under his head, his stomach quivered as his uncertainty and consciousness drifted away.

# Chapter Six

## Astor, Wisconsin
## 1853

THE BUSINESS END of a shotgun pointed at her face, but Verity didn't flinch. Jonathan could be possessive and a little mad, but he always underestimated her. Plus, he'd never blown her head off before. She supposed there were many reasons he should, but only one he shouldn't. And that reason would win.

"You've undermined my authority again. You cause me more trouble than you're worth." His eyes were spears of fire, and his knuckles whitened against the stock of the shotgun. His finger wasn't on the trigger yet. "Give me one good reason I shouldn't end my troubles right now."

Love was the right answer, family a winning second, but she was feeling extra spicy.

"You'd be stuck cleaning up the mess. And with that caliber firearm—you'd be cleaning for weeks to get all the shattered bits of brain matter out of the couch and curtains, picking chunks stuck to the fibers, scrubbing with a brush over and over." She shivered for effect. "Not a job I'd volunteer for, but if that's your prerogative, go for it." Verity placed her hands on her hips in challenge.

He growled. She didn't flinch, only waited for him to lower the muzzle.

"You know what they wanted, right?" he asked.

Perez planned to extort the family, she'd heard that much, but she shook her head to learn any new information.

"You used to get around plenty. Didn't you hear about farmer Joseph Van Cleve last year? Or Brandon O'Connell? Those men"—he nodded at the front door to indicate Perez's visitors—"are claiming to have a protection ring for the locals, but at a steep price. Van Cleve and O'Connell plus how many others refused in Bridgeport? They were all murdered—some quietly, some publicly. Everyone knows Brandon didn't commit suicide, and Perez hung Joseph at Common Square. I refuse to be bullied by thieves or my little sister."

"What makes you so confident you can stop them from killing you, too? Joseph and Brandon were capable men."

He ground his jaw in irritation. She stared down the barrel of the shotgun and tracked his trigger finger. So far, she was safe.

Verity continued, "You aren't understanding here. If we don't pay, Jaime Perez himself will come knocking to convince you. He has every reason to, because he needs commerce to continue to make his own living. So that means he'll strong-arm you into paying. As for me, you know what will happen if he finds out I'm here. The world doesn't revolve around you and your selfish pride."

"Dad would've refused."

"Dad isn't here. Mom neither. You're supposed to be protecting all of us and blowing my head off is in direct violation of that promise." Verity struck an arm out and slapped the barrel

away. She admitted her and Graham's actions stressed her big brother. But they were not Jonathan, and Jonathan wasn't Dad. She turned her back on her brother and sat at the table. The dinner she worked so hard for in the steaming heat was disappointingly cool. She tore a wedge of bread and buttered it while he trained the gun on her head again.

"Eat your food," Verity said. "Waste is unacceptable. Then find those men and agree to pay before Jaime shows up."

Jonathan roared in anger, knowing she was right. His finger found the trigger and squeezed. The bang echoed through the house. Hogs squealed in fear. Verity winced from the pain in her eardrums. He shot through the open kitchen window and across the cornfields.

She stood from her meal, and her chair scraped against the floor. Verity marched up to her brother, yanked the gun from his hands, and pointed it at him with the stock pressed snug against her shoulder.

"I don't have to aim at this distance. Now listen to me. I'm done playing little child with you. I'm a grown woman, and I'm not stupid. I don't want Perez or his men crawling all over this place any more than you do. A simple payment each week is the lesser of two evils here until you can figure out some grander plan to stop him. Sit down and eat. Then get moving."

"Next time someone comes knocking, you hide like we agreed and don't come out. Understand?" His finger pointed at her face. She wanted to shoot it off, but then he'd be less productive in the field.

"I do what's best for all of us," Verity said. "You think you can protect this farm? I just stole the shotgun from your hands.

What kind of protector are you?"

And…that was one too many of his buttons. In a guttural rage, Jonathan lunged for the shotgun. She threw it across the room, and it clattered to the hardwood floor. He'd have to reload it, anyway. She dashed to the back door before he had a chance to do something he regretted. She wished he weren't such a stubborn ass. The screen door banged against the frame, and she jogged down the wooden steps, heading for the field workers. They would sing for her until Jonathan cooled off. She'd even help them to pass the time.

# Chapter Seven

Astor, Wisconsin
1853

MATHEW'S STOMACH stopped quivering. What a weird sensation. He didn't remember dreaming at all. Guess he screwed up that experiment. Mathew opened his eyes, and straight ahead, clouds broke the afternoon rays of light. Um, where was his ceiling? Mathew craned his neck around and found himself in a corn field, knee-high plants in neat rows spanning all the way to the forest's edge. To the north stood a two-story farmhouse with shutters, either painted brown or just unpainted. So, he must be in the dream. He didn't remember falling asleep, either, which would've been difficult ¬with an intimidating woman staring at him. Exhaustion must've pulled him down. A vacation sounded great.

Mathew stood and brushed the debris off his gray dress pants and striped button-up shirt and ignored his black dress shoes. They would get dirty again before he got out of the dusty field. Besides, he was dreaming anyway. When he woke, he'd be clean—well, dusty from his old couch, but clean*er*.

He marched through the rows, passing workers, who were singing ethnic songs, and nearing the source of manure. The

telltale hog oinks came from a pen, and a small narrow barn with a smokestack—perhaps a toolshed—leaned next to it. The July heat burned the back of his neck and sweat beads formed. He rolled up his sleeves, exposing his forearms, and unfastened the top two buttons at his throat.

First, he needed directions to locate Verity Arris. All he had to do was stop her from getting captured. Sounded easy enough. He collected mental notes to report every detail to Kiko, since after waking from dreams, most of the time it was impossible to remember what had happened. No way would he do this twice.

Mathew didn't want trouble for trespassing, so he crossed toward the side of the house, hoping to remain invisible to the owners. His plan was to ring the front door's bell, ask for help, and be on his way.

An explosive gunshot shook the surrounding air, and he dove back for cover against the pigpen's fence. That was no firecracker, more like a cannon. Mathew clutched a hand to his chest, and his eyes were wide with surprise. A woman's yelling and an angry man's roar came from the house. Mathew scrambled along the fenced pen for cover behind the barn, or toolshed, that he now hoped didn't collapse on him.

Now what?

It was an open field all around. It would take all day to crawl through the squat corn all the way to the forest. Only to do what? Cold mud penetrated his clothing, and it soothed his clammy skin.

A screen door banged against the trim and a young woman, maybe mid-twenties, rattled the wooden stairs on her descent. He needed to get her out of there before the next gunshot.

"Hey!" he yelled for her attention, and her head spun, but she didn't move. Why would she just stand there when some lunatic was shooting at people? Mathew jumped to his feet and ran over to her with his head ducked low. He tugged her arm, and she wrenched out of his grip.

"What are you doing?" she asked.

"I'm saving your life. Come with me." Mathew grasped her soft hand, and she followed. A hint of amusement played at her lips while he dragged her toward the toolshed for cover. He sat in the mud and she copied without hesitating, which on second thought, was surprising. Women didn't accept filth on their clothes typically. She was intriguing.

"Why were you stalling?" he whispered. "You could've been shot."

She laughed, an easy on the ears melodic sound. "The only one at risk of getting shot was Johnny."

Her bright green eyes trained on his face. Her hair was dark brown like his, but where his was gelled, hers was wild and untamed. He wanted to touch it, to smooth it away from her face. She had freckles that glowed in the sunlight. He peeled his desperate eyes off her face and noticed her clothing was strange. She wore a full-length dress that resembled his grandmother's curtains from the sixties, and he would know, because the curtains in the common area of his apartment were the same style. Why would he dream of Amish territory?

"We need to get out of here," he said.

"Sure, tough guy. Where are we going?" Her eyes twinkled with amusement, and Mathew scanned the fields for an answer. The rows of corn led to the house, so crawling through the corn

was out, because if that angry man was a decent marksman, he'd shoot them in the ass while they crawled. There's a great way to die.

"Do you have a car? I can run ahead and come back for you."

"A what?" Her nose crinkled in confusion. It was cute. He forgot Amish communities banned technology, so...horses and buggies.

"Never mind. How do we get out of here? There's no cover."

That sweet chuckle returned, and the intriguing woman casually stood. She gave him a hand up out of the mud, and Mathew stared at the offer for a moment. She was helping *him*? He accepted, so as not to offend, but he pulled back his weight. Mathew plastered himself against the wall of the toolshed. The woman stood next to him in a relaxed position, staring at him with a tilted head.

"Come with me." She stepped out into the open air, and Mathew croaked.

"What are you doing?"

"Follow me, you big baby."

Mathew furrowed his brows in confusion. By her unconcerned actions, this must be her house, so Mathew kept on her heels, eyes scanning for any threats. The workers coming and going from the field appeared to be unconcerned as well. Maybe the shooter was scaring off a fox. They crossed the yard to the back porch, and the steps creaked under their feet.

"Come on inside. You look like you swallowed dust." She opened the door for him, and after he stepped inside, the screen door slapped shut behind them. Already on edge, Mathew jumped out of his skin. She laughed. "You are strange." They

turned around, and Mathew found a shotgun pointed at his cheek.

"Freeze," a deep baritone voice commanded. Mathew's insides turned to jelly.

VERITY SLUNG A HAND on her hip while they stood in the kitchen. Jonathan had the gun back in his hands, butted against his shoulder, and aimed for business. This time the barrel pointed at the new stranger.

"Did you even have time to reload that thing?" Verity asked her brother, whose rage festered with a twitch of his eye and taut jaw.

"Yes," he said without moving a muscle. "Who's this?"

Verity spun on the strange man she dragged into her house. So much for being careful. He had walnut brown hair slicked up in the front, a trimmed beard, and thick dark brows above wide terrified eyes. Before he danced around the hog pen, his clothes were pressed and sophisticated. The stench and caked stains killed some of his attractiveness. The man was afraid of a shotgun, which ruled out being one of Jaime's men, and he'd tried rescuing her from her own brother. It was sweet, and warmth bloomed in her chest with his innocence.

The sensitive stranger behind her cleared his throat and held out a shaky hand. He was afraid of her brother, too. It was as if he'd never had a shotgun in his face before. Verity was amused by her pondering but decided she'd had enough of Jonathan bullying people. She pushed the shotgun away, again, and squinted at her brother to act like a gentlemanly host. The weapon swung right back, and the stranger flinched, his hand still dangling in the air.

"Mathew McCall, uh, sir. I'm friendly."

Jonathan squinted at him for a beat and lowered the gun. He shook Mathew's hand. "What are you doing in my house?"

"I brought him in," Verity answered. "Looked half parched out there in the fields."

"Do you work for me? I don't remember you."

"Uh, no, sir. I don't."

"Then what are you doing in my house?" Jonathan's trigger finger shifted, and Verity prepared to confiscate the gun when he made a move.

"I'm looking for a woman named Verity Arris. I'm supposed to find her because she's in trouble." Jonathan didn't move. Verity didn't either. She could've sworn he wasn't an enemy.

"What do you want with her?" Verity asked before Jonathan said something stupid, like her name.

"It's a long story." Mathew flashed a gleaming smile and rubbed the back of his neck. "I don't mean any harm. I come in peace." He lifted the first two fingers on his hand, spread apart. What did that mean? He seemed like a spoiled city boy, so perhaps it was a sign common in Chicago. Verity's eyes lit up. Perhaps not Chicago, perhaps—California. She would be his shadow until she discovered his origins. He could be her ticket out of Astor, a repressing Podunk town filled with bad memories.

Jonathan passed the gun to Verity and patted Mathew down, searching for weapons. "Nothing," he said with disbelief and crossed his thick arms over his chest. "You have no weapons on you. What kind of man carries no arms?"

"I don't carry guns. Personal preference." Mathew shrugged.

"I'll get that water," Verity said, taking the shotgun with her. She set it on the counter and brought a cool glass back with her. She offered it to the intriguing city man.

"Thank you." He swallowed it down in a few gulps and made a strange face before passing the empty glass back to her.

Satisfied with Mathew's threat level, her brother said, "I've got work to do. Be respectful in my house. And you"—he pointed at her—"put your gun away." He spun on his heel, and the screen door slapped behind him.

Mathew sighed and chuckled. "He's intense."

"Yeah. Johnny's a stubborn jackass too. Sit. Are you hungry? I've got a lot of food and no one ate it."

"I don't want to impose or anything..."

She clenched her jaw, feeling a flash of anger and insult at his refusal. Mathew continued, "But I'd love some."

Verity smiled with his acceptance and served him a fresh plate at the table. She resumed eating her cold food. At least it was still edible.

"What did you want with Verity?" she asked between swallows.

"I guess she's in trouble—"

"What do you know about it?" she cut in.

"Uh, nothing actually. I don't know where she is, what she looks like, what the trouble is, or anything at all. But I'm here to help. I suppose I won't be very useful."

"I'll help you find her. Perhaps we can figure it out together," she suggested, hoping to stay by his side.

"Oh, no. I won't trouble you with my issues. You must be busy."

"I don't mind." She leaned in close to him. "Truth is, I'd love to get away from here."

"The farm?" Mathew forked a potato.

"Astor, Bridgeport, Navarino, Greenleaf, all of it." Mathew tilted his head. She liked when he did that. It was funny. "What?"

"Are those places? Greenleaf sounds familiar."

"You're sitting in Astor, Wisconsin. Are you lost?" Verity tore into a bite of chicken, completely engrossed with his predicament. "Where are you from?"

"Green Bay, Wisconsin."

So, not California, but Green Bay was the name of the water. He dressed odd for a merchant sailor. "Hmm…Are you a pirate?" she teased. His quizzical look returned, and she laughed. "Guess not. Is Green Bay a city?"

"Yeah. It's a city." Mathew used a piece of bread to wipe up his plate. "This is great bread, by the way. Most excellent."

"Thanks. I just baked it."

"From scratch?"

"What do you mean?" He was definitely strange.

Mathew noticed Jonathan's newspaper left on the table. He spun it toward him, while she scooped up her last bite. His eyes rounded while he read the front page.

"What is it? What happened?" It had been a while since anything interesting happened around these parts—not since the whole shakedown of Gabriel Grignon's extortion last year. His hanging made front page news, and people talked about it for weeks. Too bad all that effort was for nothing, since Jaime Perez had resumed his operations. And from personal experience, Jaime was worse than Grignon could've ever pretended to be.

Mathew's head craned around the room, taking everything in as if seeing it for the first time. Perhaps he was too frightened by the shotgun to his face to notice anything before.

"What year is it?" His face blanched like he would faint. He dug his fingernails into the wood tabletop as if bracing for balance and stared at them in some sort of disbelief.

"Last I checked, 1853. Why?"

"Wow…How the hell did she...? This is wild." He reached into his pocket and removed a small metal trinket.

"What is that?"

He chuckled in a higher pitched voice. Could men suffer from hysteria?

"I don't know. I don't know anything anymore. What the hell is going on?" He slipped the trinket back into his pocket and stood too fast. He wobbled, and Verity sensed he was going down. She dashed around the table to him and barrel hugged his chest before he cracked his skull on the floor. She guided him to the couch and tipped him just enough that he crashed on the cushions. He was out cold.

Pig mud coated his shiny shoes—shoes of such a high quality she had never seen before. He must be rich. His trousers felt like soft clouds between her fingers. His shirt was half unbuttoned, and it had the same silky quality. She noticed dark hair peeking out from a lean chest. A flash of heat rolled through her body. Verity studied his face. His angular bearded jaw and strong brow made him very handsome. She wanted to touch, to learn who he was. A wallet! He would have a wallet. She dug in his front pockets. The one had the trinket, and the other was empty. She tried to reach his back pockets, but she couldn't move him. She

snapped her fingers in frustration and retrieved a moist washcloth. Verity was fascinated by him, but she was mostly interested in why he wanted to help her.

MATHEW BLINKED his eyes open to an unfamiliar plaster ceiling in a buttery yellow color. It smelled like pig manure and boiled chicken, and his face was drenched in cold sweat. A face popped into view, and he held his breath in shock. The dream was so real he could hardly breathe.

"What happened?" he asked.

The intriguing woman, who casually stared down the barrel of a shotgun like some kind of outlaw said, "You read the newspaper and fainted."

*Talk about embarrassing.* Mathew had never touched a gun before, nor saw one in person. The Amish were amazing people with a commanding presence. This woman and her husband instantly earned his respect. They also appeared to have some serious marital problems.

Mathew cleared his throat and sat up. A cool towel fell off his forehead, and he handed to her. "Thanks." Mathew watched her lips spread into a sweet smile and a similarity struck him. "I hope this isn't weird, but you look like my sister a little." He hadn't noticed the resemblance until she'd smiled or was his mind simply manifesting a likeness to his sister because he missed her dearly?

Her brows lifted in surprise. "I didn't realize I had a twin."

He chuckled. "Well, she doesn't know how to shoot a gun, so you got her there. She also hates dresses. Blue eyes, not green,

and she doesn't have freckles. Her hair is less wild. Well, that doesn't make you sound similar. Maybe it's the bone structure." He was babbling. Her nose scrunched up and all the resemblance was gone. He shouldn't have said anything, because now he sounded like a weirdo.

"What's wrong with my hair?"

"Nothing." He smiled. "There's nothing wrong with it at all."

She was distracting. When he looked at her, he saw an assertive woman who handled herself with confidence and a baffling amount of bravery. He fought the urge to bury his hands in her hair, to tangle the waves in his fingers. But he'd already met her husband, Jonathan, and frankly, he'd appreciate never crossing paths with him again. Mathew needed to find Verity and...something. How was he going to prevent her from being captured?

"Can you take me to Verity? I assume you know who she is."

A loud pounding on the front door startled them both. The intriguing beauty next to him sprung to her feet and uncharacteristically stuttered. "I...I, uh. I have to go." She dashed into a room off the living room and disappeared into the darkness.

"When you gotta go, you gotta go," he muttered. The pounding returned. Mathew craned his neck and realized he was alone in a strange family's home with the only occupant in the bathroom. At the very least, he could ask what they wanted.

Mathew swung the door wide, and a short Hispanic man stood before him with dark eyes and black curly hair. His clothes were well-tailored—brown linen trousers with suspenders. The man assessed him back and pinched his face in disapproval.

Obviously, he wasn't looking for Mathew.

"Can I help you?"

"I'm here to see someone. Is the man of the house here?"

"He's out back." Mathew hooked his thumb behind him. "I can get him for you."

"Great. Say, have you seen a woman resembling April?"

April? An alarming jolt of nerves raced through his body. How many Aprils were there? He inhaled a careful breath and waited to ask until he was confident his voice wouldn't break. "April who?"

"April Hartley."

Mathew exhaled. Why would he think people in his dream would know his sister? He stepped aside, and the short man entered.

"Can't say I know her. Have a seat, I'll be right back."

Mathew stepped onto the back porch, and the screen door slapped shut behind him. He jumped in his shoes. That door was going to give him a heart attack one of these times. Mathew lifted a hand to shade the falling sun from his view and scanned the fields for the familiar face, the frightening man of the house. Jonathan wasn't in sight. He took two creaking steps down and heard a muffled scream behind him. Mathew spun on his heels and raced back inside. The short man tussled with the intriguing woman. His hand clamped over her mouth, as he tried to pull her across the living room. She put up a fight, but Mathew extrapolated the Hispanic man would win.

Mathew crossed to them and demanded, "Let her go."

He hissed at him like a threatened cobra, "Never!"

Mathew decided for her safety to fight the guy. He wasn't

sure how to begin without hurting the nameless beauty. He collected the shotgun from the kitchen counter. He didn't know how to use it, but the short man didn't know that. He pointed the barrel at him and repeated, "Let her go."

"You won't shoot me, you'll hit her!" The man fought and pulled on the woman, trying to drag her toward the front door by her hair. She thrashed and kicked and grunted.

True. Dammit. He turned the shotgun around, gripping it like a baseball bat. Mathew swung down hard and bashed him on the back of the neck. The man tumbled over, knocking the couch back, and his weight smothered the woman. Mathew grasped her hand and shoved the body off her, hefting her up to her feet. "You okay?"

She nodded with tears in her eyes. The strong, carefree woman was gone. She was terrified. Something primal inside Mathew woke up, and a heated rage burned against this man for attempting to hurt her. He guided her behind him, repositioned the gun properly, and aimed to use it. The short man stood up, wobbled, and rubbed his neck. He saw the gun and held up his hands, disappointment and frustration passed his features.

"I'll go. I didn't mean any harm."

"Liar!" the woman shouted behind Mathew.

"Just let me go, please?" His face shifted with fear, but something sinister lurked behind his eyes.

Mathew wasn't going to shoot him, even if he knew how to, but the intimidation worked. "Get out of here and never come back!"

The short man scurried out the door. Mathew blew out a deep breath in relief. How did people live like this? The stress

alone was enough to kill. He set the gun down on the coffee table and grasped her upper arms in support. "Are you all right?"

Her tears spilled over, and she crashed her body against his, fitting just right beneath his chin. He inhaled a deep breath and released it slowly. He comforted her with his hand making motions on her back. It felt right. Mathew had been lonely for so long, he almost forgot how nice it was to hold someone and to be held. Her arms squeezed around his body, and he hushed her quiet sobs with a gentle hand to the back of her head. "It's okay. You're going to be just fine. I won't let anything happen to you."

The front door swung open with a kick, and a pair of revolvers pointed right at them. *Oh, shit.* The short man was back. So much for having a commanding terrifying presence to chase him away. The shotgun was too far away. He had nothing—no weapons and nowhere to hide. He was going to get them both killed right here.

"What do you want?" Mathew asked, his voice less in control than he'd planned.

The short man smiled and nodded to the woman in his arms. "I want her."

"Who are you?"

"I'm Jaime Perez, and you should know it."

Mathew stiffened. His arms protectively tightened around her. She trembled beneath him like a leaf in a breezy night.

"And if I say no?"

Jaime Perez stepped closer, keeping the barrels pointed at them both. Mathew had no idea about the accuracy of pistols. They looked old, like theater or reenactment-type stuff. He

heard a story when he was a kid that said if you die in a dream, you die in real life. He wasn't about to risk testing that theory.

Jaime laughed, a horrible tinny laugh. "I will kill you and take her. Only she'll wish she was killed too." His thumbs pulled the hammers of the pistols. "Now, hand her over, and you won't get hurt."

Mathew shifted to make it seem like he was agreeing. With the reflex of a cobra, Jaime's hand snaked out and yanked the woman from his arms. She pinwheeled back and brought Mathew down on top of her.

Mathew squished her with a cringe-worthy crunch. Jaime grabbed her by the collar of her dress and tried to drag her with Mathew still on top of her. Mathew gripped her hands and spun around to gain purchase for his feet.

"Let go now, or I'm blowing your head away."

Mathew looked up at the barrel of a pistol trained squarely on his head. In his peripheral sight, a glint of a shape in the window caught his attention, and Mathew exchanged glances with a half of a face through the living room window. Before he could react, the woman whimpered beneath him, and he returned his attention to her. The fear in her eyes crushed his heart.

"It's shameful to destroy such a pretty thing. Yes, your head, not the threadbare rug. Last chance, big fella."

The hammer clicked with a squeeze of the trigger and Mathew closed his eyes. This was the end for him and the captured woman—wait!

Blackness dragged him down before he finished his thought.

# Chapter Eight

## Green Bay, Wisconsin
## Present Day

MATHEW OPENED HIS eyes with surprise. His stomach's quivering subsided. What a crazy dream. So real, so believable. He chuckled and patted his body. No holes. He shook his head to clear it and stood up. A wretched smell penetrated his nose and his face pinched. In the bathroom, he flipped on the overhead light. In the mirror he sucked in a breath and stared.

"Hey," Kiko's voice floated over from the door.

Mathew's tongue felt stitched inside his mouth. His fingers touched the caked stains on his shirt. They didn't wipe off. A demanding need to understand what just happened loosened his tongue.

His head turned, and he stared her in the eyes. "What the hell was that?"

"Please have a seat."

Mathew followed her to the couch and stiffly sat. He didn't want to shake pig shit onto his couch, not that anyone would notice a difference either way, but he also didn't trust his body's movements.

Mathew noticed a red journal sitting on his coffee table with

a pen next to it. He didn't know what to think of that. Oh, research notes? What kind of research was that?

Kiko returned to her spot on the recliner. "I pulled you back here, because you failed the mission."

"Mission?" Anger heated Mathew's skin. "What kind of dream study was that? I'm coated in mud."

"It's a special kind of mission reserved for special people. You were chosen. I knew the difficulty, but I misjudged the situation. There was something…" Kiko trailed off. She shook her head and flipped her hand back to front in a strange way, as if surprised it was attached to her wrists.

"Misjudged? I didn't get to finish the fight. How is that failure on my part?"

"The hammer was already descending when I pulled you. If I hadn't, you'd be Swiss cheese."

"It was a dream," Mathew insisted. "Or is it one of those die-in-your-dreams-and-die-in-real-life things?"

Kiko didn't respond. No matter how insane her project sounded, Mathew only thought of Jonathan's wife. "And that woman, what happened to her?"

"She was eventually killed."

"Was?" The confirmation of her murder struck him fresh.

Kiko nodded.

"Why not send her husband to save her? This school dream project mission sounds insane. Can't you reprogram the simulation?"

"Hmmm. Proprietary software?" Kiko answered with the slightest lilt in her voice as if uncertain of her own answer.

Every bone in his body tingled with hyperawareness around

the enigmatic nameless woman. Was he so pathetic that a woman in his dream could scramble his brain? Why couldn't a real woman do that to him? His gray matter refused to let her go, so he needed to try again, even if only to see her for a while before fate caught up to her. "That woman was going to help me find Verity. Can I try again?"

Kiko smiled, and it crinkled the corners of her eyes. "Yes. I recommend a change of clothes first."

Mathew glanced down at his reeking outfit. "Right. How much time to do I have?"

"All the time in the world, truthfully."

"Right, because—simulation. But your report..." Mathew relaxed with a shrug and glanced at her red journal. If she turned in her assignment late, that was on her. Being in the simulation was like virtual reality—so real, yet not, but he didn't have an explanation for the mud on his clothes.

In the meantime, Mathew planned to tackle this correctly. He could alert the authorities ahead of time, so they could meet him there. Oh, and pack pepper spray. Sure, he pestered his sister to always carry some and gifted it to her annually, but it worked when needed. Besides, no one got arrested for fending off an attacker with spray, and he had no intention of going to jail.

"But only three tries."

Mathew's head whipped around. "What?"

"Each pair is to receive three trips there and back again. You've used one, but because I made a mistake, you still have three."

"What do you mean—*mistake*?"

"There was a glitch." Kiko pressed a hand against her temple

and frowned. "It's never happened before. After all this time—never."

"Is something wrong with the simulation?"

Kiko's lips quirked into a barely perceptible smile. "No, no it's nothing. Your three trips will continue as planned."

"You keep calling them trips, but I'm only laying on the couch. How is this a simulation exactly?" Little flags were waving in Mathew's head, but he didn't know if they were red or white. Kiko was a strange woman.

"I'm going to level with you," she said carefully. "That wasn't a dream."

"What was it then?"

"I sent you back in time to prevent a woman's capture, because she is destined for greater things."

Mathew stood and backed away from Kiko. "Are you for real? How is it possible?" He glanced at the mud on his clothes and shoes. "I've heard the theories about parallel universes and grandfather paradoxes. I thought that was proven to be science fiction."

Kiko smiled. "I'm not at liberty to explain, but I can hint at quantum mechanics playing a role. My boss prefers a more mystical belief surrounding it, but like you, I'm more of a science girl myself."

"Time travel is real? Who else can travel?" Gears in Mathew's head began turning with the implications. Who else went back and changed the future already? Did he alter the future with his screw up? A headache slowed the mind-blowing possibilities.

"I cannot divulge too much information—only enough to fulfill the mission."

"Mission? Saving Verity?" If only he could find her.

"Yes. Also, this is important—do not interfere with your previous self."

His brows lifted. This sounded straight out of Doc Brown's mouth from *Back to the Future*. "Wait, I saw the movie. Are you sending me back to the same moment, and I have to avoid myself?"

"I'll send you back a short while after you arrived last time. You should have plenty of time to succeed during this attempt."

"Attempt?" Mathew's skin crawled. "Is this some sort of game to you? We're talking about a woman's life and you're so casual about it."

"I've been working missions for more years than you've been alive, Matt. I can't help if some of my thought process has become...less empathetic."

A sudden jolt burned through him. *That* was the intimidating weirdness around her. She was brilliant, but creepy weird, almost inhuman. "Are you human?" Mathew asked with a whisper. His body screamed at him to run away, but the fascination kept his muddy feet planted on the carpet.

She chuckled. "Yes. Jesus, Matt, you've known me for over a year. You crashed on my couch more than once. Think of it as a bizarre hobby."

Yeah, right. There was so much to process Mathew didn't know where to begin. A deep breath reminded him of the stench in his clothes. "I'll go change now."

Mathew switched into clean clothes—a different set of dress pants and shirt. He didn't plan on sitting in pig manure again. And he wiped his shoes clean. He groaned at needing to hire a

carpet cleaner when this was all over—another bill he didn't need.

Satisfied, Mathew stood over the once familiar, but now terrifying, woman.

"Ready?"

He nodded, and she motioned for him to lay on the couch again. Mathew grabbed a sheet off his bed to cover the dirty cushions and then laid down. Kiko slipped the trinket back into his pocket and he didn't want to ask how she'd gotten it back from him.

"Now don't forget—you can't interfere with your previous self or you can induce a cataclysmic event. Everything has to happen the way it's meant to happen. Otherwise—real nasty stuff, and I don't want my boss screaming down my neck, okay? And that trinket is a direct tunnel between times. Be careful where you're standing when you press it. You don't want to end up inside a wall or something."

"Ten-four." Just yikes. Mathew was only doing this to save Verity—and spend more time with the assertive bold beauty, but he also wanted to get as far from Kiko as possible.

## Astor, Wisconsin
## 1853

WHEN THE NAUSEA passed, Mathew ducked low in the cornfield. This time, he was confident in what to do. His legs ate up the ground to the toolshed, and he wrenched open the split doors. Primitive metal tools hung all over the walls. He couldn't

use a gun, but he still understood physics. Mathew lifted an ax and dashed across the open space to the house. He sidled against the wood siding near the front door and ducked out of sight behind overgrown bushes. His prior self would come along shortly—or he had already. Awaiting the inevitable was like waiting for Father's anger to unleash in the household. The tension and stress made his palms sweaty against the wooden handle. Two attempts left after this one. He was living a real-life video game.

Mathew shifted hand positions to wipe the sweat onto his pants. He could do this. He had the upper hand knowing the future events. The shotgun rang across the field, and Mathew swallowed a thick lump. He needed to keep his head clear if he saw himself. *Talk about literal déjà vu.*

A deep inhale and slow exhale calmed the pounding in his head. He watched the short Hispanic man ride up the front yard, and Mathew shrunk himself further.

Jaime Perez dismounted and walked up the steps. Adrenaline coursed through Mathew's veins, and he white-knuckled the ax's handle. Jaime Perez had to go inside so Mathew didn't mess up the past. He used a forearm to wipe his sweat-lined brow, and the screams liquefied his guts worse than before, because he knew exactly what was happening.

Mathew risked a glance through the living room window. Shock stopped his heart for a moment. The woman was underneath his other self. Jaime Perez was fisting her dress collar to drag her away. The other Mathew held onto her for dear life, and with the click of the hammer being pulled back, he exchanged glances with himself. It was like reliving a dream, like

watching a movie starring himself, like watching his life rewound. He ducked back before his sneak peek interfered with the future…or the past? Kiko's warnings scared him enough.

The next gunshot, a smaller caliber pistol, made Mathew jump. That was the bullet meant to kill him. If it weren't for Kiko, he would be dead. But if it weren't for Kiko, he never would've come here to die in the first place. The whole idea spun his head.

Blood-curdling screams came from Jonathan's wife. Was she afraid he died? Or was she afraid of how he vanished? When the front door opened and kicks and screams of struggle percolated the evening air, Mathew sprung from his hiding place, ax raised for battle, and rushed behind Jaime, whose head was tilted down at his target while he dragged her down the stairs.

With one round discharged, the evil little shit had at most five left, and Mathew wasn't taking chances—he needed to be within arm's reach, but he wasn't a murderer.

"Unhand her," he demanded with the blunt end of the ax raised. Both the woman's and Jaime's faces turned to him. He found a pinch of satisfaction for catching Jaime off-guard with his magical reappearance. Mathew swung down hard, smashing the side of Jaime's now-tender neck. He didn't want the guy dead, just incapacitated. Jaime pinwheeled sideways into the dirt at the foot of the wooden steps and curled into a ball, hand on his neck. He groaned with a pinched face. Although comprehension was fleeting for the dazed man, within seconds, Jaime was out cold.

"Are you okay?" Mathew asked.

Her face fell with shock.

Mathew held out his hand, and she accepted. When she stood to full length, she crashed against his chest with sobs, and Mathew breathed in her scent. Relief washed over him—relief that for once he hadn't failed to protect a woman against a brute of a man. He lifted her off the last step of the porch and over Jaime's prone form, setting her feet gently on the dirt.

"How did you do that? I thought you were dead and then I thought...I don't know what I thought. You vanished and now your clothes are different—clean, too."

"Just a little trick. It's really me. Don't be afraid." No sense trying to explain it to her, he didn't believe it himself. She released him and gazed into his face, as if trying to convince herself he was corporeal. Her green eyes were dull and wide with terror. Tears streaked her face and her hair was knotted and snarled from Jaime's vicious grip. Mathew's hands balled to fists, and he fought the urge to hit the man with the business side of the ax this time. But Mathew spent his life helping people and saving animals. *Justice will take care of him.*

"Are you an angel?" Her voice was a whisper.

Mathew chuckled. "Hardly. Let's go inside. We need to phone the police."

He wrapped his arm around her shoulders and guided her to the steps. He was so grateful he'd succeeded.

"What's a phone?"

A grunt of annoyance came from Mathew's throat. No technology here in 1853. "What happens when people need to be arrested?"

"The sheriff comes."

"Who brings the sheriff?"

"Someone volunteers to ride out there. But I wouldn't bother. The sheriff works for him, anyway." The woman indicated where Jaime was left.

A shudder ran through his body. "How do you deal with law-breaking citizens then?"

"Guns, knives, dogs, money, and keeping your nose to yourself."

No help. He would have no help in getting Jaime arrested. The sniveling man deserved to be behind bars for attempted murder at a minimum.

"So, what do we do with him?" he asked.

"Flattered you're discussing me."

Jonathan's wife gasped in terror. A chill ran down Mathew's spine at the tinny voice. Jaime Perez stood at the front door, pistol aimed and ready. How had he gotten up there? Mathew checked the ground and yep, he was no longer where he'd left him. This wasn't over yet. Mathew grasped Jonathan's wife's arm and pulled her back away from the house. Accuracy was worsened with distance.

Jaime pulled the hammer back on his pistol. "You won't manage that trick twice."

The ax in his hands was no match for a pistol, and he wasn't Paul Bunyan—capable of an accurate ax toss—by any shot. Mathew had one option. He discreetly slipped the trinket out of his pocket and lifted the lid. A small red button stared at him.

He whispered into her ear, "Hold on tight and don't let go." Her head nodded against his chest. If the pig manure clinging to his clothes came home with him last time, then in theory the woman could be transported away, too. If this didn't work, he

still had two tries left.

Jaime growled. "So that's how it's going to be? Congratulations, sir. You just earned a spot on my list."

*Oh, shit.* Mathew closed his eyes, grasped her tightly, and hoped like hell this would work. He pressed the red button.

# Chapter Nine

Green Bay, Wisconsin
Present Day

VERITY'S STOMACH SWIRLED and clenched while she kept her eyes pinched shut. She wanted to vomit, but Mathew held her tight. When her stomach stopped tumbling, she opened her eyes. Darkness swallowed them, and Verity peeked her head around Mathew's broad chest. Bright orange little suns floated in the air, shooting cones of light down on the ground. Buildings were around her, houses, some with lanterns on the porch and some without. Some windows were lit. She heard yelling at a distance and a foreign rumbling noise coming closer. She tensed in his arms as the ground vibrated under her feet. *What was that?*

Two extra bright lights flew at them, rumbling like an angry beast. She cried out and buried her face in his chest. His torso shook with laughter while he stroked her back. She smelled something on his skin, beyond the pungent pig manure on her dress. It was a musky masculine scent, and she enjoyed it very much. She was terrified of wherever she was but confident she was safe in his arms.

"It's just a car. It won't hurt you if you aren't in front of it. Come with me. My apartment is just around the corner."

Verity held herself glued to his side while they walked along a hard path between patches of grass. Trees lined their way. Where were they? She didn't recognize anything, and she didn't remember making a trip.

Jaime Perez had hunted her down inside her own home. Found her in her hiding place. Dragged her out to the living room by her hair. She'd fought enough to keep him from whisking her away to whatever hell awaited her, but Mathew had rescued her. Verity shivered at the thought of what Jaime had planned for her. She only hoped to never see him again.

Mathew's arm hugged her shoulders tight and his hand rubbed her upper arm. "Cold?"

"Just a little."

"My place is right here. It's not much, and I wasn't expecting visitors, so pardon the mess." They crossed the grass into an open space where sparse orange lights dotted an open lot. A two-story brick building stood before them. Some windows were lit and others dark. This place was huge! He *was* rich. She'd never seen any building like this before. He unlocked the front door and led them down the hallway. Two pearly cubes sat in the open space.

"What are those?" she asked, pointing.

"Washer and dryer. They save a lot of laundry time."

Verity smiled. She didn't know how they worked, but laundry was a bane in her life. This strange city sure was fascinating. "You'll need to show me how to use them."

Mathew gave her sad smile, and she cast her eyes aside. Perhaps she could not assume she'd get to stay. Verity followed him up the stairs, and he unlocked another door.

"This is me." He opened it wide, and light bathed the whole room at the sound of a click. She stepped inside and wandered around, marveling at the strange living quarters. Couch, coffee table, kitchen table, those were familiar. Wash basin, kitchen counter, familiar but much fancier than hers. The rugs underfoot extended through the whole room. How extravagant! In the kitchen she found more pearly cubes. She pointed. "Washer and dryer?"

"Dishwasher, stove slash oven, and refrigerator. You are a fascinating woman."

Her cheeks heated with the praise. The descriptors she had heard were never so flattering.

"Hungry?" he asked.

She shook her head. She had finished her dinner before Jaime showed up, and her stomach wasn't ready for food after that journey. Thinking of journey..."Where are we?"

Mathew prowled through the house and took a small black thing off a table. It lit up bright in his hands. He blew out a breath and ran a hand through his hair. "I think you should sit."

Verity adjusted her petticoat and sat on the couch, surprised at how soft it was. "This is nice."

"Nice piece of crap, you mean."

"Huh?"

"Nothing. Listen." Mathew sat in the matching cushioned chair next to the couch. "I don't know how to say this, but you're in Green Bay."

"The city you're from?"

"Yeah."

"But how did I get here? I don't even know where here is."

Mathew lit the little black thing again, and his fingers made quick work on it. He showed it to her. It was a map.

"I recognize that." She touched the spot on the map where she lived. "Astor." Words popped up, blocking most of the map. "Something's wrong with it."

Mathew relocated next to her. "The newspaper at your house, you remember the year?"

"Yeah, now you're speaking silly. It's 1853."

Mathew touched the black thing a few times, sliding, tapping and sliding. He held the image to her. "Read this date. It's a news story from today."

"July twenty-third...*What?*" Verity stood. "That's impossible."

"You're telling me," he agreed. Mathew stood and paced, speaking rapidly as if panic reared its head. "Where is Kiko? I need to get you back home. I was helping my sister's roommate with a dream project, which turned out to be a lie. I still haven't found Verity, so I guess I failed again. Kiko gave me this." He stopped pacing and held out a small trinket. "And I pressed it before Jaime blew us away. Now you're here. I'm glad it worked, otherwise we'd be dead, but you don't belong here, and I don't even know your name. Your husband will be worried sick."

"Husband?" Verity wasn't married. No one would marry her. There was a reason her brother was so frustrated with her, and why she wanted to run away to California.

"The man with the trigger finger, Johnny, isn't your husband?"

She laughed. It was the most, no second most, ridiculous thing she'd heard today. "Brother."

Mathew sighed and smiled, softening his features and bearing

straight white teeth. He looked like a hundred thousand dollars.

"I'm glad I don't have to worry about a pissed off husband coming after me. Well, a pissed off brother is just as bad, I suppose." He paused and stared off. "Yeah, just as bad." His hands balled to fists. She wondered what bothered him about her brother so much.

He picked up the black thing again and pressed it and slid his finger on it. "Just one second, okay? I have to make a call."

She heard a ringing come from the thing and she sat still, uncertain of what a call was.

"Come on, Kiko. Pick up." It rang and rang. Mathew pressed on it, and the ringing stopped. "She's not answering. It's late. I'll show you where you can sleep. I'll take the couch."

How was she supposed to sleep when she was in a different time, far away from the land she knew? It was exactly what she wanted. Excitement bubbled in her veins.

MATHEW GROANED WHILE he woke from the most insane dream of his life. It was impossible. Light broke through his patio door and blinded him. He remembered an intimidating and assertive woman with wild hair, green eyes, and beautiful freckles, and his aching morning hard-on reminded him how long it'd been since he'd gotten laid. Way too long. He debated for far longer than usual about what to do next—coffee or relief.

He sat up and adjusted himself and realized he was on the couch—the same place where Kiko had left him yesterday. Was Kiko even here? Too many drug fumes at work—they were messing with his head. Perhaps he would have Kiko or Becca fill

the prescriptions from now on. He rubbed a palm between his brows and stood for a stretch. The smartphone on the coffee table told him he would be late opening the clinic.

He turned on the coffee pot, then turned it off. It would have to wait until he got to the office. He went to his closet and grabbed dress clothes and brought them to the bathroom. In the mirror he found mud caked on his face and on the chest of his shirt. He turned around and his pants had dirt stains on them that reeked like...pig manure.

He ran back into his bedroom and found the dream woman in his bed.

*Holy goddamned shit.*

Mathew ran a hand through his hair. Now what? He stepped up alongside the mattress and leaned over. Her breathing was deep and even. With her still asleep, he cleaned himself up. He didn't want any patients at the office marking him as their territory. He washed fast and changed into clean clothes. When he stepped out, the woman was slipping into her dress. She wore a corset and long stockings with a garter belt. Mathew's face burned hot, and he pivoted for her privacy. The image of her dressed like that would forever be burned on his brain.

"I'm sorry. I didn't realize you were up yet," he said.

The sensuous laugh burst from her lips. "Nothing to be ashamed of. Don't you have a maid to help me dress?"

Mathew's turn to laugh. "No. Sorry, no maids here."

"Give me a hand then?"

Mathew cleared his throat and turned around. She had the gown covering her breasts, but it flopped open in the back. He stepped behind her and the smooth supple skin tempted him. A

heat rushed through his body, pooling in places he wanted to forget right now. Two laces dangled behind the fluffy bump of the dress and he picked them up. "I'm not sure what to do here."

"Lace me up like a shoe. You can do that, right?"

"Yeah. I can." He grasped the uppermost strap and tugged. "Too tight?"

"No. Keep going." A smile danced on her lips. His fingertips traced her skin while he grasped the next strap. He was being ridiculous touching her on purpose. Mathew didn't even know her name! But at least she wasn't married. He finished the straps and tied the laces tight. She turned around with a smile. "Thank you."

"After doing that, I feel I must know your name."

Her eyes cast aside, and the warmth drained away. She left the bedroom and went to the kitchen. "Where are your pans? We need to eat."

"No time. I'm late for work. Can you stay here until we figure this out?"

She searched the kitchen with her eyes, settling on the appliances. "I don't think so. Can I come with you?"

He smiled at her antique outfit and wondered what they girls would say. "Sure. I hope you won't be bored. I'll have breakfast delivered and waiting when we get there." Mathew collected his wallet and slipped on a belt. He ran a gelled comb over his hair and swished mouthwash. He offered her some, assuming she had nothing to brush her teeth with. "Want a swish?"

"What is it?" It would be another one of those strange days. Hopefully Kiko was already in, and he could get this mess straightened out.

"Here, I have a new toothbrush, an extra from the dentist." He unwrapped it and offered her the paste. She smiled in recognition.

"There's other stuff in here if you need anything. I have a curling iron here if you want it for your hair. Plug it in, wait until it's hot, and wrap chunks of your hair around it for a few seconds. Don't ask why I have it."

She shrugged and he gave her time to brush while he made a call for delivery to the clinic. When they were ready, Mathew locked up behind them and brought her downstairs to his SUV. He unlocked the doors with his key FOB, and the lights blinked with a chirp. The woman yelped and hid behind him. Despite his meager living, everything was amazing and exciting to her. Or terrifying too, he supposed. He wondered what it would feel like to jump over a hundred and sixty years into the future. Would they finally have hovercrafts? Or universal healthcare? That was a bill he would be glad to rid himself of.

She stepped out from behind him and held his gaze as if she searched for something. Her deep green eyes seemed to know more than they'd seen, a depth of aged wisdom in the body and face of a twenty-something beauty. He opened the door for her and held her soft hand while she sat sideways on the passenger seat. The bump of her gown fluffed up around her. The corner of Mathew's lips lifted, and he helped shove the layers of fabric inside the vehicle and shut the door. Climbing into the driver's seat, he helped her buckle in and they were rolling down Mason Street toward the clinic on the east side of the city.

Her knuckles were white with strain and her body rigid in fear.

"You're looking a little green around the gills. Should I pull over?"

"I'm not used to going this fast."

"You never took the rail?"

Her nose crinkled in that cute way. "No passenger rails near Astor."

"I'm not exactly a history buff. I guess everything around here is foreign to you. Anything look familiar?"

Silence followed. Mathew glanced her way, and she bit her lower lip in thought.


VERITY CLENCHED EVERY muscle in her body as the large black behemoth thundered down a terrifying roadway at impossible speeds. When colored lights changed, Mathew stopped, sped, and slowed accordingly. She was amazed these carriages moved without horses. She couldn't fathom all the fascinating things from the future. Some were turning out to be more terrifying than exciting, though. They turned another corner, and she certainly recognized something.

"Yes, this is Sam Hartley's place. It looks so similar. It's amazing!" The auto carriage stopped between yellow lines in front of the town hero's home. She fumbled with the tethering strap across her chest. Mathew pressed the red button near the base of the tether. She would remember that.

"His place?"

"This part here is his house. Around back is the blacksmith shop and gallery. He and April do well for themselves." Her fingers searched the door and failed to find the escape latch.

Mathew, her rescuer with big blue eyes and well-groomed hair, leaned across her lap and disengaged the door for her. An intoxicating masculine scent filled her nose and heat rose in her cheeks. She wanted to kiss him for bringing her here, away from everything. He saved her, and he didn't even realize how terrible her life would've been if she'd stayed.

"Huh. And how do you know them?"

"Small towns. Everyone knows everything." Unfortunately. Super unfortunately, which was one reason she was a prisoner at her family's farm. Verity slid out of the auto carriage and closed the door behind her. Taking a step forward, she pulled up short. Her skirts caught in the door. Her fingers found the handle, and she pushed, then pulled and smiled when it popped open. *Take that, auto carriage!* She removed her skirts and closed the door again. Mathew circled around to help her, but she stepped away with her chin held high. She went to inspect Sam's building plaque. Her fingers touched the rough cold metal.

"The old address number," Mathew said. "I left it on during the remodel. My sister always liked it."

"Not an address number. This is the plaque Sam made in his blacksmith shop, the year he built this cabin with his father, 1841. It's so worn and weathered. It's amazing."

"Later, I insist you give me a historical tour around town. And I'll show you all the fun stuff the future has to offer."

"Really?" Verity asked. An even bigger adventure awaited. She could hardly contain herself.

He smiled. "Sure. I mean, I have to find Kiko before I can get you home."

The smile fell from her face. She didn't want to go back. She

didn't want to face her angry brother. She didn't want to face Jaime Perez. Even the thought of his name made her shiver. She also didn't want to leave the man who had saved her from him. A hand jutted into her view interrupting her melancholy train, and she accepted it. His warm fingers cocooned her hand, and he led her inside the cabin.

She had been to Sam's cabin once, back when her dad drew up the contract for her brother to marry Sam's little sister, Sarah. It was large for a cabin built by a working-class family, but cozy, and it had the essential amenities: a wood stove, wash basin, and bedrooms. But now, it was simply incredible. Beautiful, modern, but cold. Gray and white with rusted metal accents. The smell was most striking, like fresh grilled meat and wet dog. She wasn't sure whether to be hungry or disappointed. A desk ran the length of Sam's living room with striped bags of steaming food beckoning her, and a woman in strange clothing sat behind it. The whole interior tugged her between awe at the modernity and disgust at trampling over Sam's legacy. At least Mathew turned the building into something useful rather than it being torn down.

Mathew cleared his throat and Verity spun. "This here is Becca. She's one of my assistants. Becca, this is…" Mathew trailed off. Awkwardness filled the air. If he knew she was the woman he was looking for, perhaps he wouldn't send her home. Besides, after all they'd been through, Verity was sure he was one of the good guys.

"I'm Verity Arris. It's nice to meet you." Verity held out her hand to the woman with striking red curls.

Becca was warm and kind with a sad smile, but her eyes

roamed Verity's clothes with raised eyebrows.

Mathew, however, stood with his mouth gaped open, catching flies. He recovered and held out his hand. "Happy to officially meet you myself, Verity Arris."

She accepted it. Like a gentleman, he bent and planted a kiss on her knuckles. Searing heat raced through her body. Nerves danced from fingertips to her toes. She ducked her head to hide her hot cheeks. No one had treated her like a respectable lady for so long.

"Welcome, Verity," Becca said, assessing her pungent stained dress with a look of confusion.

Verity compared her clothing from 1853 to Becca's floral tunic and...*pants?* Why was the woman wearing pants? Verity wasn't surprised that Becca saw her dress as strange.

"Thank you."

"Food's here, doc."

"I see that, thanks. I'll reimburse you the tip."

"There's no need."

"Help yourself," he said to Becca. "I got a bag for each of us. Where's Kiko?"

Becca lifted a bag from the top counter for herself and placed it down on the lower counter near her lap. The lower counter was decorated in strange looking pens, fancy pencils, and the rest she did not understand—long black things and more captivating squares that lit up.

"She called in. Family emergency of some sort."

"Right," Mathew said.

A note of sadness played on his voice, and Verity realized he was kind and caring with everyone he met, not just her. Verity's

heart swelled for him.

Mathew picked up a bag and brought Verity around the counter to sit next to Becca, presumably in Kiko's empty chair. "Dig in. Tell me what you think of fast food. I've got"—he checked his wristwatch—"ten minutes before the first client of the day arrives."

Mathew sat next to her and unpackaged his food. She watched him tear paper off a strange looking straw and poke it through the hole in the top of a lid. He unfolded the aluminum wrapper from his sandwich and took a massive bite with a groan of pleasure. Verity perked up, waiting for her turn at the most pleasurable sandwich she'd ever heard. She copied him step for step and took a bite.

Anticlimactic was an understatement. It was warm mush with flavors that assaulted the tongue, salt that shriveled her lips, and bread that caught on the roof of her mouth. Using the straw, she swallowed down some liquid to prevent choking. Verity coughed. The insanely sweet liquid was not water or beer.

"What is this?" she asked, lifting the drink.

"Coke."

"I see." The disappointment was thick on her tongue. She didn't mean to insinuate she disliked his food, but she couldn't lie to him.

"You don't like it?"

No lies. "I'm sorry, but it's terrible."

Mathew laughed and her chest released its nervous tension. "Most people nowadays think so, too."

"Why do you eat it then?"

"It's cheap, fast, and better than what most people can make

at home. Plus, no dishes."

True. She noticed wrappings crinkled up and tossed into the waste bin. No dishes left to wash. She wondered what it would be like to call and have hot fresh food delivered and no dishes afterward. How freeing that would be! People of the future must have so much leisure time.

The bell above the door chimed, and a small dog walked in with a tether fastening it to its owner. So many tethers, the future must not be safe.

# Chapter Ten

"HANG IN THERE, little lady. It'll only take a second." Mathew's hands palpated the furry flesh of his patient, who preferred licking its own butt to paying him a visit. Mathew wasn't that repulsive, he was sure. At least Verity hadn't run for the hills when she'd seen him. The woman he was sent to save had turned out to be the woman he'd brought back to the future with him. He didn't know how the time travel worked, but he was certain she needed to go home. He'd seen the movies. Plus Kiko had said cataclysmic events. If you mess with the past, the future becomes altered. He was afraid of the negative ramifications, but since Kiko needed time away for a family emergency, he would make the best of the situation. Verity was an innocent woman and sheltered, not because of her upbringing, but because of her world. He had the sudden desire to show her the world and watch her light up with excitement at all the future offered.

"Feels good in there, Miss Buttercup. Now I need a listen to the ticker." Mathew hung his stethoscope in his ears and pressed the diaphragm against the little terrier's chest.

Mathew smiled for this client. "She sounds good in there. Smooth and healthy. Now how about those shots?" He scratched the little dog behind its ears and turned to draw up the

dosage volume of the vaccines. Mrs. Peterson smiled and cooed baby noises at her dog. Mathew drew up the syringes and typed in the lot numbers and expiration dates into the system.

"This will only be a pinch," he assured Mrs. Peterson more than Miss Buttercup. Dogs didn't understand English, but when he pretended they did, their owners were comforted. He slipped the cover off the first syringe, grasped a handful of flesh between her shoulder blades and inserted the needle. A quick press of the plunger and it was over. He repeated the procedure with the next vaccine and patted the dog on the head. "All set today."

Mrs. Peterson and Miss Buttercup left the exam room, and his client mumbled words of encouragement to the furball. He sterilized the table and clicked the buttons to compile the vaccination documentation. Mathew washed his hands and walked out to the desk, where he found Verity scrunching her nose at the desktop screen. She glanced down at the mouse and moved it around. A smile danced on her face. The sweet innocence was appealing, and his lips pulled into a smile. She wasn't like the women in this city, literally, and he meant it.

He leaned over Becca to tell her the procedures performed, and which vaccination certificates to print. While Becca handled the payment processing, Verity walked toward him with a glint in her eye that raced Mathew's pulse and flooded his body with heat, waking parts of him that hadn't had attention in so long he hoped he remembered how to use them. He was not celibate, just busy. One brain didn't listen to the other though. Mathew cleared his throat.

"How am I doing?" she whispered, and her hot breath caressed his ear. The rushing warmth threatened the shape of his

pants. *Think cold thoughts. Think gross thoughts—dog barf, suturing wounds, emptying cat anal glands.* Stronger, he needed stronger! His dress pants were shifting. *Neutering dogs! Bingo. Neutering dogs. Snip, snip,* and crisis averted.

"You're doing fantastic. A natural. By the end of the day, you'll fit right in with Becca." He winked and her cheeks blushed bright pink. She gave him a small curtsy with her sixties-curtains fluffy dress and returned to the desk.

Mathew finished all his patients for the day and by the end, she *was* a natural. She had a surprising ability to learn foreign concepts quickly. It was like she had no fear at all. Even his own dad hated computers, and he didn't time-jump over a hundred and sixty years. She was something special all right.

He retreated to his office to compile the day's data ahead of locking up. Revenues were the same as always. They didn't increase, they didn't decrease, but...those expenses. It was a wonder he slept at night. He needed to type up a discount policy and stick to it. Scrolling through Quickbooks, he overheard the women's conversation at the registration desk.

"Hey, Verity?" Becca asked.

"Yeah?"

"Is something wrong with the toilet, because if there is, you can just tell us, and we can take care of it."

"What do you mean?"

"It didn't flush."

"Flush?"

Mathew chuckled and stepped out to rescue her from embarrassment. "I didn't mean to overhear, but is that toilet acting up again?"

"It never did before," Becca said.

"I'll get it taken care of, no worries," Mathew replied.

"Sure thing, doc." Becca crossed her arms with a frown. Her eyes raked over Verity. Mathew wasn't going to explain, not that he could anyway.

"Are we set for closing?" he asked.

"Yeah, except for the toilet."

"Punch out then. Good work today." He dismissed her a few minutes early. He would handle the toilet problem himself. Becca collected her purse, phone, and book, and clicked the mouse a few times before logging out of the computer.

"See you tomorrow." She slipped her sunglasses on and turned the Open sign to Closed as she left.

Mathew waited until the door was closed tight. "Is the toilet backed up?"

"I don't know." Her eyes were round with concern.

Mathew smiled and inside the bathroom he saw waste floating in the bowl. He pressed the flushing handle down. It swirled away with a loud whoosh. Verity covered her ears. "What was that?"

"Plumbing. When you're done, just push that handle and it all goes away."

Her face turned a shade of tomato. "I'm so sorry. I had no idea."

"It's okay. Nothing to be embarrassed about. I spend most of my days with my arms inside dogs and cats. Once you've expressed a cat's anal gland and gotten sprayed in the mouth with it, everything else is just...nothing." She stared at him with her green doe eyes. Did she not understand? "How did things

go with Becca today? I'm sorry about leaving you to fend for yourself. I can't close the clinic last second and leave all my patients hanging."

"Are you a doctor for animals?"

He smiled. That was the only thing on her mind? "Yeah. I am."

"And you own this clinic?" she asked as if the idea was unbelievable. Mathew determined she was impressed with him. Verity, the brazen woman of wonder but innocence, was impressed by his old clinic, outdated small apartment, gas-guzzling SUV, and what she didn't realize, a net worth of many negative digits. If he explained that, she wouldn't be as dazzled, and selfishly, he liked how she looked at him.

"Well, the bank does, but it's mine. Listen, how about we take a trip over to the mall? I don't want to offend you, but until Kiko returns from her family emergency, we're on our own. And to make it easier on you, I thought finding you current clothing would help."

Verity looked down at her dress and then her eyes roamed his clothing, lingering in places that caused the flash of heat to boil in his veins again. He wanted to kiss her, to take possession of her mouth, to taste her lips and caress her tongue. But he couldn't do that to her. She was probably a virgin, for god's sake.

"I think new clothing would be a proper idea. I need a bath, anyway."

Mathew was an idiot. He hadn't even offered her a shower before they'd left. They didn't have time anyway, but maybe some clients could've rescheduled. "I'm so sorry. Let's get you some clothes and get cleaned up. You like pizza?" He must've

had a credit card or two with remaining credit.

Her cute nose crinkled. "I don't know."

The woman didn't know what pizza was.

He would fix that.


MATHEW TURNED THE wheel of the behemoth until they stopped between more yellow lines on an endless lot. The building was large—two stories and as long as she could see.

"This is the mall," he said. "They were popular a few decades ago and recently started coming back. It's still the most efficient place to find clothes though. Come on in."

Verity pressed the red button to release her tether. She waited for Mathew to come around the car, as he called it, and let her out. Verity didn't want to be in front of all the cars, since Mathew said that was the dangerous side. His large hand enveloped hers, but she slipped her hand away and instead looped her arm around his. He smiled and properly hooked his arm for her. A warm rush flooded her body with the respect he showed her again. They zigzagged between parked cars, and inside glass doors that opened themselves was a sea of storefronts bathed in skylight coming through the ceiling. Scents poured over her, foreign music vibrated her eardrums, and bright colors assaulted her eyes.

It was glorious.

Mathew led her to a store with women her age browsing, so this was the correct place for her too. He held out some options, and she accepted whatever he suggested, since he knew better. He insisted she try them on in something he called a dressing

room. Wearing Mathew's selections in front of the mirror, she felt naked. Her legs were covered separately—like a man, but in torn denim with sparkles on the back pockets—not like a man. Her jeans, as he called them, didn't understand gender appropriateness, and her shirt hugged her skin very close. But breathing was much easier than with the corset. She bent, squatted, and jumped with ease. She determined that her new jeans and blue floral top were made as if only for her.

"When you're finished, I can lace up your dress," Mathew said through the door of the dressing room.

She didn't want to take them off. "Can't I just wear these now?"

"Not yet. We have to pay first."

Frowning, Verity peeled off her new clothes, slipped on the layers of her undergarments, and pulled up her dress. She held the heavy fabric in place and opened the door, exposing her back to Mathew, whose deft fingers laced both the corset and the dress.

"Next stop, shoes," Mathew said as he slid a card through a machine. It made noises, and he signed on the screen. His looping signature didn't match the screen well, but it must've known it was him, anyway. The transaction was accepted, and a strip of paper rolled out for him. She wanted to understand how it all worked. Mathew carried her bags, and she folded her arm inside his. Down the hall, he brought her inside a shoe store.

"What kind would you like?"

She saw boots in many styles, heels that she was familiar with, sandals that looked scandalous, extra tall high heels that looked illegal, and shoes that reminded her of April Hartley's. Sneakers,

she'd called them.

"Those," she said, pointing to a pair of sneakers.

"Planning on running away?" He smiled with a wink.

"April wore those," she explained. "And last year she saved the town of Bridgeport, saved Sam's life, saved Lloyd's life, and the townspeople revered her. I want shoes like hers."

Mathew cocked a brow at her. "This April, did she have a maiden name?"

"I would assume so."

"You don't know it?" Mathew looked at her feet, made a guess, and selected a box from the shelf. "Have a seat."

"I haven't met her personally, but I heard all the stories. They were in the newspaper, too."

Mathew unlaced her worn, dirty old kitten heels and slipped her foot into the sneaker like Cinderella. "How does that feel?"

"Extraordinary," she answered. He pinched the toe to judge the size, and satisfied, he laced her shoe.

"Take a small walk."

Verity stood and tried out the shoe. She walked on clouds—airy with no pressure points. What luxury! Her old shoes were like walking on wood planks. She sat back down in front of Mathew, and she caught his gaze. He'd saved her from her brother, who wasn't a threat, but he wasn't aware, and he'd saved her from Jaime Perez. She wanted to thank him forever, but she didn't know how. She had nothing of value to give him.

"I'll take these," she said.

"Great. After I checkout, we'll get you dressed in your new clothes. Sounds good?"

"Very."

Mathew's wide smile sent her heart aflutter. With a box of shoes in hand, she walked alongside Mathew down the aisle of the mall. There were people talking, laughing, and yelling. Most people were looking down at a black box thing similar to the one Mathew had, the thing he used to make a call. She wondered what was so interesting. A few people stared at her as they passed, but she would remedy that soon.

"Do you know anything else about this April with shoes like those, who saved...everyone?"

Verity considered, trying to recall details from the newspaper. "No. Nothing I haven't already said."

"Right here," Mathew pointed to the restroom door. "If you use the toilet, remember to flush." He winked and her cheeks heated with embarrassment.

She stepped inside, switching out her clothes and shoes. She poked her head out the door. "What do I do with my old stuff?"

"Up to you. If you want to keep them, put them in a bag. If not, there's a garbage can in there."

She closed the door again and looked at her long layers of bulky stiff linen. Her devil's shoes. Did she want to keep them? If anyone back home saw her wearing future clothes, her reputation would go from ruined to killed. But she already wasn't worthy of marriage, what else could they do to her? And even if she went back home, would she stay there? No. If she had to return to the past, she would leave home for good. California was still her dream. She balled up her old clothes, since she only owned a couple dresses in total, and stuffed them into one of the shopping bags. Just in case.

Outside of the restroom, she found Mathew near the sound

of splashing water. Green plants separated wooden benches. How was water inside the building? After seeing a toilet, anything was possible.

"What is that noise?" she asked.

"Step up here and lean over." He tugged her hand until she stood on the seat of the bench. Her mouth dropped open at the view of water spraying up in a majestic arch and sprinkling against the water's surface. Coins under the water glistened like gems. The pattering rhythm was hypnotizing, and the spray misted her face with cool water.

"Here," Mathew said, handing her a coin. "Toss it in and make a silent wish. They come true."

She smiled. The future was more amazing than anything she could've ever dreamed.

She tossed the coin in and watched it flutter to the bottom. Verity wished to stay here with Mathew McCall, sweet and kind doctor to animals, driver of dangerous cars, and bringer of adventure. Not to mention, rich beyond her wildest dreams. Satisfied, she sat on the edge of the water with her knees touching Mathew's. "What's this called?"

"Water fountain, but many people use them as wishing wells, as you can see. How do your clothes feel?"

"Fantastic. It's so freeing, but also"—she leaned in close and whispered—"exposed."

Mathew cleared his throat and turned his eyes away. "You're not naked, and you look great. Let's eat."

VERITY'S CLOTHES HAD morphed from Old Mother Hubbard to a trendy sorority girl. Mathew wasn't on the up-and-up with women's clothes, but he thought he dressed her like an appropriate young adult—torn skinny jeans, soft flowing floral blouse, and bright white sneakers. Now she would turn heads for reasons other than her clothes. Her wild hair and fierce green eyes and cute freckles stole his attention, but her strength, bravery, and fierceness captivated him. He wanted her naked in his bed. Mathew would settle for half-naked in the mall bathroom. But he couldn't do that to her—she deserved better. Besides, he had no idea if she'd be willing, and he drew a hard line there. With a rumbling stomach, food sounded like a welcome distraction.

"This way. I know a place that has great pizza. Do you have any food allergies?"

"What's that?"

"Adverse reactions to certain foods," he clarified.

"That sounds impossible."

"I wish it was." They reached the SUV, and Mathew loaded her bags into the trunk. She hopped inside without his assistance. "Not so scary anymore, huh?"

She buckled herself in with a smile. "No. The tether here keeps us safe, so no worries."

*If only it were that easy.*

"Right." He closed her door and slipped into the driver's seat. Soon they were rolling north on a four-lane through town and hung a left. "This is the best pizza in town, but everyone has opinions and all that, so tell me what you think."

Mathew ordered a basic pizza. He didn't know what she liked,

and neither did she. For first timers, fewer toppings were probably better. They sat in a booth and Mathew asked, "So, what is this trouble you're in back home?"

Verity's eyes widened. He didn't mean to pry, but with her in his life for at least the next few days, he couldn't resist finding out more about her. She stared at her hands fidgeting with the napkin on the table. "I...I made a mistake. The person I wronged wants to punish me."

"Well that sounds reasonable," Mathew said. Her mouth gaped open, and he backpedaled, "I mean, it sounds reasonable with the information you gave me, that's all. Tell me."

Her finger traced the woodgrain pattern on the table. "I never got along with my parents or my brothers, Johnny and Graham. They all worked the farm obediently. My job was to tend the household like my mother. I was to get married, raise babies, and tend house for my husband." She glanced aside with a face twist with disgust. "I didn't want to marry at eighteen years of age. That was too young for me."

"I understand. These days the average marrying age for women is twenty-seven." Her eyes darted to him with annoyance. "Sorry. Continue."

"After a lack of mutual interest between Bernard and I, and I refused to try again, my parents threatened a contract on me. I ran. As it was my first time outside the home, I…I got scared and went back. Shortly thereafter they died, and I was determined to make my own life with no one to stop me. For months I bounced from place to place, hitching rides where I could, scraping money where I found it, and one day in Greenleaf, I ran into a person I wish I'd never met."

Mathew was impressed she survived independently for months in that lawless time.

"Order up." The server brought a large round cast iron pan. He set down a hotplate and settled the pizza on top. He sliced the pie in front of them and asked if they wanted anything else.

"Two waters please," Mathew asked.

The server dipped his head with a smile and left. Mathew split the stack of plates and served a slice to them both. "Give it a minute so you don't burn the roof of your mouth."

"There was a bar there," she continued. "It was the only one for many miles. Travelers and drifters passed through and never returned, so the crowd on average was less than courteous, understand?"

Mathew nodded. He didn't like where this story was headed. While he waited for the pizza to cool, his hands balled into fists.

"I was minding my business, and a man wanted more than I was willing to give him. Jaime Perez. You met him at my house. I refused him and he took me to a back room. Are you all right?"

Mathew heard snarling and realized it came from his throat. He needed to calm down. It was a story, an old story, and Jaime Perez would never reach Verity again, he would see to it.

"Just fine."

"Here's your water." The server brought two chilled mugs of water and set them on the table. "How is your pizza?" He frowned at the untouched pie.

"Too hot, but we'll be digging in momentarily. Thank you."

"Great, just let me know if you need anything else."

"Thanks."

When the server left, Verity continued her rage-inducing tale.

"He demanded I dance for him. I refused. He demanded..." she trailed off and her eyes glazed over as if trapped inside painful memories. "He demanded other things, and I refused again. He used his belt against me, and I turned against him—disfigured him, but I got away, and he's angry."

Mathew's gut took a well-earned sock. He was such an asshole. "I'm sorry. I'm so sorry for saying punishing you was reasonable. I was wrong and out of line. Please forgive me."

Her eyes cast aside for just a flicker. He picked up his warm slice and dug in with a moan. It was cheesy Italian seasoned doughy softness. Pure amazing.

Verity copied his move, and she nodded and murmured in agreement. "It's delicious. Wonderfully delightful."

"I'm glad you like it."

The visual of her tale unleashed a fury he had buried since the days his father had wrongfully punished him. Mathew fought his hands from fisting and slamming the table. He pictured Jaime Perez's snarl overlaying his father's. When he returned her to her rightful time, he promised himself Jaime Perez would never get his hands on her again.

MATHEW CARRIED ALL her bags upstairs, unlocked the door to his apartment, and set them on the couch. She was very excited to explore her new clothes. Verity didn't know how she would repay him for his kindness. She didn't have any money. She didn't have a job...or did she? Verity decided to help in Mathew's clinic to pay off the debt. Brilliant.

Mathew placed the meal leftovers inside one of the pearly

cubes in the kitchen, the refrigerator or something like that. He tried to explain them all, but which one was which, and which one did what? She'd get it, eventually.

"Did you want a shower right away or how about a movie?"

"Shower?"

"It's like a bath, only you stand and hot water rains down on you."

"That sounds heavenly."

"Shower it is."

She followed Mathew into the washroom and admired the bathtub. It had been several days since she'd gotten to wash up, and an indoor rain of hot water sounded impossible. But so many things impossible to her were normal everyday things to these people. He leaned over the tub and turned a knob. Water poured in through a spigot. His hand rested inside the downpour and he said, "It'll be a minute before it heats up."

He shook the water off his hand and stalked up to her with fire in his eyes. Heat roared through her body. She wanted him so much it hurt. "I'll help you remove your new clothes, if you'd like."

"Yes, please."

His fingers slipped across the flesh of her lower belly as he tugged the fastener free. Mathew lowered his head and paused. With smoldering eyes, he waited for her response. Verity tilted her head, granting him access to her throat. Hot lips seared against her neck. Fire roared through her body, pooling at her core. Steam billowed around them as if cloaking what they'd planned to do next.

Mathew's mouth licked and sucked down her throat and

across her shoulders. With her eyes closed, her body was alive with need not knowing where the next tingle of a kiss would appear. His fingers drew her face toward him, and his lips crashed against hers. She unzipped her jeans and locked her fingers behind his neck, drawing him closer. He moaned and curled into her body. She reached down to grasp his desire and found an erection begging for release. He yelped in surprise and jumped back.

Mathew's eyes drank in her exposed skin and he spun in place.

"I'm sorry. That wasn't…proper." He pointed to soaps sitting on invisible shelves along the bath wall. "Use whatever you need. Fresh towels are here in the cabinet. Turn the knob all the way when you're finished." He stepped out and closed the door behind him.

Verity stood there in confusion while steam blotted out the looking glass. What did she do wrong? He was enjoying himself, as was she. Did he think she was unclean? Well, of course, he did. She probably smelled like a compost heap, having not cleaned since sinking into the pig's muck when Mathew first tried to rescue her from Jonathan.

Verity finished undressing and stepped into the steamy rain. All the muscles in her body eased, and she struggled to stay standing. How she'd ever lived without this, she couldn't understand. She soaped herself and rinsed. Then mucked the soap into her hair. Rinsing with rain pouring down was so much easier. She turned the knob off, and the rain trickled to a stop. Verity stepped out onto the mat and covered herself in a fluffy towel. What should she wear?

"Mathew?" she called through the door.

He responded so fast it was as if he waited on the other side for her. "Yes?"

"I don't have sleeping garments."

"Hmmm. Didn't think of that. I'll get you a shirt to wear, hang tight."

She waited, using a second towel to pat her hair dry. She found a comb and picked all the knots out. The wild waves were tame just below her shoulders.

An arm popped into the bathroom and she accepted the offering.

"Thank you."

The door closed again, and she dressed herself. It was an oversized men's shirt. Soft, warm, and hung just below her upper thighs. Not modest, but she wasn't prudish in private. It smelled just like Mathew's laundry soap—fresh and airy. Her wet hair dampened the shirt's neckline. She picked up her towels and placed them in the hamper. Then she stepped out, followed by a cloud of steam.

Mathew stood there. He scratched the back of his head and he cast his bashful eyes aside. "Matt."

"Excuse me?"

"You can call me Matt. I just realized you hadn't used my name until now. Sorry about the wardrobe options. I don't have any women's clothing here."

"I like your shirts. Far more comfortable than a corset." She tried to meet his eyes, but he kept avoiding her. Did he not approve of her clothing? He was the one who chose it!

"How about a movie?" he asked.

"What's a movie?"

"Stories you can watch." He smiled, and his hands shifted with an uncertainty, as if he wanted to do something, but fought against it. She wanted him to kiss her again. She was clean now, but she would take his lead, so she wouldn't offend again.

"Have a seat. This one is a classic and entirely fitting. *Back to the Future*." He pressed buttons on a narrow black device and the dark screen on the wall lit up with images and words that Verity did not understand. He waved her over, and she sat near him on the couch. "Do you like popcorn?"

"I don't know. I've heard of it but never tried it."

"I'll take care of that." A knowing smile crossed Mathew's face as he jumped off the couch and rummaged in a cabinet. He removed a clear covering from a small brown envelope and placed it inside of one of the pearly cubes.

"Stove?" she asked.

"Microwave."

She snapped her fingers. One of these days she'd get it right. It beeped when he pressed buttons, and it hummed while the envelope turned inside. Soon it was filling most of the microwave's cavity with a raucous popping. It beeped to signal cooking complete. He shook out the bag into a bowl and brought it back, steaming and smelling of butter. In two minutes, he fixed a toasty snack. She still couldn't wrap her brain around it. She lifted a pinch to her lips and chewed. A groan of pleasure escaped her lips.

"How is it?"

"Wonderful. How am I going to survive without all the marvelous inventions?"

Mathew's eyes cast aside again. His fingers lifted a pinch, and he didn't answer. He selected an image on the screen.

The movie was the most entertaining and frightful thing she'd ever seen. It made her laugh in many places, and at other parts she nibbled her fingernails. She hoped he didn't mind her asking questions throughout the movie, as much of it was so confusing.

"Did that really happen?"

"No. It's just a movie. It's not real. The time traveling Delorean makes you wonder though, since you're here."

"You have a car, not a Delorean."

"Right. And I didn't find you while driving. In a couple days I'll hunt down Kiko and get answers."

Verity wasn't sure she wanted answers. This new life was almost perfect. The only way it could get better was if Mathew joined her in his bed, and if she could go to California—if it still existed.

# Chapter Eleven

VERITY'S MIND BUBBLED with excitement as she worked the reception desk. She scheduled, changed, and canceled appointments. Oh, and she answered phones, placed people on hold, and asked Becca for help on more complicated questions. She had never been so excited to *work* in her life. They called this work! These modern people haven't spent time on a farm before.

After Mathew finished the last appointment of the day, they were going to a place called Bay Beach. She didn't have swim wear, but Mathew insisted she didn't need it. She was too excited to argue.

"Here we are," Mathew said as he navigated the car into a vast parking lot with a statuesque white building looming ahead. After unfastening her tether, she stepped out. Her face tilted toward the sky above, where strange bright colored metal objects twirled and spun. Fear and excitement battled in her head. Mathew extended his hand, and she grasped it tight.

"What do you think?"

"What is all this?" It looked like bright metal torture devices, but people lined up for their turn, and laughter and screaming came from the equipment. If possible, it sounded like screams

of excitement. What a novel concept that was.

"Amusement park. Let's ride. Any of these look particularly interesting to you?"

She searched for one with less screaming. She wanted to take it easy on her first ride. A wheel, larger than any house or factory she'd ever seen, towered over the whole park. Her feet ate up the pavement while her hand dragged Mathew along. "That one." She stood in line and waited her turn.

"Ferris wheel. Nice choice," he said.

"I've never seen anything like it. And people do this for fun? Whenever they want?"

Mathew chuckled. "Yeah. Well, it's not open all year round. So, mostly in the summer."

"Everyone must be so happy in the future. Work is easy. You get to have fun every day. Traveling is fast. It's just incredible."

A gentle thumb rubbed her hand. "I'm glad you're having a great time."

"I am. I really am." Verity bounced on her heels while the attendant opened the gate for her. Mathew handed the attendant the tickets, and Verity climbed onto the carriage but struck out her arms for balance. The seat moved! Mathew grasped her waist and helped her sit. His arm wrapped around her shoulders and he pulled a metal bar over their laps.

"Nervous?"

"A little."

The attendant pulled a lever and their seat moved just enough for the next carriage to unload and reload. It continued until the ride attendant replaced the whole wheel's passengers, and Verity got a bird's-eye view of the city from the top of the wheel. "It's

incredible. Look"—she pointed—"I recognize that hill! And the river. It's smaller than it looks from the banks." The park was full of tiny people walking around and seagulls scamming scraps of food. Her eyes landed on the bay, glistening under the sunlight. She couldn't see any schooners or steamboats, but she spotted familiar white sails in the distance. "It's beautiful. Thank you."

"Anytime." He rubbed his thumb along her hand again, and her stomach felt hollow and tingly before her brain registered the free fall down the wheel. Verity screamed in excitement. They lifted back up the wheel and her body pulled toward the ground, throwing her stomach all over her belly. When they passed the apex again, her body wanted to fly away. She had never experienced anything like it before.

When the Ferris wheel ended, Verity brought Mathew to several more rides until the tickets ran out. Her favorite was the Scat, a standing ride that spun like a mixer. Then he brought her inside the white building, and she tended herself in the washroom. Her hair was wilder than ever, tossed and turned by the rides, and her eyes were wide and bright. Out in a common area, Mathew waited for her, holding bags of food. Lines of bright games were chirping and ringing against the walls. Kids were laughing and playing. She was comforted knowing the future would be better than she could've imagined.

"I have one more place I want to show you," Mathew said, leading her to the car. They drove through the city and up onto what Mathew called the freeway. After the rides at the park, the freeway speeds weren't as scary. They exited and rolled through back roads. Up a hill was an empty parking lot. They stepped out

and Mathew brought the food with them. He set it on a picnic table, and she dug right in.

"Aren't you hungry?" she asked.

"Sort of. My stomach isn't a fan of the Scat. Just give me a minute." He released a deep calming breath. "What do you think of the view? This is Overlook Hill."

Verity craned her neck with a mouthful of burger and froze. She *had* been here, in her own time. Back then it was all farmland with scattered tree clusters, and small sprinklings of buildings making up Astor, Bridgeport, and Navarino. But now, a city bigger than the Chicago of her time swallowed the three villages. The view was different with freeways snaking around, and tall fingers of buildings clustered around the downtown area. Cotton balls of treetops dotted the land. And wires! There were wires strung all over. Ships in the bay were being unloaded by cranes touching the clouds. Those ships with smokestacks were nothing like the schooners and their massive sails or the newer steamboats she was familiar with.

"It's breathtaking." She took another bite.

"I thought you'd like it."

"This has been the best day of my life," she said toward the view. The picnic table shifted and Verity turned to find Mathew sitting next to her with a gentle smile. She swallowed her bite. His bright blue eyes scorched with desire, and Verity glanced around for spying eyes. They were alone, giving her a boldness that she'd learned from her brothers.

Mathew's hand reached up and caressed her jaw. "I'm glad you're having a great time. That's why we're here." His nose brushed against hers and his hand steadied the back of her neck.

"Are you not having a great time?" She set her burger on the table.

"I'm enjoying myself right now. I can't figure you out."

"About what?"

His finger stroked her ear and a tickle shifted her head.

"How can a woman, from a century of hard work and manual labor, figure out a computer in a few hours?"

Verity hadn't realized her accomplishment was impressive. With the seriousness in his composure, his compliments were genuine, and that surprised her more than anything. Once again, a roaring need for Mathew consumed her.

"There's something up here"—he touched her temple—"that I cannot get enough of."

His index finger stroked her lower lip, and a sense of urgency propelled her forward. Verity's lips found Mathew's and she fisted his soft dark hair. Her body flooded with heat while his lips begged for more. She scooted closer to him and he moaned beneath her lips. His soft hands slipped under her shirt, caressing her belly. Verity's breathing hitched at his touch.

Mathew's hand explored up her chest while he kissed her neck. Small breaths came from her mouth and Verity dared a bold move. Her fingers sought the length beneath his trousers and slid along him. His hips shifted under her palm. She went further, fighting the fasteners of his trousers. With the sound of the zipper, Mathew stopped. Again. She wanted to scream.

They both panted in each other's faces and Verity searched his eyes for answers. Had she done something wrong?

"What is it?" she asked. His face was pained, his eyes saddened. She begged, "What's wrong?"

THE SOUND OF THE zipper snapped Mathew back to reality. He wanted her so much, but her vigorous curiosity hid a childlike innocence, which was wrong of him to take. Wrong of him to want to take. Buying her fast food and taking her out a couple times did not mean he was owed anything. She deserved better than that. She deserved better than him. What was he doing? Mathew shook his head to clear the muddled mess his libido was creating.

Verity's searching gaze drove him wild, distracting him from his responsibilities. His shaking hands retreated from her sweet skin. But he feared he was already lost to her, and doing what was necessary meant causing him more pain than he could bear.

He wanted to show her all the great things the world offered. He wanted to show her—not that he was bragging—great pleasure. But then what? He'd be sending her home to her family. Not that Mathew understood quantum mechanics, but Kiko mentioned a cataclysmic event, and Mathew would do whatever necessary to keep the present as it should've been.

He needed to find Kiko. He'd already completed his end of the bargain—help her with her dream research project by preventing Verity from getting captured. In return Kiko would help him file the missing person's report. She needed to uphold her end of the deal. He hadn't heard from his sister in weeks and he feared the worst. And he should be in his office right now figuring out an answer to the financial issues plaguing the clinic.

"Matt, what is it?"

Sunlight and flying seagulls haloed her. Verity's intense gaze melted him, and he wanted to kiss each individual freckle and savor the time to find all of them. And then he admitted his

deficiency—he couldn't take her innocence away. "I can't do it."

"Can't do what?" Her hand reached down. Mathew arched in surprise and she smiled deviously. "Everything feels just fine."

Was she not as innocent as she appeared?

"Have you ever been with a man before?" Mathew asked.

Verity's face pinched in annoyance. "I'm not a virgin, if that's what you're asking." The sharp tone of her statement made him believe in her time people frowned upon the loss of the social status.

His brows popped in surprise at her revelation. "I just want to be sure you're comfortable with what's going on."

Verity relaxed and smiled. "I am not naïve to a man's body. He was Mother's choice. But things didn't work out after a devious afternoon in the barn."

Mathew's brain created an unsavory image from that. "Because he wasn't good enough?"

"Apparently, I wasn't."

He couldn't believe that for a hot minute.

Verity gave him a soft smile. Her hand cupped his wiry jaw. "Let's finish eating."

Reluctantly, Mathew resumed his seat across from her, and fisted his cool burger. His stomach was finally capable of holding food. Amusement park rides were murder on his gut and made him dizzy beyond enjoyment, but after seeing her excitement, he didn't regret the experience. He wished she could stay. He wanted to see her smiling face at his clinic, take lunch breaks with her, and go home together after work. And that reminded him of his missing employee, April.

"My sister's missing."

Verity paused her chewing and swallowed a thick bite.

"I'm sorry. Do you know where she went?"

Mathew shook his head. "Not at all. Not even a city name. April worked for me at the clinic, alongside Becca. She had a boyfriend who was kind of a jerk, and I knew she was miserable." Mathew ate a fry. "She was never going to be happy with him. After six months of dating, Levi told me he wanted to marry her. I was actually relieved, because I knew she'd freak out. So, being the overprotective big brother, I encouraged his hideous proposal idea, knowing it would split them apart."

"Sometimes we have to do things for the ones we love, even if they can't see the good in it," Verity said.

Mathew smiled. When they finished eating, he said, "Let's take a drive." They packed up their trash, and he navigated them back down the steep hill and through town to April and Kiko's rental house. His stomach knotted, wishing she'd rush out the front door with a big grin on her face. He pulled into her short driveway and unbuckled. "Come with me."

They walked up the steps, and Mathew sucked in a deep breath. What if April answered the door? What if she was home safe? Hope swelled within him, and he knocked. No one answered. He knocked again with more conviction. They waited, but no one came. Mathew used his cell and called Kiko, but it sent him to voicemail. Now he felt like an ass for trying to interrupt her family emergency. Verity wasn't in any danger here, but her family and her life were back there.

Sighing and turning around, he sat on the cement steps. Verity mirrored him.

"You miss her, huh?" She placed at hand on his back and

rubbed with a soothing motion.

He ran a hand through his hair and said, "You know, I told her to go get a life, and I guess—I hope—she did. But I haven't heard from her or seen her in weeks. Maybe she figured out what I did and hates me for it? I don't know. If she hates me forever, so be it. I just need to know she's safe. A letter, a text message, anything, just to tell me she's okay. But it's been radio silence on her end, almost like she just vanished."

"I'm sorry." Verity held his hand, and he was thankful. After his mom had abandoned them for California, and his dad moved into assisted living after a grievous injury during a drunken spat in a bar, April was all the family he had left. It tore him apart to have her missing.

"I know what that feels like," she said.

"How so?"

"I was eighteen years old when Mom set me up with Bernard—the barn incident I told you about. She passed a few days after, and Barnard left without proposing. When Dad got sick, he scoured the area for acceptable suitors for Johnny. He set up an arranged marriage for him, but it didn't work out either. Dad demanded I agree to a contract as well. I refused. I ran away from home. After that thing I told you about with Jaime Perez, I went back home like a wounded puppy to face my fate. Dad had already died, and I missed the funeral. Johnny and Graham are all I have left."

"That must've been hard, missing the funeral."

"Yeah, but not as hard as being a prisoner in my own home."

Mathew's empty hand balled into a fist. His primal protective urges fought his calm exterior. "Did your brothers hurt you,

too?" He wouldn't return her to a family who didn't treat her with the respect and dignity she deserved, cataclysmic event be damned. He'd take the risk. For her.

She chuckled. "No. They're good to me. They forced me to stay home for my own safety. I was hiding from Jaime."

"That was why you darted away when someone came to the door."

"Every time."

"Why didn't Johnny have him arrested?"

"If you have a disagreement, money or dual is the only resolution with a crooked sheriff and missing mayor. Sometimes a bride,"—Verity snorted—"But obviously that's not an option, and Johnny refuses the extortion payment. I didn't want my brother to lose a duel, because then I would be at Jaime's mercy again. He doesn't know mercy." She shuddered.

That was enough of that story. Mathew stood and brought her to her feet, intent on bringing her somewhere safe. "Let's go home. Do you want to watch *Back to the Future Part Two*?"

Her eyes lit with excitement. "There's more to the story?"

"Three parts."

"Yes please. And more popcorn."

He hadn't realized things were so life-and-death back then. History books failed to deliver the right feel. Mathew was not capable of winning a duel, whether guns or fists. He hadn't been in a fight since he was a teen. He only needed money to pay Jaime off, and she'd be safe for good. Once again, his financial mess mucked up the rest of his life.

# Chapter Twelve

VERITY HUNG UP THE phone at the clinic and typed notes in the patient's chart using her index finger to hunt down each letter. Mr. Sylvester P. Hippopotamus—she asked for spelling confirmation twice—was being treated at another clinic for a second opinion about his fatigue. The poor cat was twenty pounds, and despite what Dr. McCall had recommended, the client believed her cat was just depressed. Verity didn't understand most of that, but she transcribed the dictation as was told to her. That was the second client today that decided a hiatus was in their best interest.

Becca hung up her phone, and Verity asked, "Do clients switch doctors regularly?"

"Not really. Most clients become loyal after a few visits. If you run a special, then a bunch of new customers show up for the deal and then leave for the next one. Occasionally a new customer sticks around. Why?"

"I just had two clients call to say they were seeking a new clinic and want records forwarded."

"Hmmm. That is odd. Everyone loves Dr. McCall."

Verity understood why. He was kind and generous, smart and sexy too. She caught a few eighty-year-old Pomeranian owners

giving him the sparkle eye.

Becca smiled. "You know, sometimes I see him giving you that look."

"What look?" Verity's chest bloomed with affection.

"That same look you have right now," Becca said. "A lovey dovey dopey grin. I can see it in both of you. What's keeping you two apart, anyway? Dr. McCall's been lonely for so long. This last week, though, he's been light on his toes and lit up like the fourth of July."

"What do you mean?" Verity was jumping in her skin knowing there was a chance he liked her. She noticed that he smiled frequently around her, but she didn't have any comparison.

"Just look at him. It's obvious, and it's great to see him happy. The man deserves it after everything he's been through."

Verity gazed at Mathew's closed office door as if she could see through it, wondering if he was thinking of her at that moment. Earlier, when Verity went into his office to inform him the next client had arrived, Verity noticed a pile of mail on his desk, and when Mathew took lunch by himself, he seemed to be stressed. She didn't think his sister being missing was the entirety of his problems. Verity hoped he wasn't fretting over trying to get her home. She didn't want to go. She worked hard with Becca each day to learn all she could to convince Mathew to let her stay.

"He seems to be suffering some hardships right now," Verity said.

Becca's eyes glistened under the blinding artificial lights. Had she said something wrong?

"Yep." Her voice was thick as if fighting tears. Becca snorted and Verity noticed the woman was on the verge of sobbing.

"Are you all right?" she asked gently.

"Sure." Becca sniffed. "Why?"

"Pardon me for my frankness, but you appear to need a hug." Verity opened her arms, and tears sprung to the woman's eyes as she eagerly fell into Verity's embrace. She rubbed her palm across the woman's back in comfort. "It's all right. I've got you. Everything will be all right."

After a few minutes, Becca's shaking shoulders calmed down, and Verity held out the tissue box. Becca snapped a few out of the box and snorted her sinuses clear. "Wow, I needed that. Thank you. Dr. McCall needs me here, no matter how much he insists I take time off, especially since his sister disappeared. I couldn't leave him with no staff. And I need to be here to keep my mind off..." Becca trailed off with her voice on the verge of breaking.

"What happened?"

"I..." Her voice cracked. "I lost my baby a couple weeks ago," she said with thick emotion in her voice. Her lips twisted, threatening another fit.

Verity's chest constricted, and her hand touched her throat. She had seen the pain of a mother's loss. It was common back home, but she had never experienced it herself. Mothers mourned for weeks, tired and withdrawn, but they still functioned—shopped, washed, tended. The only thing that seemed to pull them back up was news of a healthy delivery. She couldn't imagine that kind of pain. "I'm so sorry."

"Everything was fine until the last minute and then...it

wasn't." She inhaled a jagged breath. "Now I bury my face in work to keep my mind busy, even though these waves of pain catch me off guard. Sometimes I can hardly function. I don't know what I'd do without coming here every day."

Mathew never said Verity could stay in the future, nor that he even wanted her to. Sadness percolated into her, and a spear of pain struck her chest when she faced the truth—she would be returning to the past. "Please don't worry about your job. Even though Matt...Er, Dr. McCall seems to be struggling with something, you'll always have your job here. Soon it'll be all you again until Dr. McCall can hire a replacement."

"Oh, no. Where are you going?" Becca blew her nose into another tissue.

"Home," she said simply with a tinge of her own sadness.

"I'm sorry to see you go. You're a fine worker and a quick learner. We could use you around here, but if that's the case, then good luck to you. And thank you for everything."

"And to you," Verity said. The sadness of the conversation drew her down and she fought to crack a smile.

MATHEW SAT AT HIS office desk staring at a dreaded stack of ignored mail. He opened Quickbooks to download yesterday's data since he'd cut out early with Verity and hadn't done it. Grim as usual. He selected a random piece of mail and tore it open with his index finger. Letter number one informed him Internet service was going up an extra twenty bucks a month.

Great.

Next, property tax assessment. Value increase of over a

thousand dollars, which meant a few more bucks a year for property taxes.

Great.

Next. An overdue payment notice for his SUV. Oops. Mathew logged in and set up the payment for today, plus the late fee. Ugh.

He needed a miracle to clear his mess. The idea of a lottery ticket still lingered. But the odds of winning were so marginal, the ten bucks would be a guaranteed waste.

If only he could go back in time...

Mathew patted the time travel trinket in his pocket. Perhaps he could go back in time and buy a lottery ticket and choose the winning numbers. But then he'd have to split the winnings with the true winner, and what if the true winner needed it for medical bills or something? He would feel retched for taking half their much-deserved winnings. What if he went back farther and invested a bunch of money? He didn't have a bunch of money. Catch-twenty-two. What if he opened a savings account and interest accrued over a long period, perhaps from 1853 to the present?

Mathew opened a savings calculator website and plugged in theoretical numbers to see what he'd get. To earn enough money over a century and a half to cover all his debts, he would have to invest ten thousand dollars in 1853's dollars. He didn't have that kind money, once again. Even if he did, how would he convert money from the present day to passable money in the past?

Mathew strummed his fingers on his desk. To start with, he needed cash. He locked his computer screen. Endless possibilities floated before his eyes. What would it be like to be

free of the incessant buzzing debts? Would there be silence? Would he sleep soundly for once? Seeing a solution—albeit a very slim, long-shot of a solution—had his feet moving. Before he rushed out of his office, a whiney whimper from the surgical holding reminded him of the pup who'd been left waiting.

"Oh, hey, Becca? Did Mr. Van Grunden pay for Snoopy's surgery yet?"

Becca typed in her computer to bring up his file. "No, not yet. Do you want me to call him again?"

"Give him a gentle prodding, will you? Ladies, keep my calendar clear for the next hour. I'll be back." Verity and Becca exchanged confused looks. Mathew couldn't explain the out of character change of schedule, because he wasn't sure his plan would work. He needed to visit a place that had money. Mathew entered the credit union and, finding no line, stepped up to the teller.

"Good afternoon, what can I help you with today?" A young woman with hair pulled into a smooth bun smiled politely.

"I need a business loan."

"Sure, can I have your name?"

"Mathew McCall."

She lifted the handset of a multiline phone and said to him, "Please have a seat over there and someone will be with you shortly."

"Thanks." Mathew drummed his hands on the counter's edge a couple times before plopping into plush chair in the lobby. He watched the young teller call a loan officer. She smiled and nodded as if the officer could see her. So far, so good. His knee bounced in nervous excitement. If this idea worked, he'd be set.

Debts would be gone, monthly cash flow would be comfortable, and he'd be free to buy a house, get married...

Wait. His leg stopped bouncing.

That word, *married*, popped into his head, and the first person he thought of was Verity. He pictured her screaming with excitement on the Ferris wheel. Even though his stomach took a beating, he *enjoyed* the ride. He pictured how her face lit up with eagerness to try new things, to taste new things. There was adventure in her that Mathew sorely lacked—that he didn't even know he wanted. The crushing emptiness lifted when he was with her. Was Verity the reason why his determination was finally going to succeed? What would it take for her to give up her brothers for him? He felt like a selfish bastard for even thinking it.

"Mathew?" A plump woman with smart eyes, a friendly smile, and a black suit held out a hand in greeting. Mathew stood and shook then followed her to her office. "I understand you are interested in a business loan?"

"Yes."

"Let me pull up your file and we'll get the application filled out."

Mathew gave her all the information she requested. He used the clinic as collateral. This had better pan out, or he'd just sealed the foreclosure notice on his future. His knee bounced while he watched the loan officer click away on her keyboard, eyes glued to her screen. She frowned, then relaxed. She squinted. Mathew's heart thumped erratically. It was too soon for the plan to fail. Please, please, please, he begged.

Finally, she smiled.

"Good news. You're approved. How would you like it?"

Mathew blew out a breath. "Deposit into checking, please."

Paperwork in hand, Mathew drove over to Kiko and April's house. He knocked on the door, mostly expecting no answer, but the door opened, and Mathew's brows lifted.

"Come on in," Kiko said.

Mathew entered and closed the door behind him. "I'm sorry for intruding after your family emergency, but—"

"I suspect you'll be needing some identification for Verity to fly," Kiko finished.

Mathew tilted his head. "How did you…?"

Kiko smiled but stayed silent.

"Right. There wasn't really a family emergency." She'd told him she'd been time traveling longer than he'd been alive. He wondered if she even had family, and he felt an ache of sadness for her. "More secrets of which I am not privy."

Kiko held out a small leather book, and Mathew accepted it. "What's this?" After reading the cover, his stomach sank. "How did you get this?" An edge of anger tinged his question.

"She left it behind. Since April and Verity are passable in appearance, I think it's fitting she borrowed it."

"This will work." Mathew tapped the book against his open palm. "Why would she give this to you?"

"I don't have time to chat right now. I've another client to assist."

"Okay, sure. We need to talk later. Thanks for this, ah…thanks." Mathew tucked his sister's passport into his back pocket. Something didn't sit right about April leaving it behind. Was she that angry with him? At least he knew she didn't leave

the country.

Mathew returned to the clinic with a mix of worry for his sister and excitement for his future. For the first time in a long time, he truly had hope. Mathew opened the front door and announced, "Becca, hold down the fort for a minute. Verity, come with me to my office."

The women exchanged glances again, and Becca shrugged. Verity followed him and closed the door behind her.

He leaned against his desk while she stood just in front of his door, arms crossed over her chest.

"How would you like to visit New York City?"

Verity's eyes popped wide. "The real New York City?"

"Yes," he said, a smile broad across his face.

"I'd love it. I can't even picture it. I mean, I never got to go there in my time, but I can't imagine it in the future." The woman was bouncing with that adventure he loved so much. Mathew's chest swelled. He wanted to show her the world, and he would do it.

"Great. We'll finish up here and then go home to pack."

"Yes, boss."

Mathew froze. Verity stepped out of his office and closed the door. She called him boss. She thought she worked here. Why would she *want* to work here? She had put in half a week's worth of hours already. He would get her the paycheck she'd earned, too.

The computer screen flickered to life, and Mathew browsed websites for the best price and bought airline tickets. Looks like they'd be seeing Chicago on a layover. Too bad he hadn't rolled the cost of the tickets into his business loan. Honestly, he was

surprised they'd even approved him with his debt to income ratio. He was tapped out for credit as it was. Mathew inputted his credit card and it was accepted by the skin of his teeth. He printed their tickets, as backup in case the app didn't work, just on time for Becca to knock and announce a client had arrived.

"Becca, can you clear my schedule for tomorrow and the day after? I'm taking a vacation." As the foreign word left his lips, he realized this would be is first vacation in years. Whatever it was Verity was doing to him, he liked it. Becca's eyes widened in concern, but Mathew calmed her fears. "Don't worry, it'll be paid time off."

"Thanks, doc." Her cheeks pinked with a smile, and Mathew felt like he was doing good by his people.

That evening Mathew drove Verity home and dug out two duffel bags from the top shelf of his closet. "Two days, mostly spent in the airport. Pack light and we won't have to check bags." Verity glanced down at her small pile of modern clothes. He added, "Or just pack all the clothes you have."

Late that night, they hit the sheets ready to travel halfway across the country on a whim of an idea. So many more things could go wrong before his hatched plan could succeed. Sleep was restless and slow in coming for Mathew.

TRAVELING TO NEW YORK City was such an exciting idea that Verity hadn't thought about how they would get there, only assuming a several-month trip in the car. She never would've guessed giant white bullets. Verity knew firsthand what happened when a bullet was shot through the air—it had to stop

somehow. Mathew explained pilots could control the stopping and going and that it was safe to fly. The armed guards of the future and beeping machines were scary, but she made it through with Mathew's coaxing words. She double-checked her tether, making sure it was fastened properly. Her hands gripped the armrests of her narrow seat.

"Remember the roller coaster?" Mathew asked.

"How could I forget?"

"It's sort of like that, but less windy. We'll be in New York City in five hours."

Verity spun her head. It was inconceivable. "Five weeks, you mean?"

Mathew chuckled. "Five hours to arrive at our destination." Verity couldn't wrap her brain around the idea. He continued, "And we have a layover in Chicago too. So, you'll get to see one of the busiest airports in the world, albeit briefly."

"Chicago and New York City in five hours? Back home, a trip to Chicago would take a week. The modern world sure is fast."

"Everything is fast here. If you try to slow down, you get left behind."

Verity glanced out the small round window. Even from here the road below looked far away. She couldn't imagine what it would be like from the clouds. Guilt bore down on her when Mathew insisted she take the superior seat.

"Are you sure you don't want the view?"

"It's your first experience, it should be special. Besides, I've flown before."

Because of how he tensed at the amusement park and his

delayed ability to eat afterward, she wondered if the view scared him. If flying was going to feel like the giant wheel in the sky, Verity felt less afraid. Turned out she loved roller coasters and all things high and fast. She relaxed her grip on the armrests.

Still, Mathew was treating her to this trip, and she didn't want him to feel sick, but what could she do about it now?

"Verity, there will be a safety speech. It's required for all flights. Don't worry about what they say, okay?"

"Sure."

Mathew exhaled a long steady breath.

Just as he described, a flight attendant gave the speech, and the airplane jerked into motion. Verity gasped with surprise and watched out the window as they drove around the massive parking lot and pointed toward a long road to nowhere. Within moments the airplane lurched forward, and their speed surpassed what she considered humanly possible. The ground blurred and then they were lifting above the trees with her stomach left several rows behind her. Verity couldn't process the view. Mathew exhaled another deep breath, and she turned to him. He was white as a sheet. She pressed her hand on top of his death grip on the armrest, and his hand was rigid and cold. She didn't understand his fear. The safety speech made this seem commonplace, and Mathew had flown before, so it would be safe.

Her stomach returned to her belly when the plane leveled out. The clouds floated under her window and the sun's rays shimmied across the open sky. Her eyes watered with the beauty.

"That was the second worst part," Mathew said as if convincing her that flying wasn't terrible. He didn't need to. She

loved it.

"What's the worst?"

"Landing."

"Are you afraid to fly?" she asked.

"That would be affirmative." His grip was still fastened to the armrest under her hand.

"Then why are we going on this trip?"

A corner of Mathew's lips lifted. "I want to show you the world."

A warmth spread through her like wildfire. "You did."

Mathew's strained face softened, and he grinned with those bright white teeth. One hand released its death grip and cupped her cheek. She closed her eyes and nuzzled his hand. When she opened them again, his eyes were glistening. She would show him the world, too.

Before she realized, they were landing. The overhead announcer said, "Welcome to Chicago."

So many planes swarmed around the airport. Verity's eyes popped at the airplane parking lot below. How did they avoid crashing? Inside the building, people everywhere wore sharp suits with phones at their ears. Mathew had explained the cell phone concept to her and showed her some videos of cats knocking things over and hiding in boxes. She had no idea pet cats could be so silly when they weren't mousing.

Everyone carried luggage and rushed toward their destinations. A massive board lit up with lines for the different flights, updating instantly. Life seemed so much more exciting and much easier than what she'd left behind.

They had lunch at a small airport café and boarded the next

flight with ease. After they arrived in New York City, Mathew hailed a taxicab.

"Nearest Chase bank, please."

People walked everywhere like ants marching in lines. Cars filled rows on the street, stopping and going every few feet. The life and energy pulsed through her. Everyone was amiable, and unlike what Jonathan had said, not all the men of this time carried arms. Mathew wasn't weak, he was normal.

Power lines draped across the sky like clothes lines, and rows of cars chugged along, clogging the streets. They stopped alongside a squat brick building. Mathew held her hand, and they went inside.

"What can I do for you today?" A pleasant teller with a strange headwrap asked.

"I want to buy silver bars. A lot of silver bars."

"I'll get the manager to help you. One moment."

A tall thin man with a dress shirt and tie approached. "Silver bars, eh? How many?"

Mathew leaned forward a little and kept his voice low. "Seventy thousand dollars' worth." Why was he whispering?

The manager's brows lifted in surprise. Then his lips curved with a greedy smile. "Sure thing. One moment please."

The manager carried a black bag into the vault, and the metal bars clinked as they knocked together. He returned with the heavy bag and strained setting it on the counter. He typed in his computer—she knew how to do that. Verity smiled.

"Total today is seventy-three thousand, eight hundred and ninety-eight, after tax."

"Can you remove a few? Seventy was my limit."

"Yes, sorry sir."

"Now it's seventy thousand, three fifty. Will that do?"

Mathew sighed and ran his hand through his hair. "That's close enough." He handed over a card, and the manager smiled.

"Here's your receipt. Would you like it in the bag?"

Mathew laughed and took the receipt, tucking it inside his wallet along with the card. He hefted the bag up on his shoulders. A chorus of jingling sounded from the bag.

"Wow. That's heavy," Mathew said. He didn't strain like the teller had and Verity admired the muscle under his thin dress shirt. He whispered into her ear, "Come on, we don't want to attract attention."

Verity followed him outside, and they walked behind the building near a tall private fence. "Grab onto me. Here's the next part of the trip. I hope this works."

"Hope what works?"

"An impossibility to fix my future."

Verity bear hugged his waist as she did before when Jaime had his gun pointed at her and Mathew. She closed her eyes and when she opened them, her mouth gaped open. "You brought me back home?"

She didn't know whether to be frightened by revisiting the past or amazed at seeing New York City in two different centuries. Rather than the hard streets and sleek buildings, dirt and sparse low buildings made of wood siding and flaking paint appeared. And rather than yellow taxis moving people, horses pulled carriages. Gone are the bicycle messengers skittering around cars. Instead more horses maneuvered around slower wagons filled with raw materials. And no more phones. Many

men carried newspapers, and some were reading while walking. So different, but so much the same. New York City wasn't California, but it was still better than home.

# Chapter Thirteen

Queens, New York
1853

MATHEW SLIPPED THE trinket from Kiko back into his pocket. It worked. Hot damn it had actually worked. They were back in time again, and first things first—he needed to unload the silver bars before he got mugged. He hailed a horse-and-buggy version of a cab and helped Verity climb up inside.

"To Winter Garden Theater?" the cab driver asked.

"What?"

"Your clothes resemble that of the theater."

"New York Stock Exchange."

"Hmmm. Yes, sir."

The cab driver flicked a whip at the single horse, and they jetted off west down Fulton Street. "We're not near your home," Mathew explained. "But we are back in your time."

"What are we doing here?"

"I'm running an errand to help me out in the future." He pointed to the duffel bag full of silver.

One more unbelievable step had been completed, and the most harrowing was yet to come.

"So, this trip is about you?" Verity asked with a sharp edge.

Mathew was taken aback. The weight of the black bag shifted on his shoulder and the bars clinked inside. "What do you mean?"

"You said this was a vacation to show me the world, and now it's about money? I'm not ignorant to the fact that you bought silver to sell here. The question is why did you lie to me?"

"I didn't lie. I want to show you the world, I just also happen to be doing myself a favor. We both win."

"What's winning? Is this a game? Am I a pawn in this game?"

"Whoa, calm down," Mathew said. His back ached under the weight. The bars weighed well over a hundred pounds.

"Don't tell me to calm down." A finger pointed at his nose.

Mathew's mouth dropped open and no words came out.

"Sir!" Verity yelled to the driver of the cab. "Please stop. I need to get off."

"No!" Mathew wouldn't leave her wandering New York City alone. Women were so hard. Why didn't he ever say the right things? "Stay with me. I'll finish my errand, and then we'll head back to the clinic, okay?"

The driver slowed the horse and stopped at the side of the dirt road. Verity glared at him with contempt all over her face. If she didn't want to go back to his clinic—a tornado of pain, confusion, and worry mixed his insides into a state of panic at her silence—then he'd take her home. He hated the thought, but it was her choice, and she was right to choose her home—her brothers were safe, and it was risky playing with time. Cataclysmic event echoed through his head. Why was he fighting nature?

She stood up, and he grasped her wrist in desperation. "Please

don't go. I'll take you home, back to your brothers, just as you want. But don't leave here."

"What do you know about what I want?" Her eyes narrowed in anger.

"You *don't* want to go back to your brothers?" Mathew asked in surprise, and hope bloomed once again.

She frowned. "I will not be told what to do or where to do it. I've crossed cities by myself with nothing but the clothes on my back. Don't you dare think you can tell me what I can and can't do."

"I never said that. I only want to help you. I thought the chance to see New York City would be exciting for you."

She turned her head away. "Let me go."

"Please stay with me," he begged. Pride be dammed, he begged. "I need to make a purchase, and then I'll take you wherever you want whenever you want. I promise." He released her wrist and silently pleaded for her to stay. He didn't care if he sounded like a fool, he wouldn't let her wander New York City alone with no money.

She crossed her arms and sat down next to him with her knees angled away. She was pissed, that was obvious, but Mathew wasn't sure why. They would hash it out when they got out of Queens.

"Continue, please," Mathew told the driver.

They arrived shortly thereafter, and Mathew exited, offering Verity a hand, but she climbed down alone. He stepped inside and kept glancing over his shoulder to be sure she was following. At the counter, he asked, "Where can I buy stock certificates?"

"Right here," a short, balding man said. "What stock do you

want?"

"New York Gas Light." According to his research, they would change their name to Consolidated Edison in just under a hundred years, but the certificate would retain its value.

"Good choice, young man. What is your payment method?"

Mathew slung the black bag onto the counter. "Silver bars."

The old man whistled. "How many bars you got there?"

Mathew's cheeks heated. He knew the dollar value in his time but never counted the bars. "I'm not sure, but I'd like to keep a few these for another purpose."

The balding man's brows popped and then he shrugged. Money's money. Thankfully, the balding man didn't question where Mathew got them from, because he didn't have answers. Mathew retained a sufficient number and returned them to the black bag, since he was a believer in not putting all one's eggs in one basket. They counted and stacked the rest in neat columns. The short man completed the transaction, filling out a paper stock certificate. With the most valuable sheet of paper in hand, Mathew tucked it into the bag, thankful for losing most of the weight. He turned around to leave and Verity was gone.

"Verity!" he called, running out of the building.


VERITY DASHED OFF down a cobblestone road. She expected the trip to be a fun adventure for them both, but insult cut her like a dagger knowing Mathew brought her as simply a tag-along. He used her. As if that wasn't enough, in the heat of her anger, he said he'd bring her back to her prison on the farm when he was done with her. Then Mathew had dumped a load of silver

bars onto the counter. A shifty little man's eyes perked up in excitement. She wasn't incompetent. Verity didn't know what the New York Stock Exchange was, but something nefarious was happening, and she wanted nothing to do with it. With fiery anger burning from Mathew's insult and illegal activities, she couldn't stay by his side.

Since Verity was on the eastern seaboard, her travels to California would only take longer. But she wouldn't swallow her pride and allow Mathew to bring her to the farm, making her journey shorter. Her independence was worth more than a few weeks' travel. Here in New York City, Queens to be exact, there was bound to be an opportunity somewhere for her to earn some coin.

The dirt roads snaked through tall buildings for miles in each direction. Carriages trotted along. People marched and zigzagged all over. She needed to find a place to dance. Verity could earn enough cash in one evening to find a place to sleep. Another couple more nights and she'd have enough to set off toward California for the gold rush and seek her fortune the honest way.

As she walked north, soon carriages swallowed her out of sight. She read building names, ducked under chutes pouring raw materials, stepped around stacks of logs, and avoided smacking into other pedestrians. A stumbling, laughing drunk flopped out onto the street at Verity's feet. "Howdy, miss. Care for a pint?" He hiccupped.

Verity sneered. "Yes, good sir, I would."

An obnoxious noise resembling an ass came from his throat while she helped him stand. Inside reeked of booze, coppery

blood, and urine. Smoke haze filled the space, and upbeat tunes came from a beat-up old piano in the corner. She walked straight toward the bartender to ask for an available dance stage when her hand was yanked from behind her, sending her twirling into the drunken mule's chest.

"Why's a pretty lady like you in this place?" His meaty finger slid down the fabric of her shirt. The shirt Mathew bought her. She didn't want to think about him now.

"Looking to dance," she said. "You?"

A big goofy grin crossed his face. "How much for a private session?"

Verity smirked. She'd give him a private dance and then get out. That was tame for her, anyway. "Two bucks for ten minutes."

"Two bucks is a lot of booze." He laughed, and it grated her ears. "But I bet you're worth it with clothes like them. Done!"

Verity didn't want to take him anywhere secluded, just in case, but she didn't want to be watched for free either. While she contemplated, her wrist was painfully wrenched.

"Get moving, I ain't paying for nothing." The pungent barrel-chested man dropped sloppily on a stool, but she wasn't deterred by the fool's threats.

"Let go or you'll be disappointed."

He snarled and dropped her wrist. She positioned herself over his lap and began swaying independent of the piano music across the room. If he was already this demanding, a few Peeping Toms were significantly less risky than taking him somewhere private. Maybe others would pay next for extra attention.

"Ah, that's more like it." A wide grin split his face. Spittle

oozed from the corner of his mouth. Verity turned her face with repulsion.

She wriggled her bottom and arched her back over his lap. With a crane of her neck, she angled her mouth to his hairy ear and blew softly. Verity feigned a moan. An erection poked her bottom, and Verity's face pinched with disgust. Luckily, he couldn't see it. A meaty hand jutted out from behind her and twisted her breast. Verity cried out. That was her breaking point, and she tried to run away, but his other arm grasped around her waist. "Keep wiggling or I'll take you somewhere else."

No one stopped his invasive hand. A few customers that noticed, turned the other way when Verity made eye contact. The rest were too drunk to care or too afraid to interrupt. His hands snaked into the band of her jeans and her sensual movements became jerky.

"That's right, keep going. Oh, yeah. One more minute and I'm going to show you what real fucking is like."

"Let me go," Verity demanded. "You've had your ten minutes now pay up and let me go."

"Oh, I don't think so. I can see all your curves. I know what you are. Now keep moving or I'll make you move."

"Stop!" she yelled and tried to twist herself away. It was no use. His drunken grip was like a vice.

"Let her go!" A booming voice shouted from across the room. Verity sought the source. Mathew shoved his way through the crowd. "Get your hands off my girl or lose your eye."

The drunken lout laughed his grating noise. He released Verity and stood in challenge, towering over Mathew. "That's a mighty fine threat from some small pretty boy. Money where

your mouth is, son."

The drunkard put his fists up in preparation to fight. Mathew reached over and pulled Verity behind him. "Stay close," he told her.

Mathew rolled his shirtsleeves to his elbows and slammed a right hook into the drunk's eye. It was as if he never saw it coming. The drunk spun and thumped onto a table. He didn't get up. Everyone in the room stared. Verity's face heated with embarrassment. After moments passed, and no one said or did anything, Mathew reached down and checked for a pulse at his neck. He stood, grasped her arm, and walked them toward the exit.

"He's alive," Mathew announced to the gawkers, and one by one they resumed their drinking, ignoring the limp man on the table.

"He owes me two bucks," she said, disappointed.

On the front step he yelled at her. "What the hell were you thinking? What were you doing in a place like that? Do you realize what could've happened?"

Tears sprung to her lids, watering her view. She never expected him to find out. Verity wanted to run away, but she wanted him to know the truth more. Then he would be disgusted with her enough to let her go free instead of forcing her back to her brothers. The pain of impending rejection was almost too much to bear. "It's what I am."

"What does that mean?"

"I dance." She wiped her eyes. "I *used* to dance. That's how I made money. That's how I got in trouble with Jaime Perez. That's why I was a prisoner at my family's farm."

Mathew's rigid posture softened. His voice was quieter. "I'm sorry."

She ran away in shame. Mathew called after her. "Wait. Where are you going?"

She stopped and faced him, keeping several yards' distance between them. "Don't you hate me now?"

"I don't hate you. Why would I?"

"I'm dirty. I'm tainted." Her reputation as a dancer left her unworthy of marriage according to her time.

"That's nonsense."

"I saw the look in your eye when you saw me in his hands. Don't lie to me again."

"I'm not lying. I don't care that you were dancing…Okay, I do care. But not because I don't approve, but because he was hurting you and holding you against your will."

Verity didn't move.

Mathew slowly closed the distance as if fearing she would run again. "You're smart woman. There's a reason for whatever you choose to do, and I respect that." She wanted him to hug her, to kiss her, but dirty, violated yuckiness swirled over her flesh.

Mathew closed the distance and hugged her anyway, unlocking the painful baggage of her past. Verity buried her face in his chest and sobbed.

He didn't hate what she was.


THEY STOOD IN THE middle of a seedy Queens borough in 1853. Mathew inhaled her feminine scent and held her tight while sobs wracked her body. Why had she been so angry with

him in the horse-drawn cab? More concerning was why she fled the safety of the stock exchange. His hand rubbed her back. "Why did you leave the Exchange?"

She lifted her face away from his chest and snorted. Her captivating green eyes bore into his. "I didn't want to be involved in anything illegal."

Mathew laughed at the irony. "I bought shares of stock. Perfectly legal."

"What is stock?"

"Pieces of companies. Investors—stockholders—give companies money to invest and earn profit. In exchange you earn interest on your investment. That's all. Are you okay, after that?" Mathew thumbed back toward the bar. The dirty scumbag had groped her, and it sent him over the edge. That was the first time he'd been in a fight since he was a teen. Never had he hit a grown man, and never had he knocked one out. His knuckles throbbed in a surprising amount of pain, but it had been worth it.

She nodded and sniffled. "Can we go home?"

"We?" Mathew's lips lifted prematurely.

"I don't want to stay here," she said as if that was obvious.

At least she was cooperating, so he could get her safely out of Queens. He smiled and guided her around a corner, out of prying eyes.

"Hold on tight."

With Verity's arms squeezing around his middle, Mathew pressed the button. When light returned to his vision, a car horn blared, and the driver was making angry gestures through the windshield. Mathew grasped Verity's hand and rushed them out

of the street. The driver was still yelling, but the closed windows made the sound too muffled to be bothered by it. The car roared by when they reached the curb.

"Feels good to be back," Mathew said.

"Yeah," she agreed. "Even if we had to appear in front of the dangerous end of the car."

Mathew laughed. He stuck out a hand and hailed a cab, bringing them to JFK airport in New York City. Verity stared at the exhibits inside the airport. A mini Ferris wheel lit up the center aisle, and she smiled in recognition. While they ate at a café inside, Verity remarked that the airport was similar to the mall, and he agreed, having never thought of it before.

They boarded their flight and Verity asked, "Do you want the window seat this time?"

"No, thank you."

"It's not my first time anymore. It's your turn."

"No. I insist. The view is all yours."

Verity smiled, and Mathew stuffed their bags into the overhead compartment. He sunk into his seat next to her, and Verity turned her face toward the window. To him, she was no longer the childlike innocent, marveling at modern technology and thrilled over microwave popcorn. She was a grown woman, fiercely independent, quick witted, and shockingly courageous. He burned for her even more. If his plan worked out, he'd finally feel *almost* worthy of her.

Unfortunately, the safety speech commenced, and his thoughts flashed to the emergency oxygen masks falling, alarms blaring, loud wind blasting through the cabin, and the captain shouting over the speaker…That was a path that lead to

nowhere good. He focused on breathing evenly while his hands crunched the armrests for the whole flight. When they arrived home, they were both beat with exhaustion. Mathew dumped his duffle down and set the black bag of remaining silver from the stock exchange on the kitchen counter.

"I need a shower. How about you?" Mathew asked.

"That sounds heavenly."

Mathew made a bold offer. He was no longer afraid of offending her or scaring her by offering intimacy. He only wanted to pleasure her. "How about we conserve water?"

Her cute nose crinkled in confusion. Then her crinkle smoothed, and her eyes widened. Mathew smiled when he saw the moment his suggestion registered. He guided her by the hand and brought her into the bathroom, closed the door, and turned on the hot water. The water thrummed while Mathew stalked up to her. With a press of his finger under her chin, Verity's face tilted up to his. He searched her freckles, the smooth curve of her jaw, the individual hairs of her eyebrows, memorizing them, while unbuttoning his shirt. When it was half opened, her eyes traced his hands' movements. Anticipation surged through his body.

He flipped back the fabric, baring his chest, and her eyes drank in his skin. Throbbing heat pooled low in his groin while he painstakingly awaited her permission. Her palms pressed against his chest and her mouth tipped up. Mathew's lips crashed down on hers in sweet relief. Verity's breathing was shallow, shaky, and her eyes glistened. With dew building on their skin, steam billowed around as if wrapping them in a private blanket of encouragement. Verity unfastened his pants while deep,

possessive kisses charged him. His brain tried to register what was happening, but his instinct took control before he thought twice. He drew his hands up from her waist and slipped her shirt off in a single fluid motion. Mathew's lips trailed down her smooth throat and found her breasts. He had never bought her a bra—hadn't known where to start. And right now, he was glad to have less of a barrier between him and the only woman he'd ever truly wanted—the only one who'd ever driven him to a frenzy with desire.

Mathew knelt on the floor for better access, and while he gently sucked and licked across her pointed nipples, she arched in pleasure. His deft hands unzipped her jeans and shimmied them off her glorious body. Mathew's fingers explored her cleft. It was hot and slick, hidden behind soft dark brown curls. She gasped at his touch, and his erection jutted straight out in demand. The anticipation was both exciting and maddening.

Mathew dipped his head and lifted one of her legs onto his shoulder. She was exposed to him, and he would finally show her what he offered. Verity leaned against the counter while his tongue swirled around her sensitive core. Muscles danced with pleasure under his hands, and he sucked and rubbed until her breathing became a pant. An index finger coated in her pleasure, entered her.

"Matt! Oh, that feels so good. Keep going!" she begged for the finish.

Fluid leaked from his erection and he was certain he wouldn't be able to hold himself together much longer.

Her breath hitched, and her body became rigid. She cried out again as the waves of pleasure overtook her. Mathew stood with

a broad grin of pride. Her eyes stared at his lips in—disbelief? He kissed her with want and need, his tongue finding hers. His cock nestled between her legs, ready and begging for entry. He waited for her permission once again, despite being wound so tight he couldn't think straight.

Her fist wrapped around his erection and angled it toward her opening. With her approval, he reached under her thighs, slick with humidity, and lifted her up. While suspended in the air by his hands, he leaned her against the door for leverage. Mathew entered her with a groan and carefully seated himself. His eyes closed and his head fell back. She was hot and tight, and after a moment's enjoyment, he thrusted, slow at first and then faster. His breathing became hitched as his thrusts rattled the door rhythmically on its hinges. She gave herself to him, and he was so grateful he fought tears of pleasure from forming. He wanted her so much, and it had been so long since he'd been with anyone, he would be disappointingly short today, but he vowed to make it up to her another time. Before he realized, he arched in pleasure and filled her up, waves of release pulsing through him. They both panted and gazed into each other's eyes.

"I think we should conserve water more often," she said with a devious smile.

Mathew chuckled and glanced over his shoulder at the running water. Oops.

"We have to be quick. The water heater is probably running low." Mathew scrubbed a clean washcloth with a bar of soap and set about cleaning her. The cloth glided over her skin, and Mathew relished washing every inch of her. He wanted to give certain places extra attention, but that was risking a cold shower.

Quick swipes were all they had time for, and she turned around, exposing her bare backside, and he froze.

"What happened here?" His fingers traced the white horizontal lines of old scars across her butt cheeks.

She sighed. "Jaime Perez."

Like a flip of a switch, his fists knotted, squeezing suds out of the cloth. "He did this to you?"

"He attacked me, so I maimed him. You saved me from his revenge. He intends to kill me."

A man capable of this damage was surely a monster. Plus, he technically killed Mathew when he went back in time originally. Kiko wasn't lying when she'd said Verity would be murdered.

"He won't touch a hair on your head." He glided the soapy cloth over her back, down her legs and between her luscious crevices. Mathew squirted a dab of shampoo into his hands and massaged it through her scalp and down her hair. A moan escaped her lips.

"You're good with your hands," she said.

"Surgeon's hands. Fine motor skills are required."

She snatched the cloth from him and tossed it to the floor of the tub. She lathered up a fresh one and washed every tingling inch of his body. His cock sprung back to life and bounced for attention. With soap rinsing as she wiped, she smiled at it, knelt, and before he realized what she'd planned, she accepted him inside her mouth. He grunted in pleasurable surprise. Her hands worked his sack, and her mouth sucked while she stroked.

He warned her, pushing her back before he released in her mouth. He stood her up and penetrated her, filling her a second time. Verity hadn't a single fault. High on oxytocin, his brain

swam with her scent. How was he so lucky to find a woman so beautiful yet brave and adventurous? Perhaps he found his lotto ticket after all.

"Never change. You are perfect," he said.

# Chapter Fourteen

Green Bay, Wisconsin
Present Day

THEY WERE SUPPOSED to still be in New York City, but they came back the same day, so Mathew and Verity went to the office the next morning. Verity stopped Mathew from calling Becca, insisting she could manage the front desk herself. She wanted to prove she was capable.

Verity hadn't found a single thing about the future to dislike. She filled a cup from the automatic coffee pot and marveled at its ease. She brought it to the expansive desk and sat next to Mathew, who was on the phone calling clients to reschedule their appointments for today. Most of them were grateful and accepted.

Mathew had no problem with her ruined reputation, and her heart soared at her luck. Verity's body was still singing from last night. He was so sensual, so kind, and generous—a true gentleman, and Verity couldn't wait for his proposal, unlike that charlatan Bernard. Of course, at the time, she hadn't wanted to be Bernard's wife anyway, but his refusal to propose was a horrific insult.

Last night, after their shower, they watched *Back to the Future*

*Part Three*, but Mathew pointed out the movie wasn't real. It looked real, and if that wild time traveling duo could fix their futures, then why couldn't Verity? At any moment, when Mathew proposed, her cursed reputation hanging over her head like the warning flag of a pirate's mast, would vanish, and like Doc Brown and Marty, she, too, would have her happily ever after.

After the movie, it had been late, and she stood from the couch and stretched for bed, yawning strongly enough to rattle her whole body. Mathew had leaned over on the couch, limbs splayed for sleep, but she insisted he share her sheets—his sheets, actually.

He hadn't hesitated.

Verity sipped her hot coffee and her brain snapped alert. This morning she'd awoke to a heavy arm draped across her middle, a hand enveloping a breast, and an erection perched against her butt. They fixed that problem. After the passion they shared last night and this morning, Verity was on edge waiting for her modern gentleman to pledge himself to her.

Verity set her coffee cup down, logged into the computer in front of her, and opened the correct programs like Becca had taught her. She made a few calls herself—there weren't that many, as Mathew could only see so many patients in a day. He hung up his phone and said, "I want to show you something before the first client gets here."

She followed him into his office, shaking with excitement, and he crooked his finger at her. Over his shoulder she watched Mathew point out a graph on the screen.

"This is the ticker tape for the stock I bought back in your

time. At that point, the stock was twenty cents each. Now…"

"It's over ninety dollars each?"

"Precisely. Our current money is too different from your money. So, I exchanged the silver bars to buy shares like these on the screen. I took a big loss exchanging the value from today's dollars to 1853 dollars, but this stock here more made up for it. Do you believe that I didn't do anything sketchy?"

"I trust you, even if I don't understand." She believed it was a legal transaction and that's all that mattered to her.

Mathew nodded. "You sure? You didn't seem convinced standing outside that seedy bar."

"Yes, I'm sure." She planted a quick kiss on his amazing lips.

The first customer of the day jingled through the front door and Verity winked, leaving him with a teasing smile. Mathew gave her a maudlin grin on her way out.

A younger man with a lanky Great Dane stopped at her desk.

"Good morning. This must be the handsome Duke. How do you do?"

The young man's face turned bright red. "He's good."

"Still on Ninth Ave?"

"Yes."

"Phone number ending in five-three-zero-nine?"

He nodded.

"We just need a weight."

The owner, Brandon, brought Duke over to the floor scale. His rump shimmied against the force of his overactive tail.

"Hundred and forty-two pounds. Big fella. You're all set. Doctor will be right with you."

Duke's large tongue lolled out the side of his mouth. She

smiled at the good boy, and Brandon stared at her. Verity's face flushed with his gaze. Could he tell she had intercourse this morning? It had been a long time for her, but never had it ever been so amazing and distracting, and never had it been with someone who cared about her pleasure. Verity updated the dog's weight in his chart, hiding her face behind the screen.

Another customer entered, and the elderly man with a cane shuffled over to their shelves of cat food, lifted a small bag, and brought it to the desk.

"Good day, sir. Is there anything else I can assist you with?"

"What happened to Becca?" he grumbled.

Verity kept her smile shining. Nothing could dampen her spirits. "She's got the day off."

He mumbled at her and checked out with cash. Mathew came out to take the Dane while another customer entered. The phone rang, and she placed them on hold. She checked in the beagle, here for shots, and then answered the phone. Another call came through within seconds. The rest of the day was so busy the time flew by, and before she realized, it was time to close.

"You did fantastic today," Mathew said while he wiped his hands clean on a cloth. "I've never had an assistant that could handle it all by themselves. Don't tell Becca or Kiko or even April, if I ever find her."

She blushed with the compliment. "Thank you, and I promise I won't."

"Here." He handed her a folded stack of bills. "I don't have an official check for you, since you don't have a social security number. Cash okay?"

He was paying her. Did their copulation last night and this

morning mean nothing more to him than a business transaction? A crushing weight settled on her chest. She thought she'd made it clear she was only a dancer when Mathew caught her with the drunken bar lout. Anger roared through her, tensing her body. She was not a whore, and him paying for her *professional services* was equivalent to a slap in the face.

"I don't want your money." She folded her arms, refusing the stack.

"Everyone on my payroll gets paid," he insisted.

She fumed even more. "I didn't do it for money!"

Mathew scratched the back of his head in exasperation. "You put in hours of work here at the clinic and everyone gets paid for working. I'm trying to be fair and not take advantage of you."

So the cash had nothing to do with their repeated intercourse. Why didn't he just say so? She snatched the cash from him and stuffed it into her jeans pocket.

"Thank you." She appreciated him giving her a paid job.

"I've got some work to finish up and then an errand to run. Did you want to wait here or at my place?"

"I'll wait here."

He smiled. "Great. Just give me a few." Mathew went to his office and closed the door. He was beaming with energy, and Verity couldn't help but wonder what kind of errand he had. Her anger swirled away just like the sophisticated toilet water. Quickly, curiosity turned to excitement.


MATHEW RECEIVED confirmation over the phone from the transfer agent at the currently named Consolidated Edison to

sell the shares of stock. He needed to get the certificates notarized and then place the sell order after they confirmed ownership. Should be a few days at most.

If he paid off his personal debts, then he could take a smaller salary from his clinic, thus boosting the clinic's profitability and keeping the doors open. He calculated he'd even have enough left over after capital gains tax for a down payment on a decent home—with grass and a garage—in a safe neighborhood. Then at twenty-nine-soon-to-be-thirty years old, he'd be ready to enter the dating market in search of a partner, his equal, a woman that made him want to be a better man. He wanted kids, several kids, and he would raise them better than his parents had. A sense of confidence in his ability to do a decent job had sprung up lately.

With Mathew's life on the verge of being fixed, he wanted to celebrate. He stepped out of his office ready to get the document notarized.

"Verity?"

"Hmmm?" She was nose deep into the computer screen. Mathew smiled at her and flutters of butterflies danced in his stomach.

"After I finish the errands, how about a fancy dinner tonight?"

Her face beamed with that innocent wonder. "Fancy sounds fantastic. What should I wear?" Her hands combed through her wild but incredibly soft locks.

"I'll take you out for a dress beforehand. I'm afraid the one you came with wouldn't do."

"I imagine not. I can't wait!"

"I'll be back soon. Don't go anywhere." He winked at her and

set off for the credit union. His hands gripped the wheel, but the butterflies in his gut wouldn't go away. Every time he thought of Verity—which was almost all the time—the all-consuming, beautiful insects returned.

He reached the credit union, and Mathew showed his driver's license and had the stock certificate notarized in a jiffy. Then he dialed his favorite high-end restaurant that he only ever used when he wanted to impress a woman—which was to say, not often—and made reservations. He checked his watch and calculated the local time in New York City. Inside his car, he made the life-changing call.

A couple days.

A couple more days he had to wait for the paperwork to go through and the deposit to be finalized. He could wait a couple days. After all, he'd waited the last twelve years to get his life together, and he'd waited his whole life to have stability. What was a couple days compared to that?

With everything in place, Mathew returned to the clinic to pick up Verity for a shopping trip. He found her brushing her hair in the bathroom, her hands shaking.

"Everything okay?"

She screamed and dropped the brush. "I didn't hear the bell. You startled me."

"Sorry." He smiled. "Ready to go?"

"Y-yeah."

She seemed out of sorts and damned if he knew why. Mathew drove her to a formal wear boutique, and she chose a plum halter dress with ruffles. The hue made her green eyes pop. She was simply stunning.

"What do you think?" she asked.

"I…I think you look amazing." She certainly took his breath away.

"Is this right for the restaurant? Feels too formal just to eat."

"It's perfect."

Her smile was radiant when she returned to the dressing room to switch back into her street clothes. Mathew pulled out his plastic, the one not maxed yet, and Verity pressed his arm down. "I earned money. I will pay for my dress."

Mathew bore a deep yearning to provide, but for a couple more days, he couldn't afford much. He figured Verity would be insulted if he insisted, and since he technically needed the card space for dinner, he waved his hand in acquiescence. A satisfactory grin split her face as she pulled out a stack of twenties. The cashier told her the total.

"How much?" Her mouth gaped.

"Two-hundred and forty dollars, please," the cashier repeated.

Verity flipped through the bills and counted them. "That's almost all my money," she said under her breath.

"You can go to Walmart instead," the cashier retorted.

"Do you want me to get it for you?" Mathew offered. "It's no big deal."

"No," she said, separating out the bills. "I have enough."

The cashier completed the transaction, gave her the receipt, and tucked the dress into a garment bag. Verity slung it over her shoulder, and Mathew walked her out hand in hand. After new experiences, she typically bounced with questions, but now she was unusually silent.

"Is something bothering you?" he asked when they reached the parking lot.

"I think I found a downside to the future. How can anyone afford anything around here?"

Mathew chuckled. "Most of the time, they don't."

"That amount of money, back home, is enough to live on for a year. Just one dress? I've seen the bills charged to the customers, but I guess I didn't put the two together."

Mathew unlocked and opened the SUV door for her. She set the garment bag in the back seat and then buckled in up front. It was time to celebrate. The butterflies in his belly returned.

MATHEW DROVE HER through town while she hid her shaking under her jean-covered thighs. Mathew must be rich beyond her wildest dreams to offer to buy her so many clothes, food, and this beautiful dress without even thinking twice about it. Her body trembled because they were going to a fancy dinner to celebrate. What was the occasion? Verity only guessed he was going to take responsibility for last night and this morning and propose properly. She wouldn't hesitate to accept.

Long before her reputation was tainted, she and Bernard had a short courtship. She wasn't fond of him, and maybe it showed, but he'd denied her an offer. The insult was scarring. Afterward, Verity refused to try again, stating her age as an excuse to her parents. She decided being free to explore, to travel, to make her own wealth was far more her style than being a wife anyway. And she'd convinced herself. Her attempt to take charge of her life only led to her reputation being damaged so far that changing

her mind and finding a suitable husband was no longer an option.

But now, Mathew saved her from Jaime Perez and saved her from the headache of facing her big brother. Jonathan would be mighty angry with her if she ever returned. Mathew also gave her the world—she explored, she traveled, she made her own, albeit tiny, fortune, which now she realized wasn't all that much. Verity wanted to marry Mathew and travel with him. She wanted his babies, and she wanted to take them to see the world, too. Now it was possible since a journey across the ocean took hours instead of months.

Her fingers knotted themselves together while they drove. Mathew parked at his apartment and she changed into her dress and curled her hair with the curling iron Mathew explained to her. She'd only burned her finger once before getting the hang of it, and when Mathew stepped out in front of her, Verity's breath caught. He was stunning in a sharp black suit, and her body pulsed with need. She wanted his clothes right back off.

"Come here," he said and smiled. She stepped into his arms and his hand lifted away from them. "You're shaking. Are you cold?"

"No. I'm all right." She trembled from nerves. The moment her past no longer mattered was upon her.

"You look stunning. Turn around and say cheese."

Verity spun, confused, and saw the black cell phone. Instead of phone numbers or a map, she saw herself next to Mathew, and she appeared exposed. Her arms and upper chest were bare. Mathew's suit covered him completely.

"Are you sure this is appropriate clothing? I'm"—she rubbed

her naked arm—"not very covered."

"You're striking and completely appropriate. You'll be turning heads because you're beautiful, not scandalous."

Verity smiled. She hoped to get used to modern clothing. Mathew tilted her face back to the screen.

"How does that work?"

"The camera is built in. Selfie mode."

She did not understand what that meant.

"Just smile."

She did and a clicking noise came from the phone. He handed it to her, and she saw the image. The two of them together, captured forever.

"A photograph?"

"Yeah."

"Is there anything this phone can't do?"

"Let's see." Mathew scratched the back of his gelled hair as if she had asked a difficult question, then he smoothed it. "It can't make coffee."

Verity laughed.

"But it can order a cup or a coffee pot to be delivered to your door."

Verity stopped laughing and quirked a brow. "Really?"

"Yeah. Let's go. Reservations at six."

Anticipation made her tremble more, so on the ride over, she wedged her hands under her thighs, buried in plum ruffles. Mathew turned off the car in a parking lot. They were near the East river, and it was browner that she would've preferred a river to be, but it still glistened in the fading sun. They walked into the downtown restaurant, and Verity was taken aback by the

dimmed lights, calming shades of earth tones, brick accent wall, and dark woods. It was beautiful, and the scent of steak permeated the dining hall.

The hostess brought them to a booth and Verity slid in across from Mathew. He trembled with excitement too. Any minute now he would propose. He wasn't coy about running errands to buy her a ring, leaving her behind so as not to spoil the surprise. The gesture was unnecessary, but she admitted she loved the anticipation.

Mathew lifted the menu and Verity copied. Her eyes popped at the prices. That would take some getting used to. She read the descriptions and settled.

"What are you getting?" she asked.

"For special occasions, I always pick Surf and Turf. How about you?"

"Lobster." She'd heard of it, but only as whispers of luxury.

Mathew laughed. "Go big or go home." He tugged on the front of his tie. He was so nervous, probably more than she was. She wished she could reassure him of her answer, but that would spoil the surprise. She slipped a hand down to her lap and wiped her damp palm on the silky dress. The waiter brought drinks, and Verity held her breath. Would Mathew sink down to one knee right after the waiter left? Would he wait until the end of the meal? She wanted him to do it first so the butterflies playing tag in her stomach would call game over.

The meal came out shortly. She had tasted nothing as sublime as red-tailed lobster. The buttery, flaky white lumps were just phenomenal, an explosion of juicy tenderness. Her family never afforded anything as rare as ocean seafood, even if they found

any around. Mathew didn't tell her a price limit, and it was just so delicious. Guilt nagged at her when she thought of her week's pay and the price of the dress. Where else was she going to wear this fine garment? Back home, she'd only owned a couple dresses useful for daily activities and one nicer one for special occasions. The price compared to the usefulness made the plum dress seem like a waste.

Verity polished off her two tails. She was a bottomless pit. "Can I try your steak?"

"Sure," he said with a chuckle, offering her a bite. She slipped the square of medium rare meat off the fork and was inundated with a juicy squeeze.

"May I get dessert?"

Mathew smiled and shook his head. "Whatever you want. We're celebrating."

"What is it we're celebrating?" Verity asked with a sheepish smile. Now would be perfect. Right now!

"You remember those silver bars?"

"Yeah?" Verity confirmed with a suspicious brow.

"The paper I received in exchange is worth a lot of money. Enough to dig me out of my hole. I won't have to close the clinic anymore. It's such a relief I can't even describe."

*And?* "Anything else?"

Mathew swallowed some sparkling pale drink and said, "Not that I know of. Why?"

Disappointment flashed through her and anger flared, but she kept her voice level. "You have nothing to ask me?"

Mathew stared at her, searching for the correct answer. "I don't think so?" His statement had a ring of question to it, and

that was not the answer she expected. She had already played this game with Bernard and the insult still stung. She couldn't handle having it repeated.

"Don't you think now would be a great time to propose marriage?" Verity asked pointedly.

Mathew choked on his drink. "What?"

"It is only proper for a man to make his intentions known. I hoped for a proposal before consummating the relationship, afterward was certainly expected, but not at all? That's downright cruel."

"I don't understand. I've only known you for a week." Mathew tilted his head in disbelief.

Pain speared through her chest. Once again, she'd been rejected and insulted. Pressure built behind her eyes, threatening tears. She couldn't show her face to him any longer. Verity stood, bumping the table, causing the silverware to clink. Heads turned.

"What kind of man has intercourse with a woman and doesn't commit?"

Mathew glanced around the restaurant, as if fearing the gawkers' opinions. Verity didn't care who watched, and she didn't care if she embarrassed him. The pain and embarrassment she felt from Mathew was so much worse than from what Bernard had ever done.

Mathew didn't answer.

"I thought you were different." Before he stood, Verity stormed out, covering her mouth with her hand.

She marched down the block while the tears streamed free, stray hairs sticking to her dampened face. What was she supposed to do now? Every time she strayed from her dream by

attempting a courtship, it only ended in her being rejected. California would never use and refuse her.

A small woman with sleek long black hair stepped out of nowhere and stood in front of her. Stopping in her tracks, Verity sniffled and wiped her eyes. "Can I help you?"

The petite woman smiled. "Verity, would you like to go home?"

"How do you know my name?" Verity took a step back. No one knew who she was except for Becca and Mathew.

"I'm Kiko, the one that sent Matt to help you. I can send you home."

Oh, she'd heard all about Kiko. Verity considered the offer. Mathew's mortifying rejection was too fresh. Of course, she wanted to marry him. Why was it such a startling shock? In straying from her dream, all Verity ever found was pain and humiliation. She tilted her chin up, ready to be true to herself.

"Yes, please."

The small woman lifted her palm forward as if to stop Verity from closing the distance. Her vision blurred around her and her stomach quivered in protest.

To hell with remaining a prisoner at her family's farm. When Verity got home, she would pack up for California where her dreams awaited. She'd try to avoid Jonathan though, and if she sneaked out quick enough, Jaime wouldn't even hear she was back. Verity smiled through the queasiness, confident in her choice.

Dozens of faces stared at Mathew, and his cheeks burned with embarrassment. What was supposed to be a celebratory dinner turned out to be a nightmare, abandoned at the table with looky-loos scowling at him like he was some kind of chauvinistic pig. Mathew stood and called after her, but he wasn't about to go to jail for dine-and-dashing, so he stayed put long enough to get the check. He expected her to wait by his SUV, and they could discuss the matter in private.

Once the server returned his card, Mathew rushed out the door to the parking lot, but she wasn't waiting by his SUV. He jogged out to the sidewalk and scanned all directions of the intersection. "Verity!" he called, hands cupping his mouth for extra projection. She was nowhere in sight. Where did she go so fast?

"Verity!" he shouted again and listened, hoping to hear her heels clicking. Mathew jogged to the back side of the restaurant and listened, and then the other side. He crossed the street and still nothing. An upset woman on heels couldn't get that far downtown with traffic. But she was gone. He ran back to his SUV and dialed for Kiko, while driving to her and April's house. She didn't answer the phone. He parked on the cement driveway and skipped steps up the porch and pounded on the front door.

"Kiko, open up!"

His fist vibrated the wood door. On the final knock it swung open, and he restrained his fist from hitting the shorter woman on the head.

She stepped aside and waved him in without a word, closing the door behind him.

"She's gone," he said.

Kiko confirmed with a nod.

"How is it possible this is real?" Mathew paced the living room and shoved a hand through his hair. So many unanswered questions rattled in his brain and his full stomach threatened to evacuate itself. "Where's my sister? Why did she leave behind her passport?"

"Please sit," Kiko said. She crossed to the kitchen and said, "Matt, beer?" He didn't miss the exact reversal of roles. Several weeks ago, he'd been the one offering her a beer when his sister's proposal had gone wrong. Goddamned irony.

Mathew caught the proffered beer and crashed on the couch, slamming the whole bottle down on a single breath. It took the edge off, just slightly. He set the empty on the coffee table and forced his body still.

"Why did you tell me you had a family emergency?"

Kiko smiled. "You just needed some time."

"Time for what? Tell me what's going on." Mathew's leg bounced against the floor on its own accord. Kiko sat in the recliner across from him.

"Verity returned to her time. It was her choice."

"How?"

Kiko shrugged. "She asked."

"I didn't just imagine all this. She existed, right?"

"The dream study is a fabricated story that seems to work most of the time. She did exist."

"I don't like you talking about her in the past tense. What's the truth? No more lies." Mathew leaned forward onto his elbows, dying to jump out of his skin.

"My job is to match people who otherwise wouldn't be able

to find each other on their own."

"With time travel?"

Kiko flipped her hand back and forth in the air as if demonstrating something, but Mathew couldn't see anything. "I am an agent of Chaos. We battle against the forces of Order. Personally, I think my brother-in-arms got the short end of the deal. He's the Fear Curator, but he likes it just fine."

What kind of gibberish was she saying? He didn't need to be convinced time travel was real. He knew that plenty enough. The rest of what she was saying sounded like he'd missed out on a whole other world right under his nose. "An agent of Chaos? How many of you are there?"

"Honestly, I don't know."

"Is this a government thing?"

Kiko pressed her lips together in thought. "No. Chaos and Order precede the government."

"A secret society? Like an order of crime fighters—or love makers, I suppose."

Her back was rigid straight, as if she was a guest in her own home. "Not exactly, but that's closer."

Mathew had so many questions. He believed what he experienced was real, but he couldn't wrap his brain around it.

"How does it work? Can I go back and forth whenever I want?" That would be a useful skill. His knee continued bouncing.

"I can't tell you *how* it works. But I create a tunnel through time, sending and pulling people to and from whenever and wherever I deem best in the pair's origin years only. But the trinket can only move people to the original source time and the

corresponding return, so it's best for emergency returns only. Time isn't the same on both sides."

"So, I can go to her time or my time only?"

"Precisely." Kiko stood and carried his empty bottle, setting it into the recycle bin.

"And my three trips?" Mathew asked.

"You can go to 1853 and return home one last time. Then you can never go to the past again."

"I guess all is well then. I saved her from Jaime Perez, so now she's safely back home with her brothers. No paradoxes and no cataclysmic events. But you still owe me a trip to the police station." Mathew stood and walked to the front door. His hand paused on the knob, a question dancing at the back of his mind, but he failed to tease it forward.

"If you need any more assistance, please come visit."

He nodded. First thing in the morning he would place the call to order the sale of shares, then verify with Becca that she would come in to work. How was he going to run the place without Verity?

"Kiko?" Mathew turned.

"Yes?"

"Will you be at the clinic in the morning? I'm down an employee. Again."

She smiled, "Of course."

"Thanks." He left and drove home. He'd fulfilled the promise to himself to get Verity back home to her family where she was meant to be, but no, he didn't like it.

Verity was upset he didn't plan to propose after knowing her a week. The idea was nuts to him. But now that he thought about

it, in 1853, expectations were very different. Why didn't she give him a chance to talk it through before leaving? The thought trailed off as he unlocked his front door, an empty ache settling in his chest. There was something nagging him about the whole thing. He just couldn't place a finger on it.

# Chapter Fifteen

Navarino, Wisconsin
1853

VERITY BLINKED. She stood near the East river, and now it was a far healthier shade of bluish gray. A sign by the bridge to her west pointed to Navarino. Back behind her was Bridgeport. She wouldn't go south to Bridgeport and risk getting close to Jaime Perez's estate—Grignon's old one.

So, trekking through Navarino it was. Verity held an arm out to block the setting sun from her view. A shiver ran up her skin, and she realized she was wearing her expensive plum dress and heels—trekking through dirt. Little streaks of white piled in the crevices of the road. Snow? Her body was so cold, but as long as she wasn't spotted by anyone dangerous, she should be able to make it home—and not freeze to death first. For that one week, she'd had the best time of her life. Just her luck that it didn't last. She rubbed her bare arms.

Verity climbed the Fox River bridge and dodged to the side as a horse-drawn wagon of hay crested ahead of her. The rider tipped his hat to her and did a double take at her outfit. She smiled and turned her head down, crossing her arms for warmth and stepping faster.

If she couldn't find a ride, it would take her days to get home. She wished she had a black cell phone to call a ride, or have a cab come by with the flick of a hand. Oh, how things were so much easier in the future. The amusement park rides were thrilling and safe. The food was instant and mostly delicious. Artisans had any clothing available, and now being back home, Verity thought the whole idea was unbelievable. How would society get from this—covered wagons, farming, horses, bandits, pirates—to cars that run forever with some gas and people working at a desk?

Did she make the right choice in returning? Could she have made her riches in the future instead?

Verity slipped off her heels and held them in the crook of her finger. They weren't comfortable for long periods of walking. Her calves were tight, and her ankles hurt. She would deal with the cold on her feet instead. Coming up behind her she heard hoofbeats. Finally!

Verity turned and waved a hand at the traveler, a lone male rider on a young stallion.

"Hello! Can I have a ride? My feet are terribly sore from walking."

The rider, in a leather vest covered with a brown wool coat, pulled the reins to stop his horse. His mischievous eyes roamed her body. Verity stood absolute. She was out of her element, but she was still Verity Arris, capable of traveling by herself like any ordinary man. The last time she'd ventured out alone, she'd had a different outfit on, proper shoes, and a mount of her own— that she'd stolen.

He smiled and held out a hand for her. She climbed up

behind him and he asked, "Where ya headed, miss?"

"Arris farm in Astor. Thank you."

"Verity?" he asked with surprise. Verity fidgeted with nerves and cold. She didn't like to be recognized. He continued, "You look mighty diff'rent these days."

"Uh, yeah. To the farm please."

The rider nudged the horse south toward Astor and Verity sighed in relief.

"You look ha'f frozen." The rider opened a saddle bag and withdrew a rough blanket. "It's not soft as a lady deserves, but it'll keep ya from freezing solid. You can hug my back if it helps." He passed her the blanket, and she curled it around herself. The slight warmth instantly caused shivers to thunder through her body. She pressed her jaw tight to stop her teeth from clattering.

"Thanks."

"You know," he called over his shoulder, "I always thought you's a purty lady. I didn't care what ever'one said. When you danced wit me back at The Wounded Soldier, I couldn't keep ma eyes off you. Too bad you don' remember none."

Great, he'd seen her dancing in Greenleaf in a seedy bar, as Mathew called it. She didn't recognize the rider though—a good sign.

"I'm afraid I don't, sorry."

The horse swayed as they made their way south, one painstakingly slow step at a time. "Hmmm. That's unfortunate. Whatever happened to that Jaime guy?"

Verity shivered. "I don't know. Why?"

"He was mighta pissed off that night. His legs was running blood all down 'em and he was screaming some mighta nasty

things at you. He couldn't walk out of there none."

"Last I saw, he was just fine." Verity remembered when Jaime dragged her by the hair out of her living room. "Still mighty pissed off though."

He chuckled. "Yep, that I believe."

Verity wanted to change the subject. "Where were you headed?"

"Oh, me? I was on ma way home in Navarino. But since I didn' wanna see the old lady jus' yet, I figure it was God's will that I give you a ride home first."

"It's very nice of you. Thanks." Verity relaxed just a little, while the early winter evening sent swirling chills up her bare legs. She rubbed her arms for warmth.

"I should warn ya though. Jaime's been asking around for ya. He's a reward going even. Now since I like ya and all, I won' be turning ya in, but just so you're awares is all. Be careful out there."

Verity stilled at this information. Jaime had put a bounty on her head.

"I'm so sorry but I cannot remember your name."

He laughed. "I don' suppose you do. The name's Ben Pool." The last name sounded familiar, but she couldn't place it. He continued, "You remember my brother better, I'd wager, Joe Pool. He's workin' for Jaime. That's where I get my information from. Don' be alarmed, miss. My brother's an asshole. Mama never raised us kids like that, and he should be ashamed of himself."

"Verity!" A familiar voice yelled from ahead. Verity froze while the horse continued to sway.

"Verity! Where have you been?" It was Graham. His horse slowed next to them and spun to walk alongside. He was a spitfire of disobedience, always off having more fun than working. Jonathan despised him for it. Verity was usually jealous, but tonight she was grateful.

"I'm going home."

"You've been gone for almost six months."

"Six?" She'd left a little over a week ago. How could it have possibly been six months?

"Yeah, and Johnny's worried sick. Get on back and I'll take you home."

Verity hopped onto the back of Graham's saddle, not believing Jonathan's level of worry—more like irrational anger, and she passed the blanket back to her rescuer.

"Nah, you keep it. My ol' lady needed a reason to make 'nother one, anyway. Good luck to ya and be safe out there."

"Thanks again, Ben."

The rider turned around and headed back north for Navarino. Verity held the scratchy blanket to her skin while Graham urged the horse to go faster. Apparently, he didn't want to freeze either, despite being dressed better for the winter weather. Or perhaps Graham was fibbing about Jonathan being worried. Verity suddenly didn't want to go home, but Jonathan's wrath was better than freezing to death.

# Chapter Sixteen

Green Bay, Wisconsin
Present Day

MATHEW SLUMPED IN his recliner, still wearing his suit from dinner with Verity. She'd left and he still couldn't believe it. An emptiness pervaded his heart, stronger, more devastating than he'd ever experienced before. Mathew's cruddy apartment, once good enough for him, now had its last remaining breath of life sucked away. All sense of purpose had just slipped from his fingers, especially going to work and plugging away with patients only to come home and do it all over Groundhog Day style.

Verity wanted to go, and he was trying to help her go home, anyway. Case closed. Problem solved. Now he could resume focusing on his missing sister. Soon April would reply to his dozens of messages, he hoped.

But Mathew just stared at the black screen of his TV, incapable of turning it on. He loosened the tie at his throat and his hand flopped at his side. Mathew wasn't hungry. He didn't need a shower. It wasn't time for bed, and it wasn't time for work. The hollowness pervading is body was unbelievably heavy.

There was only one thing he wanted—Verity. He wanted to

feed her pizza and fries, to take her to more exciting places just so he could watch her face light up, and to show her what a great life he could offer her. He wanted to feel alive again.

Stupid.

He hadn't been ready to be with a woman, but he'd fallen for one, anyway, one he couldn't have. Now what? First thing in the morning he'd call Consolidated Edison and finish the sale of his stock, then finish fixing his life.

In the morning, Mathew stumped to the bathroom naked and fisted his toothbrush. Next to his stood a like-new green brush. It matched her eyes. An ache settled in his heart, and he shook his head to clear it away, but the effort didn't work. Mathew brushed his teeth with the least amount of enthusiasm possible and dressed in his usual dress pants, button up long sleeve shirt, and dress shoes. He drove to work in a mindless haze, and when he arrived, he was pleasantly surprised to see Kiko and Becca ready to go for the day. He checked his watch, sensing he was late, but he wasn't.

He pushed opened the front door and plastered a fake smile on his face. "Good morning, ladies." He held Kiko's eye contact extra long. She wasn't who he thought she was. The woman was some strange entity working for *Chaos*. After his unbelievable experience, she was certainly real, but was she even human?

His office door opened, and Mathew strode over to the fax, feeding the machine the notarized documents. Then he sat at his desk and lifted his phone. A quick call to the company in New York City, and the sale was underway. The company promised the funds would deposit within four hours.

Mathew leaned back in his chair and rested his head against

his raised hands. He released a deep breath. In four small hours his life would change.

It already had changed.

Damn it. His brain wouldn't let go of her. Mathew retrieved the fake smile from somewhere handy—he was going to need it for a long time—and resumed caring for patients. He gave vaccines to a long-haired cat whose face was so flat it was almost concave. Next was a beagle in for a checkup and heartworm treatment. The third was an Irish setter in need of a dental cleaning. After those three patients left, Mathew checked the clock on his office wall and logged into his online bank account.

They deposited the funds. Sparks of excitement juiced his whole body.

He opened a new browser tab and logged into his student loan account. A click of the Payoff Quote button got him the total, and he clicked Pay This Amount. It made him confirm the payment since it was over a thousand dollars. It was over a hundred thousand dollars, in fact. A few more clicks and that noose vanished. He logged into his SUV financing account and paid that off, and then he logged into his credit cards one at a time and cleared them all. Next, he opened his credit union account that had given him the loan for silver bars. He paid off that loan too, leaving him with just over sixty thousand dollars for a down payment on a home and no debt except the clinic's mortgage. He exhaled and smiled, feeling like he won the lottery. He had been drowning, but with a bit of luck or magic maybe, he was now free to live.

Still, he wasn't satisfied.

Mathew finished the day's cases: a puppy with diarrhea, a

Corgi with an allergy he had struggled to pinpoint, a German Shepard in need of vaccines and a flea and tick treatment. The women at the desk did well, and he dismissed Becca as soon as the last client left.

Mathew leaned against the counter, facing Kiko. "Do you want to go out for dinner?" He was antsy and didn't want to go to an empty home yet.

She smiled. "No. But there's something I want to show you. Meet me at my place in an hour."

"Sure," Mathew said, confused and intrigued. He locked up and grabbed a bag of fast food on his way over to Kiko's house. The food was bland and lukewarm. The fries were that gritty texture after they had cooled too long, where one fry was one too many. Mathew set the bag in the passenger seat, downed his drink, and climbed out of the SUV. He lifted a hand to knock, but the door opened for him.

"What did you want to show me?"

She waved him inside and he sat on the couch—his sister's couch. He missed her so much, and that reminded him. "Are you coming with me to the police station to file the report?"

"That depends," she said.

Mathew's anger flared with her reneging on their deal. "But you—"

"Read this." Kiko handed him a folded piece of paper.

*Hey big brother,*

*You were right. Thanks for the kick in the pants. My ass is still sore though. I'm going away to find the man I love. Wish me luck. Oh, and I quit if you hadn't*

*figured that out. Maybe Kiko will fill in until you can find a temp. Thank you for all your help and support over the years. You are my only family and I love you. I hope you find your own happiness as well.*
*Forever your sis,*

*Meatball*

Mathew jumped to his feet. "Where did she go? What did she tell you?"

"She is here—"

"Where?" Mathew craned his neck around and ran to her bedroom. It was just as she'd left it.

"In a different time," Kiko finished.

He froze and pivoted on his heels. "You mean she went back in time?"

Kiko nodded.

Mathew ran his hands through his hair. His anger flared again. "I've been waiting weeks to hear from her. You knew this. You promised to go with me to the police station to file a missing person's report, but you knew all along where she was. Why didn't you just tell me?"

She waited for him to stop pacing the floor. He grabbed a beer from her fridge without asking and slammed it down. Then a second. Finally, he sat still. He dropped into a seat next to her and stared into her dark eyes.

"I needed you to save Verity," she explained. "Then I needed you to care about her enough."

"Enough for what?"

"Enough to go back and save her again."

"What?"

"You need to find Verity. Jaime Perez still seeks her. And now you know that April is married, safe, and happy."

She was married? April McCall was...Mathew's thoughts trailed off as the pieces clicked together. The truth of Jaime Perez's target, of Verity's praise…"Is she April *Hartley* now?"

Kiko nodded.

Mathew remembered what Verity had said about April Hartley: *She saved the town of Bridgeport, saved Sam's life, saved Lloyd's life, and the townspeople revered her. I want shoes like hers.* He crashed back against the couch. His sister was a celebrity and a hero.

He remembered the scars on Verity's delicate flesh were from a whipping. April had showed up a couple weeks ago with the same wounding, and he'd driven her to the emergency room. He remembered his sister resembled Verity. He knew them both well enough not to see it, but to a stranger, sure. Jaime Perez was responsible for them both.

A fire erupted inside Mathew, a mind-shifting, life-altering rage. It consumed him, despite the alcohol coursing through his veins. Jaime Perez was just like Dad—whipping innocent girls for his own sadistic enjoyment. Dad had claimed it was punishment, but that was bullshit. Dad had enjoyed every second, especially when Mathew stood up to him and landed his own ass in the hospital for it.

Twice.

Dad hadn't visited him at the hospital, because he had enjoyed it. After that, April begged Mathew to stop helping because the wounding on her was much less than Mathew's punishment for interfering.

Mathew's mind overlaid his father's face over that sinister curly-haired short man with the pistols threatening him and Verity. He would kill the asshole for harming his sister and Verity if he ever crossed paths with him again.

Mathew considered all the information and had one more question. "Why did you send me to her in the first place if she was destined to leave me, anyway?"

"I sent you to save her life. At that moment, Jaime Perez would've captured her. And now you realize, he has every intention of exacting his revenge against her."

"Greenleaf?"

"Yes, and I'm afraid she won't survive it again."

Mathew stalked up to her. "I need to prepare, and I'll be right back."

Kiko nodded and Mathew stormed out of his sister's house and drove perhaps a little more recklessly than he should've back home.

In his bedroom, he filled a small bag with the remaining silver bars. He slammed one more beer and paused at a kitchen drawer. Could he carry a knife on him? Could he use it against a person? Mathew didn't need a weapon. He only needed to find Verity, apologize, and see if she'd come back with him, after making a pit stop at a bank.

What if he did run into Jaime? Mathew wouldn't get that lucky. He tore off back to Kiko's house mere minutes later. She stood in the kitchen expectantly.

With sweet Verity's face on his mind, he marched up to Kiko, full of determination and impenetrable against any doubts that lingered in his mind. He'd protect her again, and he hoped for

the chance to protect her forever.

"Send me back," he said.

# Chapter Seventeen

Astor, Wisconsin
1853

GRAHAM DROPPED HER off at the front door, and Verity held a ragged blanket around her shoulders and her heels in the crook of a finger. Her little brother brought the horse to the stable around back, leaving her to enter alone. Verity didn't want to, but the snowy winter night threatened to turn her into an ice cube, so the phrase she'd learned applied here—beggars can't be choosers and all that.

Inside, Verity hovered by the fireplace, its warmth crackling and flickering light across the room. An odd hollowness seeped into her bones from disappearing in July and returning in December, as if a chunk of her life vanished in a blink. But Verity had only been gone a little more than a week. She wondered what life was like for that lady who sent her back—if she was a lady at all. Likely an angel.

She must've been an angel, for she gifted Verity the adventure of a lifetime. She experienced the future and so many wonderful inventions. Plus, there was Mathew. She figured his attitude toward their copulation was a product of his time, but his insensitivity stung too much. And now there was no use in

dwelling on her decision.

The back door opened, and Graham shoved the heavy winter door closed. "Good luck." Graham snickered and shook his head, dashing upstairs.

"Who are you talking to?" Jonathan said to Graham.

Verity sucked in a breath. *Here comes the wrath.* She squeezed her eyes shut and waited by the fire while heavy footsteps creaked across the room. She could survive this. She had many times before. Besides, she wasn't staying, anyway. No matter how upset he would be, Verity would pack and leave on the morrow, winter be damned. She squared her shoulders and faced her big brother.

"Verity?" His familiar deep voice was softer than she'd expected.

"It's me."

His face came into the light, stern and serious, but not angry. His eyes shifted from her curled hair to her disheveled blanket and bare legs and bare feet. She released her fancy high heels, setting them down on the coffee table with a light clatter. She'd expected a shotgun in her face, but his hands were empty.

"Where have you been?" His voice was soft, concerned, and with a hint of sadness. He missed her. He actually cared. Under that gruff surface was a gentle soul. Who would have thought?

"It's a long story." She chuckled as her memory flashed through all the events of her time traveling adventure. Jonathan wrapped her into a bear hug and squeezed. Verity fished her arms out of the layers of Ben's blanket and gave her brother a hug in return.

"Sit down, I'll make you some coffee. You're frigid."

Verity shivered and sat down. Jonathan brought her a steaming mug. She opened the blanket to accept it from him, but the rough fabric fell off her shoulders, revealing her fancy plum dress.

His face curled into anger. "Where did you get that?"

Here we go. But Verity couldn't muster the energy for a fight. Her limbs were stiff from the cold and after leaving Mathew behind, she was drained. "Where I spent the last six months. You wouldn't believe the tale if I told it."

"Tell me."

Verity didn't see why not. She'd be labeled as a silly woman and sent to her room. Fine. She looked forward to her bed, and she needed to pack.

"I was brought to the future by that man who was here. You remember Mathew McCall?"

"I remember he dressed odd. And what kind of man doesn't carry a weapon?"

"That's what you said then." The corner of her lips tugged into a smile. "Jaime Perez showed up. I hid while Matt went to find you, not knowing the danger. Jaime dragged me from the cubbyhole before Matt could alert you." Verity sipped from the mug, relishing in the hot liquid filling her belly. "Matt freed me from Jaime's grasp and brought me to the future before Jaime's rounds hit us. I'd be dead if it weren't for him."

"I believe all of that—except for the future part. What happened to your hair, and where were you really?"

Verity sighed. She stood up, put her heels back on and spun. "Matt brought me to a boutique where I bought this. They have dozens and dozens of gowns fancier than this. You should see

the bead work on the bridal gowns. They're stunning. And my hair is curled with a curling iron. Fancy, huh?" Her palm patted the bottom of her ringlets to show the bounce.

"You bought that dress? With what money?"

She smiled, recounting the exciting future pulsed energy back through her stiff veins. "With money I made at work."

His eyes hardened. "What kind of work?"

"A veterinary clinic. I checked in clients and patients, scheduled appointments, cashiered purchases, and later I swiped credit cards for billing." She had a smug smile on her face knowing her brother had no clue what the hell she'd just said.

"I—I, uh…" He scratched the back of his head, and Verity delighted in his discomfort. He added, "Prove it."

Verity had one piece of proof on her. She dug in the dress pockets for her remaining cash after the dress purchase. She unfolded a bill and held it out to him. "What year is on the bill?"

Jonathan accepted it and tilted it into the light of the fire. He squinted, turned it over and back again, and grunted. "It's fake."

"It's not fake. My dress, my shoes, my money are all from the future. I'm not kidding. I've seen things you couldn't even imagine. Airplanes take several carriages' worth of people in one ride and they fly. You can cross the ocean in hours instead of months. Cars run on gas and drive on paved roads. You can get to Chicago from here in three hours. Dial a number in the palm of your hand and talk to anyone in the world instantly, and if you call the right place, they will bring hot steaming food to your door!"

Jonathan stared at her skeptically, but he had to believe her. She didn't have that kind of imagination. "I went to a place called

an amusement park. There're rides and games and food. The rides soar high in the air and rip faster than any horse can carry you. It's thrilling." She stopped and waited.

"How did you get back here?"

Verity took a deep breath. "A woman—an angel—sent me back when I requested it."

"You were gone six months."

"It was only about nine days in the future. Time isn't the same on both sides."

He handed the bill back to her and stuffed his hands in his pockets. "You've always wanted out of here. Why did you come back?"

His words squeezed her throat. She didn't expect her brother to want her gone. He was always so protective and, well, controlling, but he had his reasons. Why had she come back? It was a knee-jerk decision when the angel asked her. She was upset with Mathew for rejecting her, for deciding she was worthy of the sheets but not the home. "I have my reasons."

"Are you staying?"

"No. I'm going to pack up and head out."

"Where?"

"West. I'll make my mark in San Francisco. I'll open a saloon right next to the rush of gold miners."

Jonathan's eyes glistened in the firelight. He stepped forward and wrapped her in a hug. "If I can't convince you to stay, then good luck to you. Be safe and be well. I love you, sis."

Verity's eyes clouded over in her own tears. "I love you too, Johnny."

# Chapter Eighteen

Bridgeport, Wisconsin
1853

MATHEW CLOSED HIS EYES through the nausea and dizziness of the travel, and upon reopening them, it was late afternoon. A cold wind pierced his thin dress shirt. He fastened the top button at his throat in a useless attempt at extra warmth. Stringy clusters of snow stuck to ridges in the ground. Bent, dead grasses surrounded him in a field. What in the world?

Northwest was a scattering of two-story buildings, and everywhere else was trees and fields. Mathew trudged through the bent and frozen grasses until he reached what he assumed to be a road—a wide dirt path with ruts from thin wheels and a dusting of snow at the low points. Flipping up the collar of his wholly inadequate dress shirt, he braced himself against the cold and set off at a brisk pace to keep warm, clouds bursting from his lips.

After what felt like an hour, he came upon the first building—Couture Clothing. The lights were off. He continued and saw Stanton's Spirits, Bridgeport Chemist, Porter's General Store. And there, on the right was a bank. He really was back in time. Verity had mentioned Bridgeport. A surreal strength came

over him, an invincibility.

Mathew crossed the threshold and found a man counting a stack of coins.

"Howdy, there. We were just closing. What can I do for you?" The teller's curious eyes raked over him. Yeah, Mathew was underdressed—or perhaps overdressed—for the occasion.

"I need to open an account."

"Well, you've come to the right place."

Mathew set the bag down on the counter and stacked the remaining silver bars. The teller whistled.

"We've had a lot of entrepreneurs settling around here, but none looking like you, carrying this much silver. I'd like to know what it is you've found so lucrative."

Mathew snorted. Since he couldn't tell the truth, he opted for alluding to the Gold Rush Verity had mentioned. "If I told you, it wouldn't be lucrative much longer."

The teller chuckled and filled out a card. "Hold on to this. It's your account number."

"Thank you, sir."

Mathew passed through town with a new card in his wallet and empty hands. He didn't see the need to carry an empty bag around. Beyond the town, thick underbrush crept close to the road. Daylight quickly faded. About a half mile down on his left, his ears picked up a horse snorting, and when he found the source, his back stiffened.

The unremarkable horse stood alongside a building, currently a house, that in his time was his very own veterinary clinic. The exterior logs were newer and the plaque announcing the year of construction was shiny steel—not the dull patina plate he knew.

It was a private residence, smaller, since he was the one who commissioned an addition, but since he was freezing, lights flickered in the windows, and he was nosy, he thought this would be the best place to warm up.

When the door swung open, Mathew's jaw dropped. He blinked several times as if he didn't trust his own frozen eyeballs. The woman held a sleeping baby, nestled in her arms. Her dark brown hair reached all the way down her back. Her skin aged, just a little, from working hard, and her body was a little softer.

"Matty?" The familiar voice sent warmth blossoming through his chest.

"Meatball?" Mathew asked in a whisper of shock.

She opened her free arm to welcome him in a hug and he rushed into her arms, careful to not startle the little squirt. He'd missed her so much. Seeing her safe and well returned a piece of him that had been lost. His sister pulled back first and said, "Come on in. It's freezing outside." Mathew rubbed his arms and his sister closed the door behind him.

"I don't suppose you brought me a cheesecake, chocolate bar, or a bag of fast food?"

He laughed. "Sorry, the delivery man didn't receive your order. Wow, look at this place! It's so familiar yet...Like the freaking Twilight Zone in here."

"I know, right? I had the same thoughts when I first saw it."

Mathew took a turn around the room, inspecting it as if it were a museum.

"Come sit by the fire. You look half frozen."

He crossed to the fire and held out his trembling hands. He shivered as the warmth penetrated the inadequately thin layer of

polyester.

"I haven't seen you in so long, but you look like you haven't aged a day," she said, rocking a baby in layers of linen.

"You've been gone three weeks."

"Right," she tapped herself on the forehead with her open palm. "Time is different. It's been a year and a half here but feels like five."

Mathew sunk into the recliner next to the fire. Orange light flickered over his sister's face—so familiar yet so different. "Who's the little squirt?" April smiled with a motherly glow, and Mathew knew. "Yours?"

"This is...well...we named him after you. Matty, meet Mathew Hartley."

Mathew's eyes welled with tears of pride and love. His throat was constricted, so he didn't respond.

"I hope you don't mind. I just thought since you were the best role model in my life, I wanted to honor you."

"I am honored." He swiped his eyes. The little bundle carrying his namesake slept soundly in her arms. He was only a couple months old. "Jesus Christ, April. I'm so happy for you. I didn't know you came here. What happened?"

"Kiko sent me back to save Sam's life, Mathew's father. I screwed up, but she let me try again. After that, I couldn't let him go," she said, wistfully. "He made me return home for medical care."

Mathew remembered driving her. "The emergency room." April nodded and Mathew blew heat in his palms. "Can you tell me now what happened to you?"

"Jaime Perez."

Mathew blanched in confirmation.

"He thought I was someone else. Blamed me for Greenleaf, whatever that is. I thought it was an organic toothpaste or something. Sam tells me it's a town southeast of here. Never been there."

"You've passed by Greenleaf on the highway many times."

"I have? Well, it's clearly forgettable. "

"True." Mathew sighed. "I know who he mistook you for."

"Who's that?"

"Verity Arris. She's the one Kiko sent me to save."

Fear crossed April's smooth face. "Jonathan Arris's sister. Where is she?"

"I don't know, but now that I know where we are, my clinic, and where my apartment is, I should be able to find her farm without trouble. I just hope she's there."

"No one's moving in this cold of night. I've got a spare room for you. We can give you a ride over in the morning after breakfast."

Mathew's cold bones were grateful for the hospitality. It was a culture shock going from July to December in a blink and being ill dressed for the occasion. "I'd appreciate it."

"Is it summer back home?" April nodded to his shirt.

"It was. Wish I still had my suit on anyway." Mathew's cheeks heated, which normally he'd hide, but right now it helped thaw him.

"Suit? That's not your style unless—did Dad die?" She asked with a hint of excitement.

"I wish, but no. I had a date."

April's knowing brows rose. "And I'm guessing it didn't end

well."

"I'm guessing not also. Verity had different expectations than I did."

"That's understandable." She chuckled. "Women of our time are not like this time."

"I've noticed." Mathew ran a hand through his hair, and it stood up on ends. "Mind if I use the bathroom?"

"Sorry, sport. No bathrooms here."

"What?" Mathew stood. "Where do you? How..."

"There's an outhouse out back for a toilet. Otherwise for a bath, the pantry, uh, the office bathroom, has a basin. There's a hand pump outside to fill it. You might want to heat it on the stove for a while first. A splash of that frigid Wisconsin ground water will shrivel your...Never mind."

Mathew growled in frustration and put his shoes back on. This would be a new experience. No worse than a blue porta potty at a beer and cheese festival, right?

MATHEW WOKE WITH a start and sat up. Unfamiliar walls surrounded him—a mix of dusty library and antique hotel. A gas lamp perched on an end table. And the hardwood floors were freezing cold to his bare feet. Where was he?

Then he remembered going back in time again and meeting his sister. Unbelieving his memory and his eyes, he dressed in his wholly inadequate clothes again, awkwardly overdressed for the time, and stepped out to the kitchen where his sister prepared breakfast.

Now, Mathew was very comfortable with his sexuality, so he

wasn't afraid to admit that the man standing next to his sister was a very attractive dude. Mathew wished he'd been gifted half the gene pool as this man he assumed was April's husband. At least Mathew's namesake would grow to be a dashing young man. A pang of sorrow hit him when he realized he would never see the baby grow up. All the worse when he realized he'd lost the last family member he had. April was never coming back home.

Mathew would be completely alone, and that was the most depressing way to start the day.

"Hey there," April said when she turned. "Are you okay? Matty, come here. Meet Sam, my husband. Sam this is my brother."

A broad-shouldered man capable of crushing him like a bug extended a large calloused hand. "Nice to meet ye, Matty." And he had an Irish accent. Mathew was precisely ten inches tall right now, but he was thrilled his sister had found her happiness. It was just hard to show it at the moment.

"Um, Matt is fine. Thanks."

"Veterinarian, huh? April told me ye fix animals like a doctor. I'd say, her skills were exceptional when we needed them."

The baby cried and April whisked away little Mathew into her bedroom.

"I take pride in training my employees well," Mathew said to Sam. "She was one of my best."

"Dinnae worry about her. She's in good hands here."

Mathew smiled. "Is she doing okay? I mean, it's a bit of a shock from our lifestyle to this." He waved his hands around.

"Are ye talking about cars and planes and things?"

"Yeah, have you been to the future?" Mathew didn't understand how anyone with a taste of creature comforts would reject them for—his gaze roamed over the strong jawline, trim beard, and bright turquoise eyes—never mind.

"No. Honestly it sounds scary."

"Verity was terrified at first. Thought cars were beasts." He chuckled and Sam gave him a disapproving stare. Mathew cleared his throat. "But that was understandable. I couldn't imagine jumping over a hundred and sixty years into my future. Yikes."

Sam nodded and turned back to pouring...

"Are you making pancakes?"

"April's favorite."

"Yeah, I know." There was an aura of an alternate reality around him, as if he were a ghost shifting through different times in history. How did Kiko feel time hopping for years? What an existence she must've had. Although Kiko appeared twenty, he wondered how old she actually was.

Mathew's fingers searched his pockets for his phone. He couldn't offer the man much in thanks, but he could offer a glimpse into the future.

"Sam, would you like to see it?"

"See what?" he asked and flipped a row of pancakes on a cast iron pan.

"The future."

"I'm no' leaving April. No temptation out there would ever make me consider it."

"Pictures. Movies. You don't have to go anywhere. Sit down."

The iron sizzled with each flip, wafting the scent of fresh

browned pancakes. Sam tossed a towel over his shoulder and sat at the table. Mathew woke his cell phone and tapped the photo gallery. He turned the screen toward Sam. Inane photos of him and Becca at the clinic, he and Verity, and a photo of Verity in a plum dress from the designer shop. Sam's brows where high and his mouth gaped like a fish.

"This is real?"

"Camera in the phone." He found a video he made while driving, of a motorist on the verge of total road rage. He pressed play and Sam scooted back in his chair. Music from his phone played in the background as a Tahoe swerved lanes and honked incessantly. "It's a movie I made. I was driving. Don't tell anyone, it's not safe."

"I can see that. Well," Sam said and April opened the door to the bedroom with a sleepy baby. "I'm glad my wife is here, safe with me. And I thought I had a safety problem in my town."

"This town isn't safe?" Mathew asked.

"Hasn't been for a while. Jaime Perez and his minions have taken over the Grignon estate up the hill. Some days I wonder if it was such a great idea to kill the man. Jaime's worse. We have an accord, Jaime and I, otherwise he would've been back here in a second to steal April."

Mathew's eyes widened in alarm.

"Aye, but dinnae worry. No one is dumb enough to lay a hand on her, or little Matty."

"What's going on out here?" April asked.

"I showed my brother-in-law here a video I made of a road rage incident."

"Matty! Don't scare him like that. Honey, that's not normal

driving."

"Ye dinnae go that fast?"

"We do. We don't normally swerve and honk, and film it." His sister squinted at him.

"That was enough future for me. I understand yer comment, April, about the horses. I dinnae see any." Sam got up, shaking his head, and served up the pancakes. His sister set the baby down in a bassinet and joined him at the table. The three of them ate, and Mathew watched as April threw her leftovers out the back door.

"What are you doing?"

"Feeding the dogs." She smiled and exchanged glances with Sam.

Mathew glanced around the room and failed to see any pet paraphernalia. April chuckled.

"They're strays—mostly."

Mathew reached into his back pocket for his wallet—for the account card. He'd intended to it be a nice diversified investment for his present self, but with all his problems finally cleared, he didn't need it. And just in case his sister needed help, it was one last paycheck for her.

He opened the wallet and a gunshot echoed across the fields.

# Chapter Nineteen

## Astor, Wisconsin
## 1853

VERITY HAD ONLY ONE suitcase packed for her journey across the country. She didn't own much and didn't need much on the road. The wintry morning was chilly as usual for a December in Astor. She would miss her brothers, but she wouldn't miss the farm. Verity could die happy knowing she would never see another cornfield in her life.

She had changed into practical layers of dress for the season and the cloak wrapped around her shoulders kept out most of the blistering cold. She packed her beautiful plum dress. She couldn't wear it anywhere, but it reminded her of Mathew. Her heart wouldn't let her leave it behind.

She loaded up a horse from the stable and mounted. She headed east to swing by a place in Bridgeport. The roads were clear except a few patches of snow. Most of the trees were barren, and the rest were evergreens brushed with white cotton. The once golden fields were now brown with winter hibernation and speckled with early snow patches. Cold seeped past her wool cloak, and she shivered. The saddle offered none of the horse's warmth.

At the bridge crossing the Fox River into Bridgeport, two men on horseback stood guard. She had heard Jaime's men kept the bandits at bay, but she had never seen the bridge guarded. Of course, she didn't get out much. Verity recognized these men. They'd introduced themselves while she hid in her secret cubbyhole. Joe Pool and Rob Bertrand stood sentry on their mounts. She didn't know which was which, but they were Jaime Perez's men. Her back stiffened when she approached. Hopefully they wouldn't recognize her after all these months.

"Morning, miss. Pay the toll to pass."

Since when did she have to pay to cross the bridge? If it got her through, fine. There was always more money to be made. "How much?"

"Fifty cents." The man with a raspy voice and soft jawline stared her down.

Verity dug in her dress pocket and counted out the coins. She passed them to the man with the raspy voice.

Her horse took a step forward and the other man, who was short and lean, extended a hand to stop her and said, "Fifty cents."

Verity scrunched her nose and said, "I just paid fifty cents."

"You paid *him*." He smiled and the hole where a tooth should've been gaped back at her.

"I...You can't charge me double! Your terms were fifty cents. If you wanted double, you should've asked for it. I'm not paying that much. Let me through."

"Hey, Joe." The soft jawline man, who must then be Rob Bertrand, scratched his chin. "Do you think we should let the lady pass?"

"Hmmm. I would let a lady pass, sure." Joe's smile curled into a sneer. "But this ain't no lady."

"That's enough, men," a familiar voice sprung up behind her. Verity turned to see Butch, the onion man, riding toward the bridge, layered in envious warmth with his face half covered in a menacing cloth. She didn't know whether to be more afraid or relieved.

"Says who?" Rob asked.

"Yeah, says who?" Joe parroted.

"Says Butch."

Jaime's men exchanged glances and Verity pulled her cloak closer. There was no use in trying to escape.

"Is that Butch as in Eddie Butcher?" Joe asked.

Butch nodded and slid down his face covering. "The one and only."

Verity shivered from the cold and from uncertainty. Did Butch know who she was? Joe Pool's brother, Ben, had warned her that Jaime had a bounty on her. Were all three men going to fight for the reward?

Jaime's men shared a glance and nod. Joe moved his horse over in indication she was free to pass. The glares of hatred from the two men weren't lost on her. Butch followed her across the bridge, and when they were safely on the other side of the river, Verity turned and saw that Rob was gone. She hoped he wasn't running for the cavalry.

Butch asked, "So Jaime's got it in for ya?"

"Why do you ask?"

"Any enemy of Jaime's is a friend of mine. Got any onions on you?"

Verity chuckled. "Sorry, fresh out. Why do you hate Jaime?"

"Let's just say, Jaime's been making a mess for me and my men. We were once free to move around and take what we needed, now he stops us or charges us. He's killed many of my men."

"Who are your men?"

"My men." He shrugged as if that clarified his answer. "Some people like to give us stupid names. Bandits is one I hear most often."

Verity's eyes widened, realizing the ruthless leader of the bandits rode next to her chatting casually. He had been against two men, and Jaime's men backed down like scared puppies. Verity wasn't so sure she wanted to be friendly with him, and she didn't want to find out the hard way he intended to cash in the bounty himself. "Well, I best be going. Thank you for your help."

"Now wait a minute there, Miss Arris."

Verity stopped. Her hands shook. She couldn't out-ride this man any better than the other two. She boldly met his eyes and tipped her chin up. "Yes?"

"I heard the story of what you did to Jaime Perez."

She gulped.

"And I sure would hate to piss you off. If you ever need a hand, give me a holler."

Verity smiled in surprise. She'd just made friends with the leader of the bandits. "Thank you, Butch. I appreciate it."

"Oh, and Miss Arris? If you ever decide you'd like a life more excitin' than farmin', come find me any time. I like a bold woman." Butch winked.

Verity smiled in acknowledgment. Had he just proposed? "I'll keep that in mind."

He tipped his hat to her and turned north on Adams Street. Verity kicked the horse into a gallop and traveled straight to Hartley's Blacksmith and Gallery. The doors were closed and locked. Verity cupped her hand at the window, and no one manned the desk. Curious, Verity stepped away from the building and walked her horse toward the front door of the cabin, crossing an open grassy area.

A rifle boomed from the back of the house, and Verity dashed to the front door. It wasn't deer hunting season for two more months. Another shot rang out and Verity pounded her fist in desperation and opened the front door herself. "Hello?"

Inside she found a woman, very similar in appearance to herself, staring straight at her. *This must be Mathew's sister.* "April?"

"Who are you?" April clutched the baby closer and squinted at her.

"Verity Arris."

April's eyes widened with understanding and she relaxed her posture. "It's you. The one Jaime thought I was."

"I'm afraid so. I'm sorry for what happened to you. It wasn't fair," Verity said to the woman she'd admired from afar. "And I'm sorry for barging in here, but I heard a rifle shot."

"I heard it too. You can stay until the men say it's safe. No one deserves what happened to me, except Jaime himself."

"Can I just say that I'm so proud of everything you've done for this town and for Sam? I've read the stories in the newspaper, and I've been an admirer of you since." Verity cast her eyes to her feet. "I've been trapped on a farm because of Jaime, not out

saving the world."

April smiled. "I only did what I had to do for the people I cared about. I couldn't leave them to fend for themselves, and after a while, this place was home."

Verity respected the woman's strength and selflessness. Mathew helped animals at the clinic and showed Verity a great time, despite his fear of rollercoasters and flying. So, Verity could see some of his sister's traits in him. But Mathew also dragged her along to New York City for his own selfish needs and rejected her request for a marriage proposal. Now was not the time to dwell on it.

"I'd love to stay and chat," April continued, "but someone's out there and we don't know who. Both of us have enemies. Take this bag in case my brother needs it—"

"Matt's here?" Verity's heart skipped one too many times, and her knees wobbled.

"Help him with whatever's going on. I'm going to hide with little Mathew."

Verity nodded, and mother and child disappeared behind a thick cedar door. Verity held the bag close and watched through the back window with dread. The standard game of battle—*guess who would be dead, alive, or injured.* She only hoped it wouldn't be Mathew.


MATHEW RUSHED to the back window with the gunshot still echoing across the field. A second one rattled the quiet morning and Mathew ducked. Sam jumped to his feet and closed the distance to the door. "Did ye see anyone?"

A canine yelp followed the second echo. Sam bolted out the door in only his trousers. Mathew felt obligated to follow in his thin dress shirt and pants. He shouted to Sam, "Is it wise to be half-dressed outside in the winter chasing after a gunman?"

Sam shouted back over his shoulder, "It's disappointing to see men of the future turn soft. Move yer feet. We have to catch him."

"Soft?" Mathew yelled over the din of the crunching grasses. "Some of us future men prefer to use brains over brawn. Nothing wrong with that. This is suicidal!"

An angry man's roar shook the trees up ahead. Their feet ate up the frozen ground. Mathew took care to land his feet to prevent a sprained ankle while they dashed across a field of waist-high dead grasses and into the woods. Sam followed the whimpers. He skidded to a stop, and Mathew cautiously walked up behind him. Both their chests heaved to catch their breath, and white clouds puffed in front of their faces.

"No!" Sam's outburst thundered across the fields. He dropped to his knees, and Mathew saw a mutt lying on its side with a clear bullet wound in its shoulder. A rustling ahead warned Mathew of the shooter's presence.

"He's here, Sam. The gunman. Straight ahead." He pointed and Sam stood. Mathew continued, "Go. I'll take care of the dog. You get the guy."

Sam dropped a hand on Mathew's shoulder. "I'm trusting ye with my dog. He means a lot to me. Dinnae worry about the shooter. I'll rip his arms off."

"I've got him." Mathew smiled and Sam dashed off farther into the woods. Mathew knelt and scooped the poor filthy dog

into his arms. Its tail wagged, and it tried to lick his face. Mathew's heart broke for him. He pressed the dog's wound to his chest to stifle the bleeding and ran back to the house as fast as he could without doing further tissue damage. A glance over his shoulder was all he afforded his brother-in-law on his pursuit of the bad guy. He saw and heard no one.

Mathew entered the back door. "April! I need help."

"I've got clean water here, scissors and tongs." Mathew's head spun at the woman's voice.

"Verity? How did you...? Where did you...?"

"Stop babbling and help the poor dog. Your sister gave me this bag full of supplies. She's secured in her room with the baby."

"Why?" Mathew set the dog down on the kitchen table. Verity closed the back door and latched it locked.

"There's a gunman on the loose. April has enemies. Makes sense to me."

"I meant, why are you here? But Sam's very worried about this little guy. Give me a hand?" Verity brought over a gas lamp, and Mathew inspected the red mangled patch of flesh. "Clippers?"

She handed him scissors. No electricity. Mathew pinched hunks of matted fur and cut them away. She passed him a clean towel, and he patted the wound. The dog whimpered. Mathew had no anesthesia.

"Any chloroform in there?" Although not exactly safe for pets, it was better than nothing.

"I don't think so."

How was he going to dig all the fragments out? Mathew

waved the light closer, and Verity held the pooch down. His tail still wagged, and Mathew's heart broke for the tough little guy. Mathew palpated the skin around the opening and felt the round lodged in the shoulder blade. One lucky pup.

"Any Betadine or something with iodine on the label?"

"No."

Mathew sighed.

"Tongs." Verity handed the tool to him and he went in quick and retrieved the steel ball. The dog yelped and struggled. Blood poured out of the wound. "Hold him tight." He threaded a needle and poked and pulled the thread through, making a clean line of stitches. The dog whimpered and thrashed, and Mathew was equal parts frustrated and sorry. "Gauze."

He accepted the proffered white roll and wrapped it around the dog with Verity helping to lift him. Satisfied, he cut the end and secured it with tape. "Any alcohol in the bag?"

"I don't see any."

"Well, if he doesn't succumb to infection, he'll be all right."

Mathew released the dog, and he squirmed up to a seated position on the table, holding the paw of the affected shoulder in the air. Mathew picked him up and set him on the floor. He and Verity cleaned up together.

"So, what are you doing here?" he asked her again.

"I was going to ask you the same."

Their eyes met and Verity's cheeks pinked. Mathew said, "Well, I wanted to explain what happened at the restaurant. You?"

"Came to buy a dagger."

"What? Why do you need a dagger?" Mathew set the soiled

towels in the empty wash basin.

"What kind of man carries no arms?" She spit Jonathan's line at him while packing the unused supplies back into April's backpack.

"Ouch. Listen, can we talk?"

"I thought that's what we're doing." Verity carried the soiled instruments to the kitchen and set them in the wash basin with the towel. She dipped a bowl into April's clean water supply and set it on the floor. The injured pup hobbled over and slobbered it all up.

Sam pounded on the back door and shouted to be let inside. Mathew opened it. His brother-in-law burst through the door, panting. "April?" he called.

Mathew's sister came out from the bedroom holding little Mathew. "Is everyone all right?"

"We're fine," Mathew answered.

"And Doug?"

April gasped. "Doug was hurt? What happened?"

Mathew pointed to the drinking mutt. "This little guy is Doug? He'll be fine. Could use a neuter though."

April passed the baby to Sam and ran to Doug, giving him scratches on the head. Sam passed the baby to Verity and followed likewise. April had tears in her eyes.

Verity cooed at the baby. She rocked him and tickled his nose and made silly faces. Verity looked stunning holding an infant, a glowing radiance of maternal warmth. She was perfect with children, and Mathew knew at that moment there was no other woman for him. How could he convince her to give him more time and prove he was worthy of her?

Sam stood up, satisfied with Mathew's care, and said, "Thank ye, kindly."

"That's what I do."

"So, no hard feelings about the soft comment?"

"I think we're even."

"No. I owe ye. Doug is family. But now we've got a problem." Sam continued, "I couldna catch the gunman, but I saw him. Rob Bertrand, one of Jaime's men. I'm guessing Jaime put a hit on Verity."

"I was told there was a bounty," Verity confirmed.

"Is that true?" Mathew asked.

"It's not us," Sam added. "Jaime hasn't poked his arse around these parts in over a year. You two walk in the door and now his men are sniffing around. If it's no' her, it's ye, Matt."

Mathew gulped. "He may have mentioned something about me being on his list."

All the eyes in the room turned to him.

# Chapter Twenty

VERITY COVERED HER shoulders with her cloak, thankful for the chance to thaw out inside the Hartley's home and still in awe of meeting the woman she admired so much, but she still needed to buy what she came for so she could set out toward her destination.

"Is your shop open today, Sam? I need to make a purchase."

"Uh, sure. Just give me a minute, and I'll get the door unlocked for ye." Sam stepped to the bedroom and came back out tucking a shirt into his trousers. She followed him out back to the shop and after he unlocked the door, she followed him into the front office.

"What can I get for ye, Verity?"

"I need a dagger."

Sam smiled. "Did Johnny lose his?"

Verity frowned. "It's for me."

"Right this way, then. It's dirty back here."

"I don't mind."

"Here's what I have ready made for daggers." His hands waved over a hanging selection of knives from two inches to over a foot long. "If you want something custom, it will take a few days."

Verity lifted the handle of a three-inch knife and assessed the balance of the hilt and the weight distribution of the blade. She tucked it against her forearm and swiped the air with it. Satisfied, she replaced it on the wall. "This is fine craftsmanship as always. I'm glad you're back in business."

"Thank ye."

"I'll require a custom order. My hands are too small for these."

"Do ye have a size and design in mind?"

She pointed to the three-inch. "I want a four-inch similar to this one, but I need the handle narrower."

Sam opened her palm and pressed in areas. He turned her hand over, and his eyes mechanically assessed her size and strength with murmurs and measurements. He was a very handsome man, and this felt very intimate, but there was no spark of heat, no desire or need, not like when Mathew touched her. But he rejected her. She brushed the painful thought aside. Sam scribbled notes on a pad of paper nearby and said, "I'll need two days, maybe one, but I dinnae want to promise that."

Verity nodded in agreement and she returned to the log cabin, cloak collar tipped up against the cold. Mathew came out front just as she reached the door.

"Come on, we're leaving." His bold blue eyes challenged her.

"You can't make me go anywhere," Verity said.

"They need privacy, we need safety. Let's go." His hand reached out to take her elbow. She twisted away.

"I'm not going with you and don't follow me." She didn't trust him not to bring her back to the farm. After declaring her independence from Jonathan, the last thing she wanted was to

stand on his doorstep and announce her failure.

"Where are you going? Home?" he asked.

Verity cast her eyes down. "No. I'm going out west."

"Like Minneapolis?"

"California."

"You can't go out there alone."

Verity bristled. No longer would anyone tell her what she could and could not do. "I can go wherever I want. If you're so afraid for me"—Verity fought a smile. Maybe after a journey he'd change his mind—"Come with me."

"Whoa, hold on there. You're talking like the Oregon trail? I'm not dying of dysentery or typhoid. Shooting buffalo, buying bullets." Mathew shook his head. "Nope. Not happening. Haven't you heard of the Donner party?"

"No."

"They ate each other trying to cross the Rockies. And you would willingly follow their path?"

Verity hadn't heard the story, but it sounded like poppycock, especially since Mathew had lied to her before. Out west was where adventure and riches awaited her, and if he wouldn't come, then she didn't want to be bogged down by him. Sometimes his extreme caution drove her mad.

"Come with *me*," he insisted. "I'll get us a hotel room to warm up. We need to talk."

She couldn't handle being rejected by him again, and since he wouldn't come with her, she needed to get away. "Collect my things from inside and I'll go with you."

"That's the most sensible thing you've said today." Mathew grabbed her around the neck and kissed her. Stunned for a

second, she allowed his tongue access to her mouth, her lips tingling and her legs weakening. Heat blossomed in her body, and she hated that he affected her so. Abruptly, he turned on his heels, breaking their bond. Verity blew out a cloud and her eyes pricked with tears. As soon as the cabin door closed, she mounted up and kicked her horse to a full gallop. She choked back a sob while she fled, her lips still tingling with Mathew's touch.

Icy wind stung her eyes. Staying in Bridgeport where Jaime Perez dominated was dangerous, and she couldn't stay with Sam and April, risking their lives and their precious baby. Verity wasn't ready to show up at the farm with her tail between her legs, nor beg Jonathan for her gun or his dagger—not that she could grip his effectively, and Mathew had all her essential belongings. So, she headed back west toward Astor to seek refuge until deciding her next move and kept her fingers crossed the bridge was unoccupied.

Verity crested the bridge, and her heart sunk when two heads appeared on the far side. She skidded her horse to a stop. The traitorous beast nickered, and Jaime's men turned their heads. She spun the horse around and kicked him into a new run. Galloping hooves closed in behind her and she avoided the first turn north—where the bandit Eddie Butcher had gone. But she also didn't want to keep going and run into Mathew. He didn't stand a chance against Jaime's men. She turned north on the next road, a small dirt path only wide enough for a single carriage.

The vegetation was gangly without its summer leaves, and Verity bolted uphill. She came upon a garden, hibernating for winter, with trimmed green hedges, a pergola covered in empty

vines, and steppingstones leading up to a marvelous estate.

Sunshine yellow against the gray December clouds, it was beautiful. Verity stopped the horse and her breathing quickened. Only one man was rich enough for a home like this, and he was dead. With its immaculate condition, Grignon's predecessor must've been keeping it up, and she wanted to be as far from Jaime Perez as possible. She shook her head and turned. Rob Bertrand was on her heels—the one from the bridge that dashed off into the woods and fired a rifle in Sam's backyard. He rode right up to her and pulled her from her horse before she could react.

Verity screamed. She never would've made it to the Arris farm anyway. She only hoped Mathew didn't do some stupid, if he ever found her.


MATHEW WAS EAGER to find Verity's things and get a hotel room. He didn't know what would happen, but he needed to explain himself. She was infuriatingly stubborn, yet utterly perfect. But he refused to marry someone who only wanted a proposal because of obsolete social norms. He wanted her to choose him because she wanted him. A baby's coo turned his head.

"I suppose you're leaving," April said. She stood a few feet in front of him with his chubby pink namesake in her protective arms. His sister's sullen face showed she awaited his confirmation.

"I'm taking Verity to a hotel to chat." Mathew slung the bag over his shoulder.

April chuckled. "Sure you are. I don't need details, but no need to fib."

"I'm not fibbing," he said with softness.

"So, I guess...I'm not going to see you again, am I?"

Mathew closed the distance and gave her a hug. A quiet sob escaped her lips.

"Hey, hey. I plan to be back…with or without Verity."

"Without?" April cocked her head.

"She's mad at me. I'm trying to smooth it over."

"What did you do?"

"Apparently, I failed to propose marriage quick enough. I'm trying to stop her from fleeing to California."

"You never were good at reading women."

She was right. "In my defense, I've known her for about two weeks. So, whether I succeed or not, I promise to return. We have unfinished business."

"You make it sound like a mob deal."

"I think dealing with the mob would be safer than Jaime Perez's crew."

"I think you're right." She lifted her lips in a small smile.

"I need to go. Verity is waiting for me. I promise I'll be back."

A rumble of gurgles and fluid erupted from little Mathew. Seconds later an explosive stink fogged Mathew's brain. Without disposable diapers, he didn't want to think of what his sister had to do next.

"Someone is trying to kick you out the door," she said, smiling at the little boy in her arms.

Mathew chuckled with watery eyes. He never could keep all this promises before. "I've got a woman waiting. I love you." He

leaned in, careful to avoid any baby contamination, and gave little Mathew the literal stink-eye while he patted his sister on her back.

"And you, little man, be good and stay clean."

"I love you too, Matty," she said with a broken voice.

Mathew stopped at the door with a hand on the knob and his sister waved. Tears rolled down her cheeks, and he nodded, closing the door behind him.

The blistery cold slapped him on the face, stealing his breath. Verity was not in view.

"Verity?" He wiped his eyes dry and jogged to both sides of the log cabin. He didn't see her. His pulse kicked into gear, and rapid breaths tore from his chest. *Oh, shit no.*

"Verity!"

She was gone.

# Chapter Twenty-One

BOOKS FILLED THE walls from floor to ceiling. A small wooden table for two sat on one side of the room with two chairs placed under it. There were no windows, but a fireplace crackled, sputtering the only dim light in the room. The back of her head ached, and her fingers searched her scalp. She winced at the tender spot. Someone had hit her on the head and tossed her in here. She needed to get out. Verity's heart pounded in her chest and she stood on sore legs. Her palm went to her temple to suppress her growing headache.

The disorienting pain subsided, and Verity set about escape. She last remembered was coming up to a magnificent estate and it turned out to be Jaime Perez's house. She used the wall to support her steps to the door and tried the knob. They'd locked it, as expected.

Verity pawed at the books, hoping to find a secret door or passageway. When her fingers cleared half the room, the door behind her opened. She stilled and her breath hitched. Loud footsteps clattered on the hardwood. Verity's hands trembled while she turned. She wanted to fall to pieces upon seeing Jaime Perez with a happy smile on his face.

"My, my, my, what a wonderful sight. I've dreamed of this

day for—how long has it been? Over a year now. A long time."
He strolled inside and shut the door behind him. He wore
trousers, a long-sleeved shirt, a pistol vest, and a hat, which he
removed from his head and tossed on the table. The pistol vest
was free of weapons. He didn't intend to kill her yet. She didn't
know whether to be relieved or terrified.

"Jaime," she acknowledged and stood up straight. She'd faced
him before, and she would do it again. The smile left his weaselly
face. A tremble began in her stomach, but she held firm on the
outside. Jaime stalked up to her with casual menace and stopped
at arm's reach.

A quick snap of his hand sent her head reeling. Her cheek
stung. Verity's eyes watered on reflex, and she tilted her face to
hide it from him.

Jaime chuckled.

"Never speak unless asked a question. That's how I run this
house, and you should know that by now, but I'm glad you
forgot. So, everything I do to you is your own fault. Maybe if
your father taught you some manners, I wouldn't have found
you in The Wounded Soldier in Greenleaf, and you wouldn't
have defied me." He sucked air through his teeth and rested a
hand on his hip. "Even with the damage you did to me, I still
haven't decided whether I regretted our rendezvous." Jaime
sneered.

Verity had always known Jaime was an animal. She hadn't
known how delusional he'd been. And that was a dangerous mix.
She'd always wished for a merciful death if Jaime got his hands
on her, but now that the time arrived, Verity wasn't ready to give
up.

"Anyway, down to business." He clapped his hands and Verity's eyes searched for anything to defend herself with. A book wouldn't do any damage. Across the room were chairs and a vertical basket of fireplace implements—too far out of reach.

Jaime unbuckled his belt and Verity heard the soul-sucking sound of his leather strap sliding through his belt loops. She wanted to vomit at the memory of their last encounter. This time would be so much worse.

He unbuttoned his trousers and a crooked erection pressed at his linen drawers. Verity recoiled.

"You never saw the aftermath. So, I will give you the pleasure. Perhaps you won't fight the punishment so much. We wouldn't want your discipline to get out of hand, would we?" Jaime untied his drawers and his erection sprang free. It was misshapen, like a chunk was severed off. His—she shivered at the sight—sack was also missing most of the flesh it should've encompassed. His inner thigh and groin area had several thick jagged white scars.

If it weren't for this situation, she would've been proud to give him a taste of his own discipline, but alas, she was terrified. Her self-defense hadn't scared him off, it had only angered him more. April had suffered by his hands because of what she'd done to him. Somehow, someway, she would stop Jaime once and for all. Seeing how she was trapped and unarmed, Verity hoped a knight in shining armor would come save her just like in the fairy tales, but she had more sense than that. Hope was only a distraction.

"Beautiful isn't it? If it weren't for the circumstances"—he used a hand to shift himself around, displaying her work more clearly—"I would've been impressed." Jaime lifted his belt and

said, "Turn around. The lessons begin now, and if you fight, I will knock you out. Then your lessons will only resume once you wake, and I won't be holding back."

Verity trembled while she turned around. His hand pressed her back until she folded over. Tears sprung to her eyes and her body convulsed with fear. His disgusting hands lifted her skirting, exposing her scarred bare bottom.

A snap of leather sliced across her derriere. She stifled a scream and bit into her hand. He delighted in screaming, and she refused to allow him any more pleasure than necessary. Warm liquid trickled down the back of her thighs. The snap came again and again until the screams broke free.

She begged and cried out in pain. She screamed for him to stop. Her body shuddered and tensed under the relentless agony.

"That's it, honey, now we're getting to the meat of the lesson. Stay with me now. This is only the first of many to come. By the time I'm through with you, you'll be my personal assistant."

Not quickly enough, the pain in Verity's body mercifully knocked her out.

AT A LOSS FOR IDEAS and not dressed to go gallivanting around in the winter wearing only a dress shirt and pants, Mathew knocked on his sister's front door and entered before anyone gave him permission.

"April? Sam?" Mathew's voice was steady, but on the inside, his pulse roared, and he fought to keep his breathing under control.

April stood up from the couch with concern on her face.

"That was fast. What happened?"

"Verity's gone. She said she would wait for me to collect her things and she's just gone."

Sam stepped out from his bedroom. "Is the horse here?"

"No."

"That's a good sign," he said. "It means she left. Did ye say anything to her? Make her angry? Push the poor lass away?"

Left? Of course she left. What else would've happened? Mathew cringed at his last words to her. "I may have insulted her idea of going to California."

"Oh, yeah. Oregon trail," April said. "Loved that game." Sam squinted at her with confusion. Mathew would've laughed if the circumstances were lighter. She cleared her throat. "You're right though. It's a bad idea."

"Right. Any idea where she might've gone? I'll get lost in a nanosecond running around out there."

Sam dragged a chair out from the kitchen table and fell into it. "Well, she might've gone west back to her farm, right?"

"I doubt it. She told me it was a prison for her."

Sam scratched his stubbled chin. "East would be back toward Bridgeport. There's a bar there, my mate's in fact. A general store, a clothing shop. Not sure if she was on a mission to go shopping."

"Not likely."

"Well there's the road north to Navarino. Not sure what she'd need there. Are you sure she didn't just start her travels to California?"

Mathew lifted the bag in his hands. "I have her stuff. Probably not."

"My best advice is head into Bridgeport and check the shops. Maybe she went to get a beer at Lloyd's or a bite to eat at Max's. But what I can tell ye, is between here and the bridge to Astor is a dirt road up a hill. Stay away from there. Jaime Perez commandeered himself in Grignon's estate after I killed the old man. Jaime's bad news."

"You remember when you drove me to the ER?"

Mathew nodded. He knew Jaime had whipped his sister. He knew Jaime had previously whipped Verity. Mathew had a hunch she made a dash for her brother's farm and got herself caught.

"Thanks, guys. Uh, can I borrow a horse?"

April chuckled. "It's not like a car. We only have Bucky. Take good care of him."

"Thanks. And on that note, I promise to return your Bucky."

"Good luck, mate. If ye need any more help, just give us a holler."

"A coat?" Mathew asked.

April brought over a blanket for him. "Cloaks around here. Keep it." She slipped it over his head and kissed his cheek.

"Thanks." Mathew stepped back out into the cold and trudged to the side of the cabin. He mounted Bucky, rather clumsily, and tugged the reins until the animal started moving where he wanted it to. Verity hadn't gone home, and she hadn't gone to eat. Jaime had her. He felt it in his bones.

Mathew wriggled and jabbed the horse with his smooth dress shoes and managed to get Bucky to walk lazily westward, and when he found the narrow dirt road, he stopped with a quick yank on the leather straps. Mathew craned his neck up the hill

and drew in a deep breath. He was going straight into the wolves' den in hopes of finding Verity. He imagined she was screaming for help at the mercy of that savage, and desperation moved him forward. He'd failed to protect his sister from their abusive father all those years. Now a man grown, Mathew would not fail. His hands fisted the reins, his muscles became rigid with anger, and his breathing turned into strong pulls in preparation.

At the crest of the hill he found a fresh estate, something a rich old lady would live in. He dismounted and knocked on the door. Damn, he didn't have any weapon to defend himself with. That had been a stupid idea.

Before he fled to Sam's for a weapon or two, the front door creaked open. A plump woman, gray haired and lined with age and wearing an ivory apron, greeted him with a tense voice and a fake hospitality. Something was off.

"Good afternoon, sir. May I help you?"

"I'm looking for a woman, and I was wondering if she came by this way. She has long wild hair, bright green eyes, cute freckles…" As Mathew described her appearance, longing and regret plagued him. She was amazing, and he'd let her run away. "And a gorgeous..." Mathew trailed off and cleared his throat. "A nice smile. I suppose you may not have seen her smiling. Verity is her name. Verity Arris."

The plump housekeeper flinched at Verity's name. Her mouth parted, and Mathew knew he was in the right place.

Her head leaned out and away from the door. She whispered, "Get out of here. If you want her, bring the cavalry!"

Mathew's brows furrowed. As the words registered, his eyes widened, and a shout came from inside the house.

"Millie! Allow our guest inside. It's too cold to be jabbering about with the door open."

Millie the housekeeper blanched right before his eyes. Mathew remembered that voice. Millie opened the door wide, and he saw the man waiting. The dark curly hair and evil black eyes made his anger fire on all pistons.

Jaime Perez.

"Well I'll be the luckiest son of a bitch today. Hot damn! Joe, Rob, make sure our guest is welcome." His face curled into a sneer, and Mathew realized the gravity of his mistake. Cavalry? He needed the Navy SEALs.

VERITY AWOKE IN THE estate's dim library with a small fire still crackling in the hearth. The air was dusty, stale, and now tinged with copper. She laid on the floor with her skirts flipped above her waist, the hardwood cold on her skin. Verity shivered and her whole body ached. She sat up and flung herself back with excruciating, but familiar, pain on her bottom. A swipe of her fingers confirmed the nightmare she feared had happened. Jaime had whipped her with his belt, and he was going to do it again.

Fumbling onto her feet without angering her wounds further, Verity rubbed her upper arms more for comfort than warmth. She needed to find a way out before he returned. The only obvious way was the door, but even if it wasn't locked, she believed it was guarded.

Her hands continued their search for a secret passageway, while she fought back tears and held her hands steady. As she passed the fireplace, Verity slipped the poker under her layers of

dress. With a renewed confidence, she tugged and pushed as many books as time allowed. She missed the future, where everyone was kind, where life was easy, where everything was exciting—in a good way.

Mostly, she missed Mathew. She should not have run off. If she hadn't, they could be sipping tea at The Astor House, having a heart to heart, and maybe he would've proposed. Instead, she was between torture sessions by one of the worst human beings Verity had ever met.

The deep baritone cracking of the estate's doorknocker caught Verity's ears. Who would show up at this place and *knock*? Someone who didn't belong here, because no one was dumb enough to visit. Her stomach twisted. As much as she wanted a knight in shining armor, Mathew wasn't equipped to take on an estate full of outlaws.

Verity pressed her ear close to her chamber door, straining to listen. All she heard was, "Verity is her name. Verity Arris." The blood drained from her body in a swift flush. The voice was Mathew's.

"Millie!" Jaime Perez's horrific tinny voice shouted. "Allow our guest inside. It's too cold to be jabbering about with the door open. Well I'll be the luckiest son of a bitch today. Hot damn! Joe, Rob, make sure our guest is welcome."

Tears sprung to Verity's eyes. Her knight was now her fellow prisoner. She would have to free Mathew before leaving now and this was all her fault. Pressure built in her face with sobs threatening to escape. She sniffled and footsteps climbed the stairs. The boots stopped near her door. Verity heard a familiar loud sound elicited when a person was punched in the belly. Her

palms pressed against the chamber door.

"Matt!" she yelled.

A deep jagged breath followed, and Mathew's hoarse voice whispered, "Verity?" The footsteps continued, and Verity fisted the doorknob. If she stepped out, they would attack her for her attempt, but she had to try something. Maybe she could escape another way and bring help along. Maybe even find Butch and his bandits—Jaime's enemies.

The knob was locked, and all the wind flew out of her. She slapped her palms on the door in defeat. She knew what was going to happen to Mathew because Jaime didn't discriminate against his victims. A fleeting thought questioned how many of his rogue followers were similarly scarred on their bottoms.

She heard struggles and frantic shuffling footsteps. A door slammed shut nearby and then silence. Footsteps returned to her door, and she backed away, waiting in the corner for whatever Jaime Perez intended next. Silence stretched for what felt like minutes before the footsteps thumped in descent, and Verity sighed in relief. She rubbed her arm across her damp forehead, and her elbow bumped something that wasn't a book.

A barely perceptible black strip of metal laid between books. A surge of hope rushed through her veins. Verity pushed and pulled it, but nothing happened. She removed the books on either side of it and pushed it side to side. A clank sounded from the wall and a draft of air teased her face. Verity's fingers searched for the source and she found a gap in the bookshelves.

Shoving with all her might, the door didn't move. Frustrated and panting, Verity placed her hands on her hips and inhaled a few deep breaths. She stuffed her fingers into the crevice and

yanked with her full body weight. The heavy book-lined door only shifted a couple inches. Verity removed the poker from under her skirts and used it as a lever, forcing the door open just enough for her body to fit through.

She held the poker as a weapon. Creeping through the inky black passageway, fresh air swirled around her as if coaxing her to freedom. A spiderweb caught her face and Verity shuddered while frantically wiping it away. She cleaned her hands on her skirts and at last, found the end of the narrow passage. She stopped at the edge of a small office with a sliver of a window cracked open. There was no fire, only overcast daylight. It was freezing and Verity then noticed her breath making clouds in front of her face. A broad desk and chaise lounge were the extent of the furniture. Mathew was curled up on a rug on the floor, his arms wrapped around his middle. Quiet moans escaped his lips and Verity gasped, her hand flying to her gaped mouth.

She replaced the poker under her skirts and shoved the other end of the secret passage open. She rushed to kneel at his side.

"Matt," she whispered. "Matt, wake up." Verity's breaths were shallow. The sight of him injured or dying washed away the lingering anger at his rejection. Tears flooded her eyes, and she brushed his hair away from his pinched face. He didn't deserve to die. He didn't deserve to be tortured by Jaime. What had Mathew done but try to save her? Verity's hand caressed his jaw, and she sobbed. She wished she could take all his pain away. Her bright, cheerful, and selfless man. She loved him.

Verity drew in a breath at the realization. Yes, she loved him, very much so. His pain hurt her more than anything she'd ever experienced before, more than Jaime's whipping a year ago,

more than his whipping today. She'd blocked out Jaime's anger, violence, and psychosis. He was an empty shell, a single track of hate, and Verity didn't let it inside. But Mathew? She would do anything for him.

MATHEW WISHED AT that moment he could detach from his body and float away pain-free, which would solve two of his biggest problems—crushing, immobilizing pain and imprisonment. Although, he didn't want to be beheaded, if he had the option. But the searing pain from his gut and ribs warned him he was in worse trouble than he thought. He'd made a massive mistake trying to be the hero. He wasn't a warrior, he wasn't a fighter, and he wasn't prepared to do what needed to be done. How was he going to get out of here?

When the gunshot had rung across the field, his first instinct was to collect his sister and nephew and hide. Because men like him, who generally believe people are good, aren't wired to jump into danger, risking their life to stop a crime typically covered by insurance. And when Sam had charged off after the gunman, Mathew shook his head. For that split second, he had to decide to hide or help his brother-in-law. Considering how well built the cabin was, shooting through the solid logs was unlikely, so Mathew had given chase to do what he could for Sam. Every step, every second, he'd been at risk of a single man haphazardly pulling a trigger and ending Mathew's life before it ever got started. When he'd returned to the cabin, instinct to save the Doug's life took over, and when the dog's condition was stabilized, Mathew trembled as the adrenaline rush had worn off.

That was the extent of his bravery. In a world of outlaws and bandits, what made him think asking for Verity and walking away with her unscathed was possible?

He didn't belong in this time and he had every intention of returning home once Verity was safe. The way she handled herself with poise during a stressful makeshift surgery on Doug confirmed she owned his heart—throw away the key—and that was a problem.

Mathew rolled over onto his other side, hoping for a small reprieve from the clenching pain of his gut. Every intake of breath speared him fresh. Behind pinched eyelids, imagery of Verity's face haloed by seagulls at the top of Overlook Hill brought him a moment's peace. He recalled her screaming with excitement on the Ferris wheel and her inquisitive face at the desk in his clinic—nose deep in the screen in concentration. That innocent wonder at experiencing new things, like her first flight across country and her sensual expression after her first bite of pizza, sent a pouring of affection and a desire to protect her through his body. Mathew loved how he felt around her, as if the lurking loneliness finally washed away. He wanted it back again, and he would show her the world to keep it alive. But she only wanted a marriage for the sanctity of antique religious views on sex. Even though he couldn't fault her for being a product of her time, he couldn't marry her if she didn't love him.

But all those worries and dreams meant nothing if he couldn't escape this house alive. Mathew groaned under the pain of his ribs. Shallow breaths helped a little, but each involuntary drag of a deep breath brought temporary relief and more pain. He was certain he had bruised ribs. If he couldn't get his breathing steady

soon, he'd be sure of a collapsed lung too. Just great.

A whisper of an angelic voice stopped his heart.

"Matt."

Through the diminishing pain, his lips lifted into a weak smile. Was he dying?

"Matt, wake up."

His heart skipped at the feminine voice, spreading heat from his torso to his fingertips and toes, warming his chilled skin. Mathew cracked open his eyes, and through small drags of breath, the haloed face of Verity floated above him. She was a beautiful relief from the agony. He'd only wished he wasn't hallucinating, because that would mean he was alive and able to plan an escape route. He remembered approaching a sunny yellow estate, stark against the dreary overcast winter sky. A knock on the door...oh, he remembered! Mathew had been escorted up a set of grand stairs where he'd heard a voice through a door, a voice that caused him surprise and panic. Before he could call out to her, Mathew had been sucker-punched and tossed into a nearby room like a disobedient slave.

It had been Verity's voice.

A tug on his arm shifted his eyes. He blinked. And he blinked a few more times. "Verity?" Mathew coughed and dragged in a searing breath.

Her face shined with wetness. Her cheeks and tip of her nose were rosy from the cold, but the resilient woman of his dreams smiled. His hand reached up and cupped her jaw. She was just a beautiful woman. Every ounce of his injured body wanted to crush her against him and whisk her away from all the dangers out there. He wanted her to be his and his only.

"I love you," his faint words popped out with a smile. Her face fell with comprehension. Had he just said those words out loud? Heat rushed his foggy brain, and he leaned to stand. Pain jabbed him and his face pinched closed. Hands grasped his arms and pulled, and with her help he managed to get to his feet.

"Verity?" he asked again, unbelieving his eyes.

"Hi there, handsome." Her voice was quiet and kind. Tears rolled down her face, and he held out his arms. She rushed into his embrace, and he pressed her tight, shushing her hair while she sobbed. He flinched with frequent stabs of pain.

"Are you okay?" he asked.

She sniffled. "Much better now. Are you?"

"I'll live." Although at the moment he wasn't so sure.

"We need to get out of here," Verity said.

"Agreed. Any idea how many are out there?"

"Three for sure. Jaime, Joe, and Rob. Not sure how many others, but Jaime typically has ten or more men roaming around him. They're armed—modern six-shooters and daggers."

Mathew sighed at their odds. The reality was neither of them would escape alive. But a plan was better than none. "Well, whatever we decide on, I have a horse waiting outside—Sam and April's. To make our escape as efficient as possible, I need to know something." Mathew paused and collected himself. This was the question that would determine his future, however long it lasted. "Are you coming with me to the hotel or are you leaving for California?"

The pause while she considered was the longest moment of his life. Time around him froze, and his essential brain functions shut down. Would she give him a chance at a future or dash all

his hopes for good? What would he do if she chose California? Could Mathew live in this time—give up his clinic and live in a rugged era? The idea was so foreign to him that a knee-jerk answer was no. He had a duty to his patients, to his clients, to his employees. No matter how much he loved her, he couldn't survive in 1853. Sam Hartley was right—Mathew was soft. With the press of a button, he could whisk them both back to the safety of the future, but then she could never return. He couldn't make that choice for her, either. Anxiety rippled up his spine as her mouth opened to answer. *Please, please, please come with me.*

"I'm going with you to the hotel."

Mathew blew out the breath he hadn't realized he was holding. Pain spiked up his rib, and his face pinched in pain. She had given him a chance to explain himself. The future held in her hands wasn't dashed away yet.

Verity pressed against him for stability. "Are you sure you're all right?"

"I'm great." Better than he thought possible at this moment. "It's just breathing that's difficult. Don't worry about me." He smiled to prove it to her, and she smiled back, but the worry on her brow told him she wasn't convinced.

"So, what's the plan?" she asked.

The doorknob behind them turned and both their heads spun. "Get out of here, Verity," Mathew demanded. "If you're caught, we're both dead."

"I'm not leaving you," she whispered. Her arms were still wrapped around him and clasped behind his back. With his injuries, he couldn't force her to do anything.

The door opened just enough for a head to pop in. It was the

housekeeper Millie. Verity relaxed against his body, but Mathew didn't.

"If you two want to live, you flee on my command. Understand?" The plump woman whispered across the room. Without waiting for answer, her head disappeared out the door. Mathew and Verity exchanged glances just as Millie popped her head back in again.

"You have only a few seconds' window to make your escape. Get ready. You'll know when to go when I make a signal." Her head left again and didn't return.

"Do we trust her?" Mathew asked.

"Millie is a good woman. She's as much a prisoner here as we are."

Mathew hadn't thought of that. He wished he could save her too.

MATHEW SAID HE was fine, but Verity didn't believe him. Worry wracked her body while hot breath escaped her frozen lips in a small office of the estate.

Mathew slung an arm across his middle, and she heard his breath hitching with pain. Verity lifted his loose arm over her shoulder and wrapped her own arm around him for support. Her limbs jerked and trembled while she helped him toward the chamber door—he needed her aid as much as she couldn't bear to release him. Mathew hadn't declined her help and that scared her more. She hoped Millie's plan worked out, otherwise the poor old woman would be killed too, just for trying. Mathew placed his hand on the knob, and they waited for whatever signal was coming.

Verity only cared about being happy, about making Mathew

happy, and that began with love. Her heart sang when she heard the words, even if Mathew didn't remember saying them, and she knew at that moment, she had made the right decision in following him.

An evening tray of tea clattered down the hallway. Footsteps rumbled and several thundered downstairs. Verity thought Millie was collecting all the house inhabitants into a room, clearing an exit path. A loud knocking came from the front door again. She heard it creak open and closed. Within moments, several masculine voices cheered, and they were suddenly cut off—a closed door, Verity assumed. That must've been the cue.

Verity opened the chamber door and popped her head into the hallway. The exit appeared clear. She supported Mathew's weight while they descended the stairs with quiet steps. Verity understood the wretched implications of escape. Jaime Perez would stop at nothing to hunt her down and this time, he wouldn't be subtle about it. Mathew's condition concerned her. She'd never seen him in so much pain. And what Millie had done for them might save their lives, but when Jaime figured it out, Millie would be subjected to his wrath. The burden of guilt and worry strained her, while perspiration coated her face with the effort of Mathew's weight.

At the bottom of the steps they shuffled straight to the front door. A raucous flurry behind a closed chamber door in the foyer told Verity where Millie had ushered everyone. They were hooting with delight in there. A door opposite the party room opened with a small squeak, and Verity's breath caught. She craned her neck to see their fate and exhaled a breath of relief. Millie dashed up to them, silent with her slippers.

"Oh, thank heavens. Get out of here before the women are no longer distracting enough. I've never organized such an event. They will get suspicious soon." Millie's hands folded and refolded with worry.

"Come with us, Verity said. "We have two horses for the three of us. We'll take you as far as you want to go."

"It's a wonderful offer, dear, but I need to stay for Audrey. I can't leave the poor maid alone with a handful of ruffians. I've always served this house and my services will end in this house. Now, get out of here before my efforts have been in vain!"

Tears wetted Verity's eyelids. She was gutted to leave Millie behind, but instead of arguing, Verity nodded. Mathew's face was soft and sad with understanding, and Verity supported him while they shuffled out the front door.

A horse snacked on the dead grass, and Verity released Mathew long enough to guide the animal to him. He lifted a leg into the stirrup, and Verity shoved with all her might to get Mathew up. He grunted and situated himself. His rapid breathing troubled her.

Verity dashed to the side of the house and found her mount. She flung herself onto the saddle and arched her back in sharp pain from her bottom. Verity bit her hand to stifle the shout of agony begging for release. She'd forgotten her own wounds. She bunched her dress underneath her for extra cushion and trotted over to Mathew's horse. She grasped its reins and held it close, walking both horses together. Mathew's hands crossed his middle, and his legs shifted to hold his weight in place.

"Go to Sam's," he said. "I need to see my sister."

Always the kind man. "We need to concentrate on getting

away from this estate alive first. Then we can return our borrowed mounts. Can you handle moving faster?"

Mathew shook his head no and said, "Yes." He chuckled. "Pain is temporary, death is forever. Let's go and I'll deal with it."

Verity kicked the horse to move faster and Mathew's copied. She swung them east, and before long they reached Sam and April's log cabin. The door opened after a single knock, and April's eyes flicked between the two of them. The softening lines of her face showed her relief.

"Told you I'd be back. Brought Bucky, too," Mathew said with a pained smile.

"Matt's hurt," Verity said. "Can we come in?"

"Oh, yes. Yes, come in," April said, moving aside. "What happened?"

Verity helped him inside and set him on the couch. April closed the door behind them, and Sam entered through the back door.

Doug barked at the return of his owner. The mutt lounged on a bed on the floor, tail wagging with the excitement of the crowd—the gunshot not getting his spirits down.

"I see horses. How did things go? Oh…" Sam trailed off, concern knitting his brows while his eyes assessed Mathew's condition. "Well, I dinnae know anything about doctoring, so I'll let April tend to ye." Sam addressed April with pain of regret in his eyes. "I knew I shouldna let him live."

April's face darkened. "Don't pin all this on me."

Sam's hands went skyward in surrender. "I'm not saying it's yer fault. Just telling the truth of it."

April asked Verity, "Can you help me? Take off his cloak and dress shirt. I'll do what I can."

Verity helped Mathew remove his garments while his sister set out an array of supplies. The pain inflicted on his face tore her heart. She exposed his bare chest and Verity both admired it and searched it for damage.

April rubbed her hands together and blew on them. "Just gotta warm my hands first. I don't need you flinching more, but no promises."

Mathew attempted a smile. "I probably won't feel temperature anyway. Try not to enjoy this too much."

"I never liked seeing you in pain." She touched his chest and pressed in places.

Mathew twitched and flinched. "That's true. Ow. But…inflicting pain on one's sibling is a rite of passage into adulthood. You were deprived of that experience. Ow."

"There was enough pain to go around. No sense in adding more unnecessarily."

"Bingo. Take it easy there, Hercules."

"There's no compound fracture, obviously." April's fingers kneaded along his flesh and Verity watched to learn.

"No shattered bits anywhere. Sounds scientific, huh?"

Sam brought over a bottle of bourbon and Mathew drank heavily—half the bottle—before handing it back. Verity hating being helpless.

"That's me good stuff, Matty. A kick arse in a bottle. Go easy on it." Sam said, agape at the half-empty bottle.

"I'll reimburse…you." Mathew paused with a pinched face. "Write off…expense. Insurance…" His eyes glazed over, and

Verity worried more about his failing lucidity.

"No stark edges," April continued her assessment.

"Are ye understanding any of this?" Sam asked Verity.

She shrugged. "I know what shattered bits are."

"How's Johnny doing, ye know, after the contract terminated?"

Sam's little sister, Sarah, had been contracted to marry Verity's elder brother. Jonathan was not thrilled but willing to do his duty. Lloyd Stanton had surprised them with the termination payment. Sarah had found a man to love her, and Jonathan had received cash to float the farm.

"Johnny's grumpy as usual. He wasn't excited about the contract in the first place, not that he had anything against your sister."

"Aye, the feeling was mutual."

"There is either extensive bruising or a simple hairline fracture," April concluded. "Either way, all I can do is bupkis."

"Is that going to hurt more?" Verity asked.

April glanced at her and smiled. "I can't do anything besides wrap it for support, maybe. Nothing from the future can help either, except stronger meds. Matty, do you want to be wrapped?"

Mathew nodded, so Verity helped him lean forward while April wrapped a white strip around his torso several times.

"I've got some ibuprofen. Still in date, too. Take some. It'll help with the swelling."

Mathew shot her a look of annoyance. "Med…school."

"But you already know that," she mumbled.

Mathew followed the pills with more bourbon, and he sighed,

leaning back against the couch cushions.

"There's…strong possibility…houseful of pissed off dudes…searching for us soon," Mathew said and his words were alarmingly slurred.

April and Sam exchanged glances. Sam said, "I have prepared for their invasion for over a year. And now they have two, possibly three, reasons to come."

Sam's eyes tracked to Verity, Mathew, and finally to his wife. Verity swallowed a thick lump. Mathew's face softened as he dropped off to sleep.

"Is he going to be all right?" Verity asked the happily married couple.

"He's not a drinker," April added. "So, he's probably going to be fine, but he's got one hell of a hangover coming."

Sam lifted the corner of his lips. "My strongest whiskey. I consider myself a cultured drinker, and that amount woulda knocked me on me arse. Not a wise move for a novice."

Verity hoped he rested fast and sobered even faster with the impending arrival of Jaime's men. She needed to get herself in top shape, too.

With Mathew asleep, Verity asked, "Is there any way I can bother you for wound care of my own?"

April said, "Sure, where's the hurt?"

"I've heard you're aware of Jaime Perez's preferred method of punishment."

April cringed. "Yeah. Lean over the table here, and I'll get you stitched up. This way they won't tear when you sit. Not that you'll want to."

Verity leaned over the kitchen table and swift hands lifted her

skirts. April shook her head and stitched up the long slices in her flesh. A few swigs of Sam's bourbon and fancy white pills eased her pain, and suddenly Verity was no longer capable of staying awake herself.

# Chapter Twenty-Two

MATHEW AWOKE FROM the most blinding pain he'd ever experienced in his life. When those assholes had captured him, they'd given him a jab with the butt of a pistol straight into the rib and another into the gut until he folded in half. After they'd tossed him into a room, they added a few choice kicks with their heavy boots. Mathew had been left incapacitated, gasping for breath.

Moving caused pain, breathing caused pain, and as of right now, even thinking caused pain. He was grateful for the whiskey, drugs, and rest. He was almost functional. Mathew remembered little about waking up in an office-type room and Verity finding him.

She was curled up on the recliner next to him, face soft with asleep. She was a marvelous wonder of bravery and courage. With help from a little old lady they'd left behind, Verity had rescued him. He would never find that in a woman again. Love bloomed in his chest while he watched her peaceful sleep.

"Hey, you're awake," his sister said.

"Yeah. Not sure if I'm happy about it yet."

"Here." She offered him a glass of water and more ibuprofen. He gulped them. His ribs were a dull ache, and he drew in a deep

breath. Soreness, no pain. Mathew smiled in relief at his luck.

"So, I see no one broke down the fort last night," he said.

"No one was smart enough to find you or dumb enough to show up here."

"That's a good sign, I suppose."

The sadness was back in his sister's eyes as if she knew their end was coming, the final goodbyes. Mathew's eye caught on his sleeping Verity. "Can I ask you something?"

One corner of her lips lifted. "Sure."

"How did you know he was the one?"

April's small smile rose to a broad grin beaming with affection, the type he'd always wished to see on her. "When his needs are more important than your own, and his opinions truly matter. When his comfort is more important than your own and his stress worries you. When you find The One, he becomes more important than yourself and someone you can't live without. Your best friend." The baby cooed in his bassinet as if agreeing. "Why do you ask?" Her eyes flicked to Verity.

Mathew nodded to confirm. She smiled in silent approval and patted his shoulder. The cooing flipped to crying and April sighed. "Time for baby's second breakfast."

Crying baby Mathew woke Verity moments later, and she stretched freshened up. April tucked the baby inside her shirt and got him settled in. Verity returned to Mathew's side as if signaling she was ready to go.

"We're going to head out. Thanks for harboring fugitives," Mathew said.

"Ye willnae stay for breakfast?" Sam asked, strolling out of the bedroom and stuffing his thick arms into a shirt.

"No. You've done enough already. We need to be on our way to return a horse to Johnny and settle some business at the hotel." Mathew knew his sister and Sam were more than capable of returning a horse, but Mathew had something he needed to ask the man, and he could only do it in person. In Mathew's time, the gesture was antiquated and unnecessary, but in Verity's time, it was done for respect, and he had to honor her.

"There's only the one—The Astor House. Ye need deep pockets for that place," Sam said.

"Hey, how many trips do you have left?" April asked and shifted the baby to the other breast.

Mathew shifted his gaze even though she was covered. "My last one."

"Oh." April stared at the floor in sad contemplation, and then like the flip of a switch, she brightened and waved her arms. "I'll leave you notes about us and baby Mathew. You can find them in that secret drawer in the fireplace." She pointed. "That's how Sam apologized so I would return here."

"I'll check it, but I don't have any way of writing back."

"I understand. One of the downfalls of the choices we make."

He would love to come back for a visit before returning home, but a niggling sensation told him it wouldn't happen. He would never see his family again. Life was too short, too unfair, and too hard.

It was worth fighting for.

He glanced at Verity, having just verbalized his intentions to leave, but her face gave nothing away.

"Looks like you don't need me anymore." His heart squeezed in a fist. Mathew had to let her go, but he was comforted

knowing Sam Hartley was watching out for her. "You've got this big lug instead."

"Of course I need you. You're my big brother." She sniffled. "You just can't give me any more horrible advice."

"Horrible?" Mathew feigned shock.

April chuckled. "Use my heart, not my head. Don't you remember? I would've been a starving artist rather than working for you and earning a paycheck. I can't believe you were telling me to quit. I couldn't have left you in a lurch like that."

"That wasn't terrible advice, and I was talking about love."

April squinted at him while processing the information. Her temper rose right before his eyes. "You were encouraging me to answer Levi. You knew about his proposal before I did."

Now he'd find out if she actually hated him for it.

"He came to me and asked to marry you. First, the guy sent red flags all over that somehow you missed. Second, when he told me his plans for a public proposal, I knew you'd hate it, but I encouraged him anyway. That's on me."

"What?" April placed a hand over her mouth. Was she was pissed off or grateful?

"He wasn't right for you," Mathew continued. "In my defense, if the guy didn't know you'd hate a public proposal, then he wasn't the right guy for you."

"I had no idea."

Mathew had later heard about the details of her horrific proposal at the casino, and it was worse than he'd figured Levi was planning. "So, you don't hate me?"

"Hate you? No, I only hate country music. Couldn't you have nudged him in a better direction? Something less ear-bleedy."

"Aren't you glad I didn't? It seems like you're doing okay for yourself now."

"Yeah, it's great. Sam's great." April observed her house as if assessing her current quality of life. There was misty nostalgia mixed with warm affection while her eyes roamed. Little Mathew whined with a quiet warning tone.

"And you're doing well for yourselves." Mathew glanced around at the furniture and weird wood oven. "So, you listened."

"If I agree that you were right, will you stop rubbing it in my face?" Her tone was light and playful.

"I won't be able to even if I wanted to." Because he'd never see her again.

Shines of tears rested under his sister's eyelids and she shifted the baby on her hip.

He added, "Any messages for back home?"

"Yeah. Tell Becca it was great working with her, and I hope her baby is well. Say hi to her husband Brad for me." Mathew would not tell her what really happened. It wasn't worth crushing her. "Tell Kiko thanks. Oh, and my next-door neighbor Ms. Lewis, bring her a muffin. Did you get my parting gift? Kiko was supposed to give it to you."

"I'll ask her. She only gave me the note."

"Make sure she gives it to you, and don't say no."

"Any messages for Mom or Dad?" April glared at him with the hatred of a thousand suns. He put up his hands in surrender. "It didn't have to be a kind message, but point taken."

Mathew stood, only mild discomfort radiating through his whole body. Verity helped steady him.

"We best be going," Mathew said.

April tossed a cloak each over him and Verity, and Sam gave Mathew a masculine hug, careful to not anger the wounds again. Sam kissed Verity's knuckles. "I should have yer order ready tomorrow, if you still want it."

She curtsied. "I do." Verity sent Mathew a glance and he tried not to read into that.

Just like that, Mathew was out the door, aided by Verity, and waving to his sister and brother-in-law one last time. She helped him up on Jonathan's horse and climbed up in front. He didn't have the arm strength to control the horse anyhow. Mathew itched to get out of his dress shirt and pants, take a shower, and wear some comfortable jammies in his heated mangy apartment on his dusty old couch. He shivered with the cold December air penetrating his insufficient cloak. Verity steered the horse down the road, and when they approached the entrance to Jaime Perez's estate, they became far more cautious, craning their necks around for threats. The passage was clear, and so was the bridge. Millie must've kept those men entertained.

Verity knew the way to her family's farm, and they rode as comfortably as they could in the winter. She shifted a few times as if trying to find a comfortable seating angle.

"Everything okay up there?" he whispered into her ear.

"It'll be better when we're done with horses for a while."

"Why?"

Verity used a free hand and shifted her outer dress layer up, revealing stained underskirts. Mathew's mouth gaped open. "What happened? Are you all right?"

The corner of her mouth turned up. "April stitched me up well. Still hurts though." Mathew sucked in a breath. Jaime Perez

whipped her, just like he'd done to his sister, just like he'd done to Verity previously. Imagining her fear at reliving that torture made him sick, and a fiery rage pushed all his pain and discomfort away. He wanted to turn around and beat the bloody pulp out of every one of those disgusting monsters.

"I'm so sorry," he said. "I wish that never happened to you." His hand reached her forearm, and she patted his hand.

The wind kicked up when they reached the open fields of hibernating husks. Mathew lifted his shoulders to cover his exposed neck. Verity steered them to the familiar farmhouse, and they dismounted at the stable around back.

Verity hugged his arm again, and he wanted to pick her up and carry her inside. She shouldn't be walking around with wounds like those. He remembered April's and the excruciating pain she endured. He pulled her to a stop. "Are you sure inside is safe?"

Her face crinkled in confusion. "Yeah, why?"

"April and Sam didn't see Jaime's men at all. Neither have we, so far. Is it safe to assume they aren't inside?"

Verity considered for a moment and then shook her head. "If they came near, we'll encounter my brothers and dead bodies."

"Sure?"

"Completely. Johnny's a ruthless, stubborn asshole who doesn't tolerate trespassers. He also hates Jaime Perez for his attempted extortion. If Jaime's men appeared, Johnny wouldn't give them another chance. The only consequence is dealing with Sheriff Clint, Jaime's ally."

Mathew glanced at the quiet unpainted farmhouse. There were no lights flickering and no sounds. "Not that I don't trust

you, but how about we check through the back windows before announcing our presence, just in case?"

Verity shrugged and she helped him across the back yard to the window of the kitchen. Mathew steadied himself for what they were about to see.

THE PAIN IN HER derriere had subsided with the drink and magic pills followed by a long night's rest. She had awoken warm and comfortable for the first time since sleeping on Mathew's bed in the future. Verity couldn't believe their dumb luck in not being chased or followed by any of Jaime's men. She wondered what had happened to Millie. Perhaps they'd busied themselves with her punishment first. Verity shuddered at the thought.

She and Mathew trekked toward the old farmhouse. What was once a prison, had now become just her family's home. Not hers though. Perhaps she'd had enough adventure to wash away the dreary thoughts of being caged.

Before they reached the house, the crack of a shotgun echoing across the dead fields stunned her in place, shaking her to the core. She stilled to assess if it struck her, and finding no wounds, she craned her neck to Mathew. "Are you all right?"

He nodded. Quietly and cautiously they continued up the wooden steps and through the creaking screen door. Mathew held it as they passed through so it wouldn't slap behind them. Whoever had a shotgun in their hands didn't need to be startled.

The house was empty. A fire burned in the fireplace for warmth against the winter winds. Dishes dried on a rack. Verity checked the food cabinets. They were stocked. Mrs. Cottlewood

must've been back to routine again. She fisted an apple and bit off a generous hunk. She tossed one to Mathew who copied her.

"Thanks."

The front door opened and slammed shut. Mathew shifted out of sight while Verity ducked behind the couch, since her secret cubbyhole was known to Jaime now. She sucked in a deep breath and peeked over the backrest. Verity smiled and stood. "Wayward deer out front?"

Jonathan's serious eyes flew to her. "Everyone all right?"

"We're fine," she said.

Mathew shifted back and waved toward the front of the house. "What was the target practice?"

Jonathan stalked over to the counter and began reloading the shotgun.

"Well?" she prompted. Always a man of few words.

"I warned them twice. I don't give third chances."

The hairs on the back of Verity's neck raised. "Who?"

"Rob Bertrand. He'd been sending me threats for months and breeched my property for the last time."

Verity's eyebrows rose. "Did he say anything?"

"Didn't get a chance to. Why?"

Verity crossed the kitchen to the front door.

"The body can stay out front for a while until we're sure no more are coming. Then it needs to go to the pigs."

"The pigs?" Mathew said, lips twisted in disgust. "You can't feed a man to the pigs. We need to report this."

Verity turned the lock on the front door and sent him a look that meant don't be ridiculous. "There's no reporting and no trustworthy sheriff. If you try to raise awareness, you'll only get

yourself targeted even more than you are now."

"Jaime's men are sensitive." Jonathan finished reloading the shotgun, and he carried it to the coffee table and sank into the couch. "You snub them once and they'll kill you for it."

"Rob was likely here for us, not your extortion," Verity told her brother. "Are you sure he's dead?"

Jonathan's face darkened. "You run off to the future for a few months—not that I believe that, and the moment you're back, you bring trouble with."

Mathew stepped forward and answered before she said anything. "Jaime Perez is a sick bastard who wants unwarranted revenge for an act he caused. And since we both escaped his grasp, her not for the first time, he's now gunning for us both. So, like she said, Rob was probably here for *us*."

Verity's chest expanded from him defending her. Mathew stood by her side, stood up to her brother, and made it clear he would protect her.

"Fine. If he wants you dead, why did you come back here?" There's the cold jackass brother she missed.

"Returned your horse."

"And?" Jonathan knew that wasn't the only reason they came all this way.

"I'd like to have a word with you, if I may." Mathew asked her brother. Jonathan's squint assessed Mathew and slowly softened. He nodded, and both men crossed to his bedroom.

"I'm going to pack some food for the road," she added, expecting the hotel food to be too expensive. She could also take extra time and pack more of her belongings. She wondered what Mathew was going to say when they reached the hotel. Verity set

about the kitchen, taking inventory and planning a feast of a final breakfast—whether she went to the future with Mathew, or left forever to California.

MATHEW DIDN'T LIKE Jonathan too much. He respected him, sure, but liking was a whole different beast. He was intense, very intimidating, and stubborn like his sister. Mathew's stomach had perched up in his throat when he asked for a private moment. He'd rather be anywhere else, but he needed to do this right.

He hadn't planned when he would propose to Verity, but he would soon enough. To have a clear conscience, he wanted permission first. Jonathan closed the bedroom door behind them and lit a gas lamp on an end table.

The larger man planted himself on his bedspread and crossed his bulky arms. Mathew found his voice, lifted his chin up, and his voice caught when he saw a twelve-gauge shotgun mounted on the wall and under it hung a massive knife—bigger than his head. Mathew swallowed the lump in this throat.

"What is it you want?"

Mathew gulped. He never had issues communicating with people at work. Both Sam Hartley and Jonathan Arris were so much more...intense than he expected. Men were different back then, er, now.

"I wanted to inform you I care for your sister very much, and that I have every intention of asking for her hand in marriage, but before I do so, I would like to have your permission."

"If you're determined to ask her anyway, then why ask for my permission?"

Mathew groaned inwardly. Nothing was ever easy, was it? "I just wanted to be sure that her family approved of the arrangement."

"Care to elaborate on the details of Perez?"

"Not really, no," Mathew said.

"That wasn't a question."

Sounded like one.

Mathew squared his shoulders and clarified, "Verity met Jaime Perez, and he told her to do something she didn't want to do."

Jonathan chuckled and the tense air around him dissipated.

"Jaime hurt her," Mathew continued. "And when she fought back, Jaime ended up maimed in an area that he was very upset about."

Jonathan grunted.

"So, he's been hunting her for revenge ever since. She ran away from my sister's house and Jaime's men captured her. I went to the estate to find her and they—"

"You went to the estate alone? On purpose?" Jonathan interrupted.

"Uh, yeah."

Jonathan shook his head with a small smile.

"They knocked me around some, but with the help of the housekeeper, we both escaped. We hadn't seen a sliver of his men until now." Mathew tilted his head toward the front yard where Rob's body laid. He waited for Jonathan's response. The seconds ticked by like hours and his brow perspired.

"You, unarmed, went to the estate on purpose." Jonathan repeated his own question as a statement.

Mathew waited.

"I guess I can't say no to that. Good job, man. You've got some brass balls on you. Welcome to the family." Jonathan stood and gave Mathew a regrettable slap on the back.

"Thanks," Mathew said, strained. "Listen, is there any chance we can get a ride over to The Astor House? Verity and I need to have a discussion. She's either going to come home with me or she's leaving for California."

Jonathan pressed his lips together. "Understood and good luck."

The big man snuffed the lamp and opened the door. Glorious smells of bacon and eggs wafted in, and Mathew's stomach growled.

Jonathan chuckled. "Come eat. Men shouldn't be starving when there's food available." He turned to his sister. "Go easy on the supply, Verity. Harvest wasn't good this year with the drought."

"Oh. Well, make sure none goes to waste!"

Mathew offered to help Verity, his future fiancée, and the thought made his insides jelly with excitement.

She brushed him off. "You have a seat and just wait. I need you all rested up."

Mathew parked his rear at the kitchen table and her brother passed him the newspaper. Mathew interested himself in the headlines of the old days. *Jorgensen Robbed Last Night, Struggling Commerce: Theft of Goods in Transit Reaches All-Time High, Perez Fights Off Bandits Again.*

"Looks like Jaime's playing the good guy to the public."

"He always did, but most of the public knows better," Verity

said.

Did he own the newspaper editor and publisher too? This guy was bad news in all the ways.

A steaming plate thumped on the table in front of him, and Mathew folded the paper, setting it aside. "Smells wonderful."

"Everything smells wonderful when you're hungry," she said, and placed a plate in front of Jonathan, who collected the paper and opened it.

"Should I set one out for Graham?"

"He's upstairs getting dressed, I believe. Graham!" he shouted for his little brother and turned the page. "Breakfast! Verity's here."

Boots thundered down the stairs. "All right, grub." Graham was a spitting image of Jonathan, only in his late teens, Mathew guessed.

"Hi, I'm Graham." The boy held out a hand to Mathew. They shook and Graham dug in with no other formalities.

"Nice to meet you." Mathew stifled a chuckle and dug in himself. The eggs were so much bolder and better than he'd ever had.

"So, are you with my sister?" Graham asked between mouthfuls.

Mathew so didn't want to be having this conversation right now. His face heated, and he caught Verity's face across from him. Her eyes stayed on her plate, but her cheeks pinked. Not knowing what she would decide gnawed at him.

"This is superb." Mathew lifted his fork to change the subject and Verity smiled.

"Don't praise her too much. We don't need that going to her

head," Graham said.

"Hey! You appreciate what deserves appreciating," Verity retorted.

"Calm down you two. Eat now, while it's hot," Jonathan said.

"Look who's talking. Drop the paper and eat what I slaved to make you."

"You volunteered," Jonathan reminded her.

"Doesn't mean it wasn't work."

"No one said it wasn't," Graham chimed in.

"Hey," Mathew cut in. "Cooking from scratch is a lot of work, and the food is amazing, just like the chef."

"Awe, thanks Matt."

Jonathan and Graham both groaned.

"If you like her so much, just marry her," Graham said, rhetorically, probably. Mathew hoped.

Verity paused her chewing and glanced at Mathew, but he couldn't read anything from her expression. Heat crept up his neck and face. He enjoyed their family antics, and now he wondered if Verity preferred to stay instead. Since Jaime knew where she was and her brothers were capable of making pig food out of Jaime's men, Verity would have her home and her freedom back. A small part of him felt like a selfish asshole for wanting to tear them apart just to make a new family for himself. Had Verity changed her mind about going with him to the hotel?

"What's from scratch mean?" Graham asked, scooping more eggs onto his fork.

"It's a phrase," Verity explained. "Means that I did more work than some people choose to do."

"That doesn't make sense."

"Still going to the hotel with me?" Mathew said, trying to steer the subject away from his time travels. He needed the answer to calm his worries. If she declined, he had no reason to stay and continue to interfere with the lovely family. He'd just walk outside and press the inevitable button.

"Yeah, I'm going."

Mathew released a shallow sigh of relief.

Mathew and her brothers helped Verity clean up after the meal. There was a complete warmth of family in this old house, where the men assisted their sister, seeing her duties as not less than but different. There was a respect among them. No matter how much they'd bickered, Mathew could sense they all loved each other. He blinked back misty tears, and the guilt bore down harder. Without knowing if Mathew would be heading home alone or not only added to the emptiness creeping inside him.

"Graham," Jonathan said. "These two need a ride out of here."

Graham nodded and strolled out the back door to fetch a pair of horses. The screen door slapped, and Mathew flinched, but he was getting better at it. Verity crossed to Mathew with her bag in hand, but she stood stiffly as if she, too, didn't know how they would end up.

Her bright green eyes and golden freckles stared back at him. "You ready?"

"As ready as I'll ever be." Butterflies returned to his full belly, where guilt, worry, loneliness, and hope waged war.

# Chapter Twenty-Three

GRAHAM DROPPED THEM off on the front lawn of The Astor House. Verity had heard stories when they were building it, but she hadn't seen it finished. The majestic three-story building, glistening with white paint, had two upper floors full of identical windows with bright green Venetian blinds. It had a pair of matching chimneys—one on each end, a crowning cupola in the center, and a large weathervane at its peak. The bottom floor hardly had walls at all. The giant windows showed the luxury interior, and she was far out of her comfort zone.

"No one can afford a night here," Verity said.

Mathew nodded to her brother in dismissal and carried her bag for her. "C'mon."

Graham said, "Good luck you two. Happy trails." Graham turned his horse around and took the reins of the other she and Mathew shared. He trotted back toward the farm.

Verity watched her brother shrink down the road and knew she'd never see him again. She should be more affected, but she just wasn't. Graham was a good kid, but they'd never been close.

Mathew hooked his arm for her. She accepted, and he led her inside the luxury accommodations like a proper lady. Both the luxury and the proper made her uncomfortable. Bright soft

lights and large fireplaces bathed them in warmth, and fresh pine boughs scented the air. A few pairs of well-dressed settlers socialized in the open lounge. Mathew set her bag down and found the hostess. Verity's hands knotted together. When he returned, his face was as bright as a Christmas tree.

"What happened?" she asked.

"Got us a room." He jingled the keys and led her upstairs. When they entered the room, splendid furnishings awaited her—a four-poster bed, Persian rug, and hand-carved wooden table with matching chairs. The craftsmanship was exquisite.

Verity set her bag on the table and waited for Mathew to take the lead on his talk. The bed called her, and her chest bloomed with affection when she thought of her and Mathew together under the sheets. She brushed those thoughts aside.

Mathew crossed the room, fidgeting. He still held his arm across his middle as if his ribs were in pain.

"How bad are your wounds now?" she asked.

"Uncomfortable." Mathew sat on the bedspread with a wince and patted a space next to him. She sat very gently on her own wounds, and heat radiated off his skin. Was it lust or pain?

"I'm here. What did you want to say?"

Mathew cleared his throat. "I took advantage of the situation with time travel. I used it—I used you—to fix my situation in the future. I'm not rich. In fact, I'm the complete opposite, and I'm sorry. I shouldn't have withheld the truth from you no matter how desperate and ashamed I was."

"Don't deny you're rich." She ticked the items off her fingers. "Air conditioning, hot water with a turn of a knob, flushing toilets. That is rich."

He shook his head and smiled, "No, your bar is just way too low."

A sadness formed on his face, and Verity wanted to make promises to ease his suffering. Instead, she let him continue.

"I was on the verge of closing the clinic."

Verity pinched her face in confusion. There had been customers coming and going every day, and so many praised Mathew.

"Why did you feel you had to close?"

"There's no feel about it. When revenues stagnate but expenses keep climbing, eventually the money runs out. Hundreds of patients would've been short yet another practitioner in the area. In my desperation, I saw a way to change things, to keep the clinic open, so I did." Mathew shook his head. "When April's roommate needed help...She told me it was for a school project." Mathew snorted and his hand pushed hair off his forehead. "But it was magic or a science beyond human comprehension. I screwed up. Or maybe I succeeded as she'd planned."

Verity wasn't sure she followed. But she suspected he was taking about his future. He'd already told her he loved her, even if he didn't remember saying it. But if he wouldn't give her the commitment she required, she'd still go to California, wounded but stronger. "What do you mean?"

"I didn't know the point of Kiko's project until now. Verity, what I'm trying to say is I can't go to California with you."

After his tirade about crossing the Rockies, she hadn't expected him to join her, but the statement still stung.

He continued, "I can't leave behind my patients, my clinic,

my dream of helping people and animals. But the goal I'd set for myself long ago—becoming financially stable so my family didn't suffer—has been met, now that I used the time travel opportunity. Do you follow?"

Verity nodded, but she wasn't clear.

"What I'm inadequately asking you, Verity Arris, is will you return to the future with me?"

Her body tingled with excitement as images of everything she'd ever enjoyed in life would soon return to reality.

"I know it means leaving behind your brothers, giving up the life you've known. I feel incredibly selfish for asking, but I couldn't live with myself if I didn't. I have a disclaimer first. If you come with me, you can never return." He held out his hands. "Not my rules."

Never return to the past of bandits, tyrants, outlaws, prisons, and cornfields? "I understand."

"You're okay with skipping 1853 California?" His question was careful, gentle as if he extrapolated the answer but couldn't believe it.

Her bag was packed with essentials and food, ready for whichever path awaited her, and this was the moment she made her choice: Mathew or California. He'd told her it was one or the other, since he declined to accompany her across the country. Her current life left her two options and the first of which was simple unfathomable only a few weeks ago—waiting for Jonathan to kill the outlaws hunting her and stay on the farm while sharing her kitchen with a future bride, or traveling across an unknown terrain to seek a fortune of her own at the Gold Rush. Mathew's offer left her one option—helping people and

animals with a generous and kind man, who loved her as his equal, treated her with respect and dignity, and showed her the world. His world, where food was delivered and laundry was easy, and the biggest danger was whether to eat the salad or the burger. The choice was simple. Her eyes misted. "I've already found my fortune. I love you."

"You do?"

Verity nodded and the tears wavered her vision.

"Well, that's good news. Because I love you too." His hand reached for her chin and his fingers caressed her cheek.

"I know," Verity said, quietly.

"Is it that obvious?" Mathew chuckled.

"You told me. Back at Jaime's estate. I think you were delirious though."

Mathew inhaled and blew out a long breath as if steadying himself for something. "I have something else to ask you then. I didn't screw up when I fell for you. We were meant to be, like peanut butter and jelly. Cookies and cream. Beer and cheese."

Verity crinkled her nose, understanding the meaning without understanding all the words.

"Will you marry me?"

Her mind blanked. Had she heard him correctly? Was the one thing she wanted from him the same thing he'd just offered? Her whole body hummed with excitement. There was only one answer. "Yes. Of course yes!"

His smile was broad as hers, and she crashed against him in a fast embrace. Their lips locked, and carefully, Verity helped her fiancé undress and settle under the sheets. She explored every inch of his skin under a new—albeit, delicate—light. A light of

a promise of respect and wanting, of a future of wonders and excitement.

How had she gotten so lucky?

# Chapter Twenty-Four

IN THE MORNING, Mathew was sore all over again but this time for all the right reasons. He hadn't had so little sleep in a night since college, but he regretted nothing. Mathew promised her the world, and now he had the rest of their lives to fulfill that promise. A growling stomach woke him.

"Here," Verity—his fiancée—said, wearing only a bed sheet while she crossed the room to her bag. She tossed him an apple, and she bit into another.

"Let's go home," Mathew said. "But we need to get outside first. Kiko warned me about tunneling back to the future and ending up inside walls or furniture of future buildings."

"Home sounds great, as long as we arrive safely." She helped Mathew slip into his pants, shirt, and cloak. Mathew laced up her dress. Each morning the aches and pains receded, and he was now certain the damage was more bruised ribs rather than fractured, since his ego hurt more than his body.

Verity hugged his arm while he carried her bag downstairs. He felt ten feet tall now with his fiancée by his side. In a few moments, they'd return to the future, leaving the chaos of the past behind forever. Near the bottom of the carved wood railing, he froze. Verity kept moving and tried to tug him to continue.

"What's the matter?"

"There," he whispered. "That's a stick up. Back up the stairs and they might not notice us."

Men crowded around the hostess. The scruffy man in the lead aimed a pistol at the frightened woman's face. They were filthy, rugged, armed, and sure-footed. Mathew was none of those things.

Verity craned her neck and did the exact opposite of what he asked. "Butch?"

Five heads turned their way, and Mathew's ten-foot invincibility shrunk back down to ten inches. A tall waif of a man with a crooked nose and hard black eyes turned his head. How did Verity know him?

The leader's eyes squinted in their direction, and Mathew tugged on her arm to retreat. She stepped down two steps and pivoted, taking her bag from his arms. What was she doing? Who were these people? This had bad news written all over it.

Verity unzipped her bag and fisted something. She tossed it through the air and the waif caught it. He inspected her offering, bit off a chunk, and nodded with a smile. "Howdy, Verity! How've you been?" The waif lowered the gun, and the hostess darted for safety.

"I've been better. Jaime got his hands on both of us." She waved her hand to include Mathew. At least she hadn't forgotten him already. "But we survived. Rob Bertrand is dead."

The waif named Butch nodded his approval. "Excellent work, my dear."

"It wasn't me. Johnny did it."

His smile widened, and he bit off another hunk. It flaked off

in his palms and Mathew recognized a raw onion. He wondered for a moment what the man's breath was like, and then pushed the thought away before he gagged.

"I'll pay him a friendly visit then. After all, he did us a solid favor."

The thugs robbing the defenseless hostess weren't enemies. That thought made Mathew squirm.

"He might like that, Verity said. "Be cautious though. Trigger finger."

"Any good man would be."

Mathew cleared his throat, wanting to know what was happening here.

"Oh, Butch, this is my fiancé, Matt. Matt, this is Eddie Butcher, leader of the bandits."

The warmth he felt at being introduced as her fiancé whip lashed against the sudden fear of who stood before him. Butch nodded and tipped his hat. Mathew's jerky motions tried to mirror his, sans hat.

"What are you two doing in these parts?" Butch asked.

"We are on our way home to celebrate our impending nuptials."

"Well, congratulations. Where's the celebration, if you don't mind my askin'?"

Mathew tried to cut in, but Verity answered too quick. She glanced at him with a look that said she had this handled.

"Stanton's Spirits."

Wait, she wanted to stick around to celebrate? This was madness. Butch smiled and several of his followers grinned and smacked each other on their shoulders. What the hell just

happened?

"Hello there, lass," a familiar friendly voice said.

Every head turned and Sam Hartley stood just inside the front door, alarm and caution in his demeanor. If it were possible, even more than in Mathew's. His local brother-in-law must know more about these men than Verity had led on.

"Sam!" Verity said. "How are you?"

Sam cleared his throat. "Mighty well, thank ye. I have yer order ready."

"Brilliant." Verity fished in her bag again and made the purchase with the watchful eyes of bandits next to them. Mathew would rather have fleas than stand here any longer.

Sam and Verity completed their transaction, and she inspected her custom blade. "Sam, meet Butch. Butch, this here is Sam, the finest blacksmith in the tri-village area."

"Howdy. Will you be joinin' us for fun at Stanton's Spirits?"

Sam's brows lifted in surprise. "What's happening at Lloyd's?"

"These two are celebrating their impending nuptials," Butch answered. "And beers and dancin's on them," he said with a slight question in his voice.

Mathew nodded, resigned to being roped into a public party. After Verity's fear of Jaime and his men, and her openness with the bandits, Mathew concluded that the bandits were friendly, but he didn't trust them.

"I cannae turn down a free trip to Lloyd's. When does the party begin?"

Mathew spoke up, "After we get checked out, but we need a ride. Does anyone volunteer?"

Sam eyed them both critically. "I'll take Verity. Butch, can you give Matty a lift?"

Mathew hid his groan. He trusted his sister's husband more than the bandits' leader, but the unusual kinship between Verity and Butch made him both jealous and suspicious.

"That I can do. Load up, partner, we're having a party," Butch announced, and then said to his companion, equally filthy as his leader but much plumper, "Fingers, come here. I've got an errand for you."

Butch and Fingers chatted in hushed tones, and Mathew hunted down the hostess.

"I'm sorry for the terrible inconvenience." He handed her some cash he'd withdrawn after making the deposit of silver bars.

The hostess sat on the floor with a shaking rifle aimed at the ceiling. "No, no. I should thank you. Thank you for interrupting the robbery. Get the bandits out of here, and I'll give you a free night stay next time."

Mathew smiled. "I'll do my best."

He crossed the lobby, and finding it empty, stepped outside. Sam already had Verity and her bag up on his horse. Butch offered Mathew a hand up. Reluctantly he accepted, and for the painstakingly long trip across the river, Mathew learned just what Butch's onion breath smelled like.

Mathew noticed the plump man named Fingers broke off from the group shortly after crossing the bridge. Butch and his crew were ecstatic at free booze, so why the change of plans for Fingers?

VERITY HAD LIVED with a ruined reputation for too long. So when Butch invited himself to a celebration of her and Mathew's proposal, Verity jumped at the chance to snub her nose at those who tarnished her, and with Butch and the bandits at their side, Jaime wouldn't dare come near. She needed this.

Verity tucked her shiny custom-made dagger under her skirting for safekeeping, and Sam helped her dismount in front of Stanton Spirits. The bar had faded wood siding, a long wooden porch, and on the face of the second story, red-painted lettering showing the name of the business. She smiled, feeling relaxed in public for the first time in a year. After everyone had gotten their fill of booze, Verity then planned to have Mathew return them to the future.

Butch and her fiancé arrived moments later, and Mathew hopped down from his ride. With a small flinch, he embraced her, and they opened the solid oak door. Their whole party entered, less one plump man named Fingers, and dozens of patrons turned their heads. Verity basked in the attention while she removed her cloak. She made a motion to take Mathew's off, but he declined.

Candles decorated small round tables, low hanging gas lamp fixtures cast a soothing yellow hue, and black and white photographs of the town hung on the walls. A sprinkling of abstract paintings in bold colors stood in contrast to the neutral palate—those were new since she'd last been here. Tricky floor planks creaked under their feet while they all made their way through the crowd to the bar. Only three people were women and Verity suspected they weren't customers.

"Sam," Lloyd greeted. He was stacked like a building himself,

and no one to mess with. Verity sensed his suspicion and hesitation. He added, "What brings you and your strange party here?"

"Well, my wife's brother is here to visit. This is Matty McCall, and he's getting married to Johnny's little sister, Verity. So, we came to celebrate. Beers all around!" The crowd roared with excitement.

Over the din, Sam leaned over the bar to ask Lloyd, "Where's Sarah?"

"Upstairs with the baby." A glowing smile crossed Lloyd's lips.

"I'll have to visit another day. Make a tab, would ye?"

Lloyd nodded and busied himself with lining mugs on the bar for filling.

Butch climbed on a stool and shouted, "Matt and Verity are getting' married! Let's have ourselves a party!"

More cheers and hoots erupted. Lloyd smiled and shook his head. Beer splashed all over. Everyone laughed.

Mathew squeezed Verity's hand and whispered into her ear, "Are you okay with all this?"

Verity nodded, ecstatic. She was used to the raucous bar scene, and as a prior dancer, she'd also been the center of attention. It had been a long time since eyes gazed upon her without any intentions, and right now, she relished it.

"How do you know Butch?" Mathew asked in her ear again. His tone had an edge to it, as if he didn't trust the man. She couldn't argue. At first glance the rail-thin rugged leader of the bandits with a nose that appeared broken many times was someone to fear, but intuition said he wasn't as bad as everyone

made him out to be. At this point she trusted him as Jaime's enemy.

"He borrowed an onion from me once, and he helped me escape Jaime's men not long after."

"One of those things differs greatly from the other. They captured you before I arrived?"

"Jaime's men were blocking the bridge when I was leaving..." Verity paused, not wanting to tell him she had already been traveling to California before he came back.

"To buy a dagger?"

"Yeah." A man bumped into Verity and knocked her down. Mathew shoved the pungent man off her and helped her up.

"Shall we partake in the festivities before the bar runs dry?"

"Yes, please."

Mathew fought his way through the crowd, and it took him some time to flag down Lloyd for two beers. Meanwhile, Verity scanned the patrons, checking faces. She recognized several people from newspaper stories or in passing. Not that she was paranoid, but not everyone was friendly.

A drunken man stumbled out the front door, and when he dropped his mug, glass shattered. No one bothered to check on him.

Beer splashed her chest, coating the front of her dress and soaking through to her skin. She sucked in a breath with the shock and shoved the drunkard away. The moron laughed rather than ask if she was all right or apologize. She hoped he cracked his head on a table. Served him right.

Verity fought her way toward the bar, intent on finding a cloth to clean with, content to find Mathew so they could leave,

but found herself immobilized. A thick meaty arm grabbed her around her waist and yanked her back, feet slipping out from under her. When she tumbled over, a second arm scooped her up and carried her outside. It had happened within a few seconds, and Verity hadn't even caught her breath to scream for help.

The December air bit through her wet dress in a flash and Verity gasped at the cold. A fat hand covered her mouth, and an icy cold metal circle pressed against her neck. She froze—from the temperature and from the pistol pressed against her flesh.

Her heart hammered her ribs and a gust of air made her body quake. Why didn't she and Mathew return to the future to celebrate? Why was she so desperate to repair a stupid reputation that didn't matter?

The meaty-armed man stepped around to show himself. He lifted her around the waist up onto an occupied horse. Her bottom howled in pain, but she suppressed sound from escaping her lips. The plump man who captured her confused her more than anything. With the twist of her brows, Fingers released her mouth.

"What's going on, Fingers?" she asked as casually as possible.

The round bandit smiled up at her and showed many teeth missing.

"Well, there's my purdy lady," said a familiar voice behind her ear.

The man who sat behind her made her eyes water with betrayal.

"Jaime promised me 'nother dance wit you if I's captured you for him. Generally, I don't agree with my brother's going's on,

but I couldn't turn down Jaime's offer like that. So, this is what's gonna happen. I'm gonna give you a ride over to Jaime, and he's going to make you dance for me. Then after that, he's going to do whatever he wants wit you. I suggest you do as he says, miss. The man's got a few screws loose, if you know what I mean."

Verity fought the tears from falling over. Ben Pool had given her a ride home, so she wouldn't freeze to death in her plum dress and high heels. He'd claimed to be a good man and against the actions of his brother, Joe. But here he was, turning against her like a rat for a bounty she'd completely forgotten about.

"Here's the reward. Nice doin' business wit you," Ben Pool said and tossed a weighted cloth sack to Fingers. He checked the sack's contents and nodded both of his chins.

"Deal's a deal," Fingers said and strutted inside the bar for a moment and returned without the sack. He mounted up.

She trusted the bandits. Thinking about it now, how stupid was she?

With Fingers alongside her and Ben Pool behind her, she had no chance of escape, but with Jaime's purchase of her, they wouldn't kill her. "Help!" she shouted. "Help! Matt, Sam, Lloyd!"

The bar noise of cheers and hollers drowned out her pleas for help, and a sudden spark of pain flashed white before her eyes. Her vision dimmed to black.


HOPS AND VINEGAR and sour breath permeated Mathew's comfort zone. Warm bodies and dusty linens brushed against him. As a veterinarian, he was used to working in less than savory environments—illness, injury, surgery, but after days

wearing the same clothes and surrounded by people who didn't know what a bath was, Mathew wanted a shower more than anything right now. He wanted to press the button and take a steaming shower with his fiancée. Alas, Mathew cringed at the smell and fought his way through the crowd.

"Lloyd!" Mathew shouted through the noise. "Lloyd! Can I get two glasses of beer?" Hands were reaching and grabbing across the bar, greedy with the free-flowing offer. Lloyd made eye contact and nodded in acknowledgment. Mathew drummed his fingers, not with impatience, but with discomfort. He didn't like this place. Perhaps it would be less unsettling if the bandit party hadn't accompanied them.

Lloyd made his way across the bar toward him, pouring and handing out mugs. He marked a tally just under the bar. "Congratulations are in order. Verity is a fine woman, if you can handle her." Lloyd winked and Mathew's cheeks heated.

"Yes, I can handle her. Two beers please, one for me and the future missus."

Lloyd poured out two and passed them over. Mathew nodded his thanks rather than shout over the commotion.

Mathew zigzagged through the rowdiness, careful to not spill. Unlimited for them, sure, but Mathew didn't want to be wasteful to his sister's livelihood. Guilt wracked him at Sam's offer to pay, but Mathew realized too late, he hadn't withdrawn enough local money to pay with—not planning to throw a massive party. Lloyd would laugh at his twenty-dollar bill and scoff at his credit cards.

With beer mugs in hand, Mathew's head craned around, and he stepped up onto his tippy toes.

"Verity!" he yelled through over the noise. Where did she go? He spun in place and fought his way closer to the door, stepping over downed stools, puddles of alcohol, and downed people. Mathew craned around again and still nothing. His pulse kicked into overdrive.

"Verity!"

A few heads that listened, or had their ears cleaned by his shouts, turned toward him.

"Have you seen Verity? She's missing!"

They shook their heads and resumed their partying. Mathew fought his way outside and passed the lounging horses. Blistering cold wind nipped at his face. In both directions of the dirt road, he saw nothing. No one walking, no one riding. Just nothing. He dropped the mugs into the dirt and rushed back inside.

His cupped his hands around his mouth and shouted, "Verity!"

Half the bar turned toward him for just a moment, and then they ignored him. Frustrated, he wound his way through the crowd to Sam. Beer splashed on Mathew and he cringed, but nothing would stop him from finding Verity.

"Sam!" Mathew shouted when the statuesque blacksmith came into view. "Verity's missing. Have you seen her? Is there a bathroom around here?"

"There's an outhouse around back ye might try. Through that door, down the steps."

"Thanks." A sliver of relief flowed through him while he followed Sam's directions. Perhaps she just needed to use the…outhouse. Mathew opened the back door. The winter air

seeped to his skin, and he shivered while crunching across the dead grasses of the narrow path made by previous feet. At the wooden shack, he knocked.

"Verity? Are you in there?"

A shockingly deep baritone voice responded from behind the door. "No, but if she's offering, send the lady in." He chuckled, and Mathew's face contorted in disgust. He dashed back inside and found Sam chatting with the bandits.

"Where's Verity?" Mathew interrupted them. Sam's face paled, and the bandits watched with quiet reserve. "What happened? Where's my wife?" The word came naturally to him, even if it wasn't official yet.

"No one has seen her. Did ye two fight?" Sam asked.

"Fight? No. She was waiting for me near the bar while I got us drinks."

Two of the unnamed bandits—a redhead and a man with a pockmarked face—solemnly shook their heads, eyes on the floor.

"What? What's wrong? What happened to her?"

At that moment Fingers entered the circle. He and Butch traded a whisper.

Butch spoke up. "I'm afraid she's been kidnapped again."

"How do you know? Is it Jaime?" Mathew asked.

"I had Fingers here keep an eye on her, and he saw one of Jaime's men take her. Fingers followed them and returned to report her location."

"Where?"

Butch folded his arms. Mathew's protective rage made him want to knock the man out, just like Verity's attacker in the seedy

Queens bar, and ride off armed to the hilt.

"She was taken to the estate. Jaime, indeed, has her."

"I have to go. Can I borrow a horse and a gun?"

Butch laughed. "Boy, I'll do you one better. Come on with us, and we'll storm the estate together. A real force to reckon with."

Mathew's eyes lit up with appreciation, but he squinted with suspicion. "Why?"

"Why what?" The bandits shifted their position to leave, and one drunken bar patron slammed into the pockmarked one. The bandit picked him up and tossed him away.

"Why are you offering to help me? What's in it for you? How do you really know Verity?"

"Nothing to alarm yourself with, boy," Butch said. "Jaime interferes in my business. Call it a conflict of interest. You understand?"

"And Verity?"

Butch smirked and Mathew wanted to slap it off his face. "I didn't know she was already taken when I offered her my hand. She's a good woman—very talented. And Jaime really, really hates her."

"That's it?"

"Righty so." Mathew wasn't convinced, but it was enough for now.

"Let's go then. We don't have time to waste."

The bandits and Sam mounted in a hurry with Mathew riding shotgun on Sam's horse. They rushed through town with hooves thrumming against the frozen dirt. Ice picked at Mathew's face and his body was just as cold while he fought his brain from

imagining what Verity's already injured body was enduring at this moment. He failed to keep her safe.


BEN POOL AND FINGERS had deposited Verity at the front door of her worst nightmare. Dusk fell early in the winter, and warm lights glowed through wide open curtains—the inviting coziness a Venus flytrap. Verity didn't bother to scream. She saved her energy for when she needed it. With the shake of hands for business well concluded, Fingers had departed back down the narrow road. Ben grasped her upper arm and led her inside.

Verity wondered if anything happened to Millie for releasing her last time. With a quick flash of dread, she wondered what would happen to *her* for escaping again.

The foyer was expansive with a curving staircase leading to the second floor. Doors studded the foyer on both sides. A Persian rug centered the room and budgies chirped their happy tweets in an adjacent room. Grignon had expensive taste, and it would make a beautiful home if it weren't for the miscreants currently occupying it. Verity noticed mud on the floors, dust on the furniture, and detritus collecting at the corners of the foyer. Something had happened to Millie. The housekeeper would never let the place become filthy.

Thundering boots collected from above, and a handful of men descended the stairs. They formed a half moon in front of her and Ben. A lightheadedness threatened to drop her to the floor. She inhaled deep and tilted her chin up. A single set of boots came from a side room, and the curtain of men parted for him to step forward, revealing Jaime Perez with a sneer on his

face. Verity trembled.

"Good work, Ben. Here's a token of my appreciation and please show yourself out." Jaime extended an arm with a pair of coins. Ben Pool's features pinched into anger.

"You promised me a dance. I don' want your coins. I's want time wit her." Ben flung a hand toward Verity and she flinched.

Jaime didn't dignify Ben's response with an answer. He waved his hand in dismissal, and a pair of his men captured Ben's upper arms and dragged him outside.

"You promised me! Jaime, this ain't how business's done! Jaime!" The door shut behind them and a blast of cold slithered across her skin. She shivered from the wintry air and from what fate awaited Ben.

"Now we can finally finish this," Jaime said, pacing in front of her while three of his men stood back. None of which were Joe Pool. They all were taller than Jaime, built like locomotives, and armed like soldiers. She wanted to spill into a puddle and sob for pity and mercy, but that would affect nothing in him besides annoyance, and she needed him to stay as pleasant as possible.

"I don't…" Jaime paused and laughed. "I don't know what to do with you first. I never expected this luck. I expected you to catch a ride out of here and never return. I'm glad you didn't. Carl, Frank, take her to my room."

Verity gasped and her eyes darted to the two named soldiers marching toward her.

"Not the solitary room, boss?" one of the men asked.

"Did I say the solitary room?"

"Right, boss."

As their thick crunching fists squeezed her upper arms, the door behind her opened wide with another gust of wind. A glimmer of hope threaded through her. Mathew would rescue her just on time. The door slammed shut and she craned her neck over her shoulder. Jaime's two other men returned, and Ben was not with them. Tears welled in her eyes, and she tried to blink them back but failed. The looming end was crushing her spirit.

The men forced her up the stairs to the room at the end of the hall. When they opened the door, they shoved her painfully inside, and Verity crashed to her knees on the hardwood. The door slammed shut behind her, and the lock clicked into place.

Her eyes adjusted to the dim firelight. Jaime had claimed the master bedroom with a four-poster bed, canopy, fluffy rug, and mahogany wood furnishings. The fireplace crackled softly. A sob escaped feminine lips, and Verity realized it wasn't hers.

"Hello?" she asked into the expansive but darkened room.

The sob became full crying, a girl's crying, and Verity pulled her feet under her and sought the source. In the far corner a small girl sat on a pile of blankets on the floor. Verity cautiously approached, not wanting to scare her.

"Hi there. What's your name?"

The girl's face tilted up. Her brown eyes were sunken in and her cheeks hollowed. Tears streaked dirt down her face. Verity thought she was a teenager, but the fear and weakness made her appear much younger. The girl rubbed her eyes, and with a movement of her feet, chains rattled.

"Audrey," the girl replied through quivering voice. The scullery maid. Millie had mentioned her. The poor thing was

now a prisoner instead of a servant. Verity would do everything in her power to free the girl as well.

"That's a pretty name. How old are you?"

Audrey wore a stained and torn plain servant's dress, her bonnet was missing, and her long blonde hair was snarled and knotted in a nest around her head. Verity didn't like what she thought was happening here.

"Fifteen."

Verity exhaled a deep breath. "Do you have any parents around?"

She shook her head.

"Grandparents?"

Audrey tipped her head down into her hands and sobbed, shoulders shaking.

"Grandma Millie is gone."

Millie? The housekeeper was her grandmother? Verity knelt by the girl and inspected the chains. They were thicker than her finger, and the bands were too tight around her delicate ankles. There was no hope of slipping them off, even if Verity found soap. The chains were fastened to a loop in the hardwood floor. Verity could not free the girl.

"Are there keys around?"

Audrey nodded. "He's unlocked me a few times to bring me to his bed, but the keys were always in his pocket."

Verity snapped her fingers in frustration. "I'll get you out of here. I promise."

Audrey's weak smile crushed Verity. She could see herself in the girl. A prisoner of her familiar world. Mistreated by men and left to wilt away. Verity would never leave her behind.

The lock in the bedroom door clicked. Verity spun to protect the girl and waited as the door swung open.

THE HORSES SPREAD into a two-by-two formation to fit up the narrow dirt path leading to the estate. Darkness descended upon them, and the once cheery house now loomed overhead with glowing yellow windows like a scowling jack-o'-lantern. Mathew was storming a mansion filled with unknown numbers of Jaime's outlaws, and his only help was a group of five bandits whose loyalty he didn't have, and his brother-in-law, whom he felt guilty was walking into the same death trap.

Once they crested the hill, a shape of a man shifted in the shadows. Butch stopped all the riders with the lift of his arm and said, "Identify yourself or we fire."

Fingers and one other man drew weapons and aimed. The bandits spread out behind their leader, keeping their weapons trained on the target, as if intimidating the man into submission. Mathew hung back with Sam, unwilling to get between the crosshairs of the bandits.

Hands from the shadow bolted skyward. "Don' shoot me. I's Ben Pool."

"Ben Pool, as in Joe Pool?" Butch asked with a gravelly warning tone.

"We have the same momma, but I don' agree wit what he does. I's promised a dance, and it was taken away from me."

Butch dismounted and approached Ben Pool, and as if on a practiced cue, the remaining bandits copied and stayed on his toes. The wind tousled Butch's cloak. Mathew and Sam

exchanged glances and dismounted. The cold finished numbing Mathew's discomfort, so he was back to his capable self, on time to get himself killed.

"Join us in taking down Jaime's men." Butch commanded.

Ben shook his head. "They's lots of ya, but Jaime's got lots too. I don' like those odds. I's not a fighter and I only wanted a dance. No, I can't say that I can help ya."

"Is there anything you want in exchange for your services?" Butch asked.

Ben Pool's eyes searched the faces of the mismatched cavalry. He nodded. "I's wanted a dance wit' Miss Verity for the last year. I almost got it, too. Promise my dance and ya got yourself a deal."

"No way!" Mathew shouted. All the heads turned toward him, and Mathew's height returned to a few inches again.

Butch answered Ben. "It's Verity's call. She can say yes or no, and you'll respect it."

"Yes, siree."

"Are your arms ready?" Butch asked.

Ben Pool unholstered a pistol and checked it against the pale yellow light of the windows.

"Ready as I ever be."

Butch nodded his head and the misfit group followed him to the front door, weapons drawn and ready. The leader made motions that Mathew didn't understand, while Sam tapped him on the arm and handed him a knife. Good ol' Sam—he figured out Mathew was useless with a gun.

Mathew nodded his thanks, and the front door opened. Two of the bandits slipped in first on silent feet. Butch and Fingers

followed next. Ben and another bandit entered, and Sam and Mathew took up the rear. The men spread wide, hunting Jaime's men. Knives were the first used, creeping through the estate like ninjas. The bandits slaughtered men where they sat and others shortly after standing up to defend themselves. Mathew's stomach heaved. In moments, the misfits reassembled in the foyer, and Sam stayed behind him to pat Mathew on the back.

After a few moments bent at the waist, Mathew recollected himself and stepped away from his mess, wiping his mouth.

"Didna want ye to get shanked in the back while heaving up yer lunch," Sam said.

Mathew paled. "Uh, thanks."

He and Sam joined the bandits, and the men quietly discussed the count. "One back here is down."

Another one said, "One sleeping over here is dead."

"How many are left?" Butch asked Ben Pool.

Ben shrugged. "He's always got five or more 'round 'im and ten loungin' around these walls."

Butch motioned for half the group to continue combing the first floor and the second group to head upstairs. Ben led Mathew, Sam, and Butch up the stairs. Fingers led the other three bandits around the stairwell to the maze of rooms.

At the end of the hallway, Ben said in a hushed tone, "Here's his private room. He keeps 'em locked in here sometimes."

The men shifted their feet for an offensive charge. Mathew held Sam's knife extended, hoping that if he had to use it, the death would be quick and clean, or even better—the man would simply surrender.

After a swift kick by Sam, the door creaked open. Ben entered

first, and a woman's scream tore through the mansion. Shouts and yells permeated every room in the estate and boots pounded across hardwood floors. Mathew shoved his way through the group and sought the scream of his fiancée.

"Get away from me, Ben!" she yelled.

"Verity!" Mathew shouted.

"Matt! We're in here."

We? Mathew lifted his knife in case Jaime showed himself. The other men spread out and Mathew dashed to his love. Their chests crashed and arms wrapped around each other in panicked relief.

"Break it up. We still have to get out of here," Butch said.

Verity pulled herself back from his arms and he reluctantly released her.

"What is he doing here?" Verity asked, pointing at Ben.

"He's helping us rescue ye," Sam answered.

"He's the one who brought me here!"

Sam, Mathew, Verity, and Butch turned their heads toward the traitor. Mathew couldn't zap Verity away to safety yet, because he couldn't abandon his sister's husband in the middle of the tyrant's estate. The three of them needed to escape alive together, and right now, he wanted to punch the man who'd given Verity to the enemy.

"Is that true?" Mathew asked, taking a step forward. Verity's hand gripped his arm.

Ben stepped back. "I...I was offered a dance wit the kind lady in exchange for bringin' her here. I didn' know anything's bad was gonna happen. Jaime assured me she'd be jus' fine. I only wanted a dance. I'm sorry." He took another step back as

Mathew found himself prowling closer, fist clenched.

A gunshot rang through the room. Verity folded down with her hands on her ears. Mathew flinched from the pain in his eardrums, but Sam and Butch didn't move at all. In the moment of silence, chains rattled from the corner of the room, but rather than inspect the source, they watched Ben Pool crash to the floor. Jaime Perez stood in the doorway, pistol smoking. Boots thundered up the stairs and two more men flanked him. Mathew's heart sank. Two of Jaime's men came, but where were Butch's?

Three men to three men. Butch and Sam were tense but calm as if they'd done this many times before. The standstill caused restless nerves in Mathew, turning his insides into sparking wires. He was afraid, he was nervous, and then he reminded himself this was the man that had abused the woman he loved simply because she'd defended herself.

He was going to prove to Verity he would protect her forever. Mathew stepped forward to line up with Sam and Butch in a challenge.

VERITY HELD HER BREATH. The man she loved shifted forward to challenge Jaime. Despite her affections, she wasn't so sure of his ability to handle a dagger. Then she remembered Mathew performed surgery, so he was well-skilled in knowing how to do fatal damage to living tissue. The thought wasn't reassuring because Jaime packed firearms, but it helped her keep her composure. She didn't want to trigger an accident or frighten Audrey.

The scent of cordite lingered, and coppery blood quickly mixed with it. Jaime was almost a full head shorter than everyone else and, in this room, he would not be intimidating at all if it weren't for Verity's horrible memories of him. Her bottom had stitches along her raw wounds. She fought a strong urge to vomit.

A sputtering came from Ben Pool, who was left splayed on the floor. Blood oozed out of him, but Verity's focus returned to the pure evil before her.

Jaime spoke first, facing Butch, "I thought we had a deal."

Verity's face pinched in disgust, and her head swung over to Butch. What did this animal mean by a deal?

Butch answered, "We *did*. The deal is done. Now my men and I are free agents once again."

Butch betrayed her. The thought cozied up in the back of her head while the enraging conversation continued.

"In that case, I have another deal for you." Jaime pointed his pistol straight at Verity, but with all she had done to him and having escaped him, his rage wouldn't be satisfied by a quick death. That was the only thought that kept her on her feet.

"Name your terms."

Verity sucked in a breath. She, Mathew, and Sam had no chance of escape if the bandits aligned with Jaime's men.

"Five hundred."

That was enough for a whole group of men to comfortably live for a year. She didn't believe he would turn down the deal. Verity discretely lifted the back of her skirting and her fingers searched for her custom-made dagger.

"Hmm," Butch muttered.

The pockmarked man giggled. Mathew and Sam remained silent but calculating. Jaime's men didn't move a muscle as if they only responded to commands, and Audrey kept quiet like she must've been taught. Verity hated what the girl must've suffered.

"What did you want for it?" Butch asked.

"You and your men to walk away."

Without the bandits, their odds of escape would improve, but not by enough.

"Cash in hand first."

Jaime's cold eyes searched Butch for a long, strained moment.

"Whiskers," Jaime said, "Collect it from my office."

"Yes, boss." The minion named Whiskers left, and his boots thundered down the elegant steps. Jaime's group was down a man now. Verity's surprise was kept hidden like the blade's handle in her grip.

"I've waited a long time for my chance at revenge," Jaime said to Verity. "I had it not too long ago, but then it slipped from my fingers." He paused. "It didn't take long for me to figure out the traitorous mouse in my house, and Millie has been under my secured watch ever since."

The girl gasped behind Verity.

Jaime paced the expansive bedroom, finding a boldness with only Sam, Verity, and Mathew still standing against him. "What you've done to me is unacceptable. I didn't want the sheriff to take you. What fun is there in that? Rotting in a cell doesn't teach you anything, and it doesn't make me feel better. After all, you maimed me permanently. So, *an eye for an eye* as I've been taught."

Mathew and Sam shifted their weight, ready to spring into action. Butch stood resolute, a businessman waiting to finish his

new task.

A loud thump echoed from downstairs followed by a grunt. Butch reacted as if it were a signal and leapt at the remaining soldier of Jaime's with surprising agility. Sam dove for Jaime. Whiskers hadn't returned, freeing Mathew, and he dashed to Verity. His hand enveloped hers and he pulled. Around her, fists flew, jaws crunched, and skin thumped with impacts. And then the grunts came.

"Let's get out of here while we have a chance."

"No," Verity said. "We can't leave Audrey."

The girl whimpered, and Mathew's eyes searched the darkened corner.

"Oh, shit." He knelt by the girl and inspected her restraints. "Damn. Do you know where the key is?"

"Jaime has it on his person," Verity said.

Mathew turned toward Sam and Jaime's fight. He cringed. Arms swung and legs thrashed. Groans speckled the air. Mathew joined the fight and yelled to Verity, "Stay where I can see you!"

Verity nodded, not willing to leave the girl's side.

Sam had Jaime on the ground. They rolled and punched. Fists locked across necks. Sam had considerable size on Jaime, but the smaller man was slippery. Mathew reeled back for a kick to Jaime's side, helping Sam. When the opening came, his foot slammed into the smaller man, and Jaime let out a heave of air. Sam stood, panting.

"Thank ye. I suppose ye owe him a few slugs yourself." Jaime laid flat on the floor, trying to suck in a breath.

"I need his key for the girl's restraints. You can do whatever you want with him. When we get outside, we will disappear."

"Back to yer time?"

"For good."

Sam clapped Mathew on the shoulder. Jaime inhaled a ragged breath, regaining control of his diaphragm. Mathew leaned down, and Verity covered her mouth with her hand. The rage that festered behind Mathew's eyes came out just like it had at the seedy Queens saloon. A fast strike twisted Jaime's head on its axis. Mathew shook his knuckles.

"You deserve so much worse than that," Mathew spat. Verity's heart warmed at her love protecting her, and then she remembered her dagger. Verity strode over to Mathew and Sam, and Mathew tried to pull her back for safety.

"No. I need this," she insisted.

"Ye've earned whatever ye need to do, lass."

Verity waited until the spark returned to Jaime's eyes and fixed on hers. She took the dagger and knelt next to him. "This is for Greenleaf." She plunged it into his crotch, properly destroying any intention he had of hurting women and girls ever again. He folded with a stunned scream, and Verity retrieved her blade to a second wind of screams.

"Fine craftsmanship, Sam. Thank you."

"Yer welcome."

Butch stood and stretched after his opponent had given up fighting, and a dagger was wedged in the downed man's chest. The bandit leader fisted the handle and lifted, but the man's body followed, so Butch used his foot to hold the body down while he wrenched his dagger out.

"Jesus, Verity," Butch said as he inspected her handiwork. "If you weren't already betrothed, I'd be marrying you myself.

You're one hell of a woman. By the way, if things don't work out between you, the offer's still on the table."

"Uh, thanks, Butch," Verity said with a twist in her stomach. She decided remaining civil was for the better until they escaped. The bandits weren't trustworthy.

Jaime roused again with his hands in his crotch. His eyes were coated in tears and his face puffy red from exertion. Verity remembered Sam explaining how he carried guilt for not stopping Jaime last year, so it surprised her none when Mathew passed the torch to the blacksmith.

"Sam, end this," Mathew said.

Sam nodded and knelt by his head. "Jaime, ye were my kin and ye betrayed me. I only did what I had to in order to earn yer sister's hand in marriage. When I found out about the terrible things Grignon was doing, I refused to continue working for him. Grignon killed Issy, but not before Dennis raped her. It broke me. I didn't allow it to happen, and I didn't cause it to happen. Whatever animosity ye have for me is unfounded. Ye beat my wife, because ye thought she hurt ye. She didn't touch ye. Then ye go around beating Verity here, and I was told she did hurt ye, but ye deserved it. Ye're not the man I thought ye were, and it's time for ye to stop once and for all."

Jaime lifted his hand and stared at the bright blood coating his fingers. There was no likely way he would survive those injuries, but if he did, he deserved them. Jaime's eyes welled with tears. He choked out a raspy reply. "I'm sorry. Sorry to April, Verity"—he sobbed—"to you Sam. I'm sorry."

Sam nodded with watery eyes and plunged his own blade into Jaime's chest. They waited until the last of the light in his eyes

blinked out.

"If I'd have done that last year, Verity, this wouldna happened. I'm sorry too."

"Don't be. I got my revenge, and all these events brought me Mathew. On that note, we need to get out of here." Verity dove for Jaime's pockets, not remotely disturbed by the blood, and searched for the key to Audrey's prison. She found nothing. "They aren't here. The keys. We need the keys."

Grunts of fighting echoed from down the stairs.

"Then we find them," Mathew said.

MATHEW WASN'T SURE what to feel about Jaime's death. He should be elated, ready to throw a party. The evil had been defeated, his fiancée had been saved, the world would continue as normal. Mathew didn't feel like celebrating. A life was wasted. The man needed help, but in this time, what help was there?

Too many things had happened to allow Jaime to live, but still the guilt nagged him. The grunts of fights downstairs snapped Mathew back. They still needed to find the keys to rescue the girl and get out of the mansion in one piece.

Butch exited the master bedroom first. Mathew was right on his heels with his hand on Verity. Sam took up the rear.

"Don't leave me," a small voice pleaded from the corner, and Mathew stopped.

"I'll watch her, find those keys," Sam said.

Mathew nodded, and he and Verity searched room by room for any clues. Most rooms had sheets draped over the furniture as if they hadn't been used in years. The last one they checked

on the second floor was nearest the staircase. The door was locked.

"I've been in that room. There's a secret entrance," Verity offered.

"This is faster," Mathew said, wanting the opportunity to kick it in just like in the movies, just like Sam had earlier. His arm motioned Verity to stand clear, and he rushed the door and threw up a kick. The door didn't budge. Mathew held in a yelp of pain and slowly released a deep breath. "Well, that didn't work."

Verity sighed. "Follow me." Mathew limped behind her while she led him into the room next door. He stilled. A single window alongside a fireplace. A table and chairs, bookcases. He remembered this room.

"Right through here is how I found you." She stood in the corner and her fingers searched the edges of the bookcase. "Here." With the strength of her body, she pulled the secret door aside just enough for them to squeeze through.

The breeze rolling through the tunnel kissed their faces. On the other side of the tunnel was a small room with another table and chairs, a large fireplace, no windows and floor-to-ceiling books. Verity dashed to a corner. Mathew followed her and his jaw dropped open.

"Millie. Can you hear me?" Verity asked. The woman was half naked and bruised. Her eye was completely swelled shut, and her lip was split. Jaime took a lot of time to do this. Mathew's rage burned in him again, but he controlled himself with the memory of Jaime's life blinking out.

Millie moaned.

"We're going to get you out of here," Verity said. "Audrey is locked in another room. Do you know where the keys are?"

Millie opened her good eye and tears welled. "She's alive?"

Her weak hoarse voice crushed Mathew. What a horrible monster Jaime must've been to do this to a woman, to anyone. He was disgusting. Mathew wanted to vomit, but he put on his veterinarian hat to think more objectively.

"She's shaken, scared, hungry, but alive," Mathew said. "We're getting you both out of here. Where are the keys? Jaime didn't have them on his person."

Millie tilted the non-swollen corner of her mouth. "End table, downstairs, next to the bird cage. Follow the tweets."

Mathew and Verity exchanged surprised glances. "We'll be right back for you," Verity said to the battered woman.

Millie wheezed a grunt, and they left, feet stepping down the stairs quickly but as silently as possible.

The tweets came from a room on the right and Verity followed it. Mathew stayed close on her heels, watching their backs. Both of them only had a knife each, and untold numbers of Jaime's men were still around, armed with pistols.

Inside what appeared to be a study was a thick comfortable chair, a large fireplace, broad windows overlooking the darkened woods, and a round birdcage. Mathew's brow furrowed. He reminded himself that the inappropriate cage was all that was available at the time. They didn't know any better. Next to the hanging cage was a recliner, and the end table was within arm's reach. Books stacked on top of it, and Mathew searched the top while Verity opened the drawer.

"Got 'em," she said, dangling the keys in the air.

"I see you got yourself out of this pickle," a strange voice said behind them.

Mathew and Verity spun, and Fingers loomed near. Mathew swallowed a thick lump caught in his throat.

"Fingers," Verity acknowledged. Her body stiffened next to his, putting Mathew on alarm.

"No hard feelings, eh?" Fingers asked.

"Hard feelings! You sold me to Jaime. Why would you do that? You hate the man."

At the sound of their voices, Butch entered the study. "Yes, he did."

"How could you, Butch?"

The leader of the bandits shrugged. "Jaime wanted you. I wanted money. We made a trade, and then we came to rescue you. If we just showed up to kill Jaime, the money could've been locked at the bank, doing us no good. We needed assurance the money was accessible."

Fire burned in Mathew. All of this could've been avoided had Butch not sold them out.

"And Ben Pool, what was his hand in this?"

"Ben was the delivery boy."

Verity growled with anger, and Mathew squeezed her hand to calm her. The bandits admitted betrayal, and they were still trapped in the house with them.

Another bandit entered the room, one that hadn't spoken before.

"I think we got them all, Butch. Searched every room. No one's left."

"Good work, Brawley."

Verity gasped. "What about Millie and Audrey?"

Butch smiled with dark menace, turning Mathew's stomach. "Where's Sam?"

The leader's head turned to Brawley as he answered. "Upstairs, where you left him."

Did the bandits really kill Sam? Why had he left Sam alone? Mathew pulled Verity between the group of three and straight upstairs. The door to Millie's room was open, and the housekeeper was slumped over in her corner. Mathew checked for a pulse at her neck. Her head lifted. "I'm not dead yet, son. Did you find them?"

Verity handed Mathew the keys, and he checked each one until the cuffs opened. He helped the woman stand and used what rags were still attached to her to cover her top. She took his weight, and he set her in a chair at the table. "We'll be right back. We're getting Audrey."

"Don't worry about me. I'll be right here." She chuckled lightly, and Mathew led Verity out of the room.


THE BETRAYAL AMONGST the bandits shouldn't surprise Verity, but for some reason, it still stung. The leader *had* proposed to her way back when he assisted her crossing the bridge guarded by Jaime's men. She wouldn't say yes, then or now. Especially now. He'd sold her to the enemy twice for money and then rescued her, but why? What was his end game in all this? She could only figure it was his genuine affection for her that lead to the rescuing and his genuine hatred of Jaime's outlaws that lead to the slaughtering.

Mathew followed on her heels toward the master bedroom where Audrey was chained. They stepped cautiously. The bandits declared the house was empty of everyone, but she didn't trust their word. Verity opened the door while standing to the side, uncertain if Sam was alive and trigger happy.

Silence followed and Verity popped her head into the doorway. She stepped inside to find Sam cuddling the girl, keeping her warm and safe. Verity's heart melted for them. The girl deserved so much more than her prison. Mathew stepped past her, over Jaime's body, and knelt by the two of them.

"It's going to be okay. I've got the keys. We'll get you out of here soon."

"Where's grandma?"

"She's in another room. We'll bring you to her." Mathew tried key after key and finally, the last key turned the tumbler, springing the girl free. She rubbed her ankles, but an excitement didn't come.

"How are you doing, Sam?" Verity asked.

Sam stood up and stretched. "I'm fine. What's going on with the bandits?"

"We don't know what side they're on, only that they wanted Jaime and his men out of the picture. The sooner we get out of here the better. Let's get this little lady to her grandma."

The four of them exited the room, leaving behind the bodies of Jaime and Ben Pool, and returned to Jaime's punishment room where Millie was recovering at the table. Sam entered first to check for any more threats and waved them all inside. Mathew guided the girl to her grandmother and his gentleness with the girl melted Verity's heart. He was good with kids, and she smiled

with affection at his profile.

"Grandma?" Audrey asked and reached a gentle hand out to Millie's forearm. The housekeeper's head rested on her arms. Verity wasn't confident the old lady would pull through.

"Grandma?" she repeated. Millie hadn't moved. Verity knelt by Audrey and touched the old lady's throat as she'd seen Mathew do before. Verity caught his eye and shook her head. Mathew reached down to check. He blew out a deep breath. Millie was gone.

"Audrey, honey, your grandma isn't feeling well. Maybe we should come back later."

Verity guided her away, and the girl asked, "She's dead, isn't she?"

Startled, Verity's mouth popped open. "It appears that way, honey. I'm so sorry."

"Where will I go now? She was my only family."

Verity glanced at Mathew and Sam. She didn't know what to do with the girl, but Audrey could not stay in the house. Before Verity made a suggestion, Sam knelt down in front of her and said, "Dinnae worry, lassie. You'll have a home with me and April. You'll have a little brother and a dog named Doug."

"Your dog is named dog?" the girl asked.

Verity chuckled and Mathew smiled.

"D—o—u—g," Sam spelled.

"Oh, that's sounds like dog."

"I suppose yer right. Let's get out of here." Sam stood and took the girl's hand. The four of them left the house without any trouble. If any of Jaime's men survived, Verity didn't care. She was going home.

The night sky blanketed them all in a freezing chill. Extra horses were lounging in the front yard from the bandits, Sam, and Jaime's men. White clouds came from all the animals, and the people. Audrey rubbed her bare arms.

Sam rifled through the horse's sacks until he found some warm garments to cover the girl. She curled them up to her quivering chin.

"I guess this is it," Mathew said. "Mind if we steal one of these? I'd like to arrive home in a safe location."

"I dinnae think they'd notice," Sam said.

Sam helped Audrey up onto Bucky, and Mathew helped Verity climb aboard a healthy horse and dull pain lashed against her bottom anew. Mathew mounted behind her. They strolled down the narrow path to the main road, swinging left back toward Sam's cabin. No one said anything on the ride. They were lost in their thoughts, just like she was. The images of Jaime's death flashed before her eyes followed by all her previous interactions with him, all the way up to him beating her with his belt. She shivered and Mathew held her closer.

All four of them dismounted at Sam's cabin.

"Sorry for all the trouble," Mathew said, "But I offer you a horse as a peace offering."

Sam chuckled. "Thanks. I could always use a spare. Bucky's getting up in age these days."

"Someday soon, little Mathew will need a horse to get to work…er, run errands?"

Sam smiled. "Someday."

Silence filled the gaps between their sentences. The final goodbyes were on everyone's tongues, but the idea of saying the

words out loud had everyone doubting their voices.

"Well," Sam said, "It's been a pleasure meeting ye. Thank ye for the opportunity to end this whole mess, and now we get to add a new member to our family. No regrets here."

"Yeah," Mathew agreed. "No regrets here either. I'm honored to have met you. I know you'll take good care of my sister." He paused, and Verity squeezed his hand. "Tell her I love her, and she'll always be my meatball."

"Ye dinnae want to say goodbye to her yerself?"

"I did already. Anything more would be waterworks."

Sam nodded and Verity said, "Your knives are the finest craftsmanship I've ever seen. Thank you for the weapon that allowed my retribution. I no longer have to live in fear, and for that I thank you again." Verity's eyes watered, but she hoped in the darkness no one saw.

Sam and Mathew shook hands and clapped backs. Verity gave Sam a hug and then gave little Audrey a hug. "None of this was your fault, you hear? Your grandma knew you were alive and escaping. She was able to pass on in peace. Your new family will take excellent care of you."

Audrey nodded. Verity embraced Mathew. They watched Sam and Audrey enter the cabin and close the door behind them.

"Let's go home. Ready?" Mathew asked.

"Yes, please."

The press of a button sent them through quivering, nauseating darkness, and Verity held on for her love, for her future, and for the rest of her life.

# Chapter Twenty-Five

Green Bay, Wisconsin
Present Day

WHEN THE NAUSEATING quivering in his stomach stopped, Mathew opened his eyes. The smell of Verity enveloped him with a peaceful calm. Warm summer air teased his face and Mathew sighed.

Verity released him and vomited in his clinic's parking lot. He reached over and held her wild hair out of her eyes and away from her mouth.

"Are you hanging in there?"

She wretched until she dry heaved. Verity straightened and nodded. "I'm just glad it's over. I'm glad to be home."

Mathew smiled and his chest warmed with the brilliant green eyes, bold freckles and tousled hair shifting in the summer breeze. He pressed her body against his and leaned down for a kiss. Verity turned away.

"What's the matter?"

"I just vomited."

Mathew laughed. "The ride across is rough on the stomach. Let's go home and get cleaned up. I've been wearing this outfit for days and I think I never want to wear it again. We can spend

some time saving water."

Verity's eyes sparkled, and Mathew used an app for a ride to his apartment. He unlocked his door, and they collapsed on the couch. They both fell asleep before getting a shower.

Mathew woke up to aching ribs and a pounding head. It still smelled like pig manure in here. He lifted himself off the couch and downed some ibuprofen. His breath rivaled dogs who drank toilet water, and he freshened up before returning to his fiancée.

Verity was still asleep, draped across the couch, wearing layers of ancient linens and wool. He opened his dismal fridge and collected a few things to make breakfast. Verity woke once the eggs began to sizzle, and she stood and stretched like a cat. She strode over to him and wrapped her arms around his middle.

"Good morning, honey," Mathew said. "How do you like your eggs?"

"Cooked is best."

Mathew chuckled. "Always so picky."

She kissed his neck and freshened in the bathroom. While waiting for her to return, Mathew called a carpet cleaning business who would be by later to scour the floors, and then dished out an amateur spread of eggs and pancakes, promising to buy everything Verity wanted at the store later.

And still Verity was in the bathroom, so Mathew knocked on the door. "Everything okay in there?"

No answer.

Mathew tried the knob, and the door opened. "Verity?"

His fiancée leaned over the toilet bowl and a sheen of green covered her skin. He rushed to her side and flipped her hair back just as another wave of vomit came up. He needed to get her

help. She hadn't displayed any symptoms of illness until right now. What was wrong with her?

"Come on up. I'm taking you to the hospital."

Verity stood on wobbly knees.

"Wait."

Mathew gazed into her eyes. She was scared, and panic threatened to scatter his logical thought process.

"I need to clean up first. I'll feel much better. The eggs are getting to me. For some reason the smell of them..." Verity folded over the toilet and vomited again. Mathew agreed with her clothing and cloak, the hospital would be asking questions he wasn't at liberty to answer.

Mathew collected the clothing she had left behind. He stacked them on the bathroom countertop. He cranked the hot water, and while they waited for the heat to steam the room, Mathew returned to the kitchen and disposed of the eggs and opened the windows to vent the smell. They'd grab something on the way to the office instead.

In the bathroom, he helped her undress. The hot water caressed her skin, and she smiled. A pink blush returned to her cheeks, and Mathew found his hands massaging her scalp with soap suds within moments.

"You're so good at that. Come in here and I can help you wash."

Mathew's heart thrummed in his chest. A hot shower would do them both good. Verity perked up just getting washed. Mathew stripped down, and they spent a while saving water together.

MATHEW HAD DRIVEN them to urgent care since Verity vomited again after he disposed of the eggs and their odor. Verity insisted she didn't need to go to the emergency room after Mathew explained its purpose, but she was worried. She sat on the exam table while Mathew stood beside her, holding her hand. Bleach turned Verity's stomach and concern knitted Mathew's brow.

"What are the symptoms so far?" The nurse asked while shining a light in her eyes.

"Upset stomach. The smell of normal things can make me retch. Tender breasts and dizziness."

The nurse nodded.

"I think a blood test is in order to check your hCG levels. When was your last period?"

"Uh, I don't know?" Verity answered. She'd never heard of a period.

"Your menstrual cycle?" the nurse clarified. Although Verity knew what that was, she still didn't know the answer. Even if she'd been paying attention, the time travel scrambled her.

"I don't know."

The corner of the nurse's lips lifted. "I'll have the lab come and do a blood draw. We'll get to the bottom of this shortly."

Verity nodded and Mathew squeezed her hand. As soon as the nurse left, a woman from the lab brushed passed the curtain carrying a tray full of glass tubes. Verity swallowed a thick lump.

"Hi, I'm Ashley. hCG today, huh? I'll get it drawn for you quick here."

Mathew had warned her about possible blood tests, and the modern syringes were definitely less scary than the glass ones of

the past, but Verity still didn't like the poke or sheath of metal shoved in her arm. Moments later, the nurse returned with a bright smile.

"What is it?" Mathew asked, his voice an octave too high. "What's wrong with my fiancée?"

"Well, Verity, you're pregnant."

Mathew's jaw dropped and Verity gasped. Her hand covered her mouth, and they both stared at the nurse while she crossed the room to the chair and sat at the computer. Her badge beeped in her access to the system and she clicked away at the keys.

Mathew's eyes glazed over while the nurse asked for primary care information, a preferred obstetrician, last vaccine dates, and to set up initial appointments, including the first ultrasound. Verity had no idea what the nurse was talking about.

Mathew didn't say anything. What did that mean? Verity turned to see his reaction, and he was way too pasty for her liking. Their eyes met for a moment before his rolled back.

Mathew fell back and landed on the cushioned chair. Verity and the nurse crowded over him, but he woke seconds after.

"What is it?" he asked, confused.

"You fainted," the nurse said.

"I what?"

"Her hCG level indicates Verity here is about six weeks along. Congratulations."

Verity hoped for a good reaction this time, but instead, Mathew passed out again.

MATHEW WAS BUZZING when he drove over to his sister's old house to deliver muffins to little Ms. Lewis next door. They had only been in 1853 for one day's worth of modern time. It felt like weeks! He pulled into the driveway in the historical district and killed the SUV's engine. Mathew smiled at his sister's rental house. She was never coming back, but she was in better hands where she was. April had a great husband, a business to help him run, and two lovely kids to look after.

He was going to be a father soon, too. It hadn't sunk in yet, but the excitement rumbled around in his brain. Mathew climbed the steps next door and rang the doorbell.

An elderly man opened the door just a crack. "I don't want anything you're selling." He eyed the muffins in Mathew's hands.

"I'm not selling anything. Is Ms. Lewis here?"

"Who?"

"Ms. Lewis," Mathew said much louder.

"Never heard of her. I've been here for thirty years."

Mathew cocked his head to the side in confusion. "Sorry to bother you."

Ms. Lewis didn't exist? The old man closed the door, and Mathew gazed at April's house again. Mathew met the old lady before, so something else had happened. April's front door opened and Kiko beckoned him inside.

"What's the deal with Ms. Lewis?" he asked her, standing in her living room.

Kiko smiled. "She wasn't born in her time."

Mathew stared, processing the small woman's words. "You mean she is the great, great, great, granddaughter of someone who no longer lived in the past?"

"Precisely."

Mathew plopped onto the couch. "Whoa."

"My work alters current and future events. Most of the time harmlessly. Sometimes for the better. I don't ever make matches that will harm future society."

"And you can tell ahead of time?"

"Yes."

"All right then."

"Here," Kiko said, patting a box on the coffee table. "This is stuff I think you'd like to have."

Mathew opened the box top and found April's copy of *The Count of Monte Cristo*, followed by photos and her old portrait drawings. His eyes misted. Kiko handed him a stack of different sized documents.

"Verity will need these," Kiko added. "Perhaps have her go through the channels to legally change her name to Verity. It would be easier for both of you."

Mathew accepted the documents. Birth certificate, social security card, passport. All April's. Verity was similar enough to his sister. This could work.

"What about my parents listed on the birth certificate?"

Kiko smiled. "Already changed."

Mathew unfolded the certificate and found the information had changed. "How?" Kiko didn't respond, so he added, "Got it. Us mere mortals can't know everything."

"April wanted you to have this too." She handed him a folded wad of cash and…a check. Mathew turned the check over and his mouth gaped open.

"What's this?"

"April insisted I give you her emergency savings. She said she won't be needing it anymore."

Mathew was floored. The kindness of his sister made him drop onto the couch. "I wouldn't take if it she was here."

"I know."

"I can't believe she just handed me this much. I knew she was saving for whatever she decided to do with her life, but this is just too much." And Mathew then realized he forgot to give his sister the bank account card in his wallet. He surmised she didn't need it anyhow. What was he going to do with it now?

"I know."

"Thank you, Kiko. You've saved my life in more ways than one."

"I know."

"Right." Mathew stood and gave Kiko a tight hug. Tears formed in his eyes and he used a hidden hand behind her back to wipe them away.

"As someone with far more years under her belt than usual, do you have any pointers for us regulars?" Mathew asked.

"Pointers, no. But I was very surprised to find out that after age thirty, you don't change much. Your body does—not mine exactly, but you get the idea. Your mind is still just you. The ability to learn more things, gain more empathy, understand patterns of history, to care about the future, all comes with time. But you and your personality, stay the same."

"Makes all those 500-year-old vampires who fall in love with twenty-something women stories seem more plausible," Mathew said, remembering his sister going on and on about books like those. "Not that I read any of them, you know. April

was a fan."

"Right," she mimicked him.

"Am I going to see you again?"

Kiko smiled. "I may steal away one of your assistants."

Mathew quirked his brow. "I hope you're talking about Becca."

Kiko nodded and covered her lips with her index finger in a hush.

"Well, good luck to you and your matching. I've got another errand to run before I can return to my future bride, oh, and my lips are sealed."

"Good luck to you, Matt."

"And to you."

Mathew pulled out of the driveway and went straight to the jeweler. After logging into his bank accounts this morning from his phone, he found balances as expected. It was surreal to see zero balances for his student loans, SUV loan, credit cards, and the seventy-thousand-dollar gamble loan. It had all paid off and now he was set. Mathew chose a beautiful ring that still didn't compare to Verity's stunning uniqueness. And he had more plans to come.

On his way home, Mathew unlocked the clinic to check the hidden fireplace drawer. It had creaked open without a fuss, which supported April having broken it loose already. Inside was a stack of fragile papers and a dusty current-model smartphone. Mathew had brought the phone to the desk for charging and unfolded the papers with care. They were aged, worn, and dusty.

The first one was a portrait of little Mathew snuggling his family, including Audrey and Doug. A letter describing his first

teeth, first steps, and first words. Mathew's eyes had watered. Turned out little Mathew sounded like his mother, but occasionally used some of dad's words, like lass. Mathew smiled. April wrote that a happy and beautiful Audrey stayed with them for almost a year before leaving home. The blacksmith business was booming, and they were doing great. Some droughts gave them setbacks, but they weathered on. The letters had stopped after a family portrait where little Mathew, a spitting image of his mother, was a teenager.

Mathew wondered what had happened to them after, but he didn't have the strength to find out, since they had lived over a hundred years ago. Mathew had brought the papers and charged phone home and digitized and preserved them. When he had a moment, he turned on the phone. It was dead—a paperweight.

Disappointed, Mathew remembered her android had a micro SD card. He disassembled the case and ejected the card. He scrambled for a card adapter and attached it to an old laptop he kept at home but rarely used. He scrolled through the photos. There was no trace of Levi, her ex-boyfriend. Instead, he found dozens of photos of her and Sam, Audrey and little Mathew. She made videos. Mathew's eyes watered when his sister used selfie mode to film her own family. The kids weren't fazed by the technology, but Sam's face and April's speech made Mathew chuckle. What a treasure. Mathew made copies of the all the files to keep forever.

VERITY RODE IN Mathew's SUV with excited anticipation until…they passed endless rows of *cornfields*. How disappointing

to find out cornfields surrounded their new city of Green Bay. Mathew explained corn was used for much more than eating, which Verity rejected.

They pulled into a long gravel driveway of a two-story farmhouse. It had a long front yard, woods behind it, but no farms in sight. It quiet except for the birds chirping, and off into the woods, frogs sang their mating calls.

A sign in the front yard had someone's name on it with a phone number, and a bright red car was parked in the driveway ahead of them.

"What are we doing here?" Verity asked.

"We are house shopping. Remember that trip to New York City saved the clinic? I had enough left over so I can buy us a house."

"You want to live *here*? What's wrong with your house by the clinic?"

Mathew chuckled. "So much. There is so much wrong with living in a dingy one-bedroom apartment on the second floor of a neighborhood I wouldn't raise..." He cleared his throat. "I want something better for us, for the baby."

Verity's hand instinctively covered her lower belly. Mathew had already given her more than she ever deserved, and he wanted to give her more. But living in isolation brought back memories she didn't want.

"Can we pick something in the city?"

Mathew's brows rose. "Sure. I figured something resembling a familiar landscape would be preferable to you. But if you'd rather live in town, that's fine with me. Great, actually. Less commuting means I'll be home more."

Mathew apologized to the realtor and backed down the driveway, answering a call on his phone while driving. He navigated the car through the city, and they pulled into another driveway. This time the house was one story, small, with a driveway wide enough for two cars and a garage stall for each. The front yard was small, but she would have to see beyond the wood fence to see the backyard.

Something about the house drew her in. Its bright blue color reminded her of a summer sky. The wooden fence was painted an inviting white, and the flower beds in the front reminded her of a smile. Her hand opened the car door, and Mathew exited on her tail.

She paced the front yard, looking it over, while the engine of a car rumbled by her at the curb, and Verity turned. The same red car from the first house had followed them here. A woman slipped out of the driver's seat and came around with her hand extended for a shake.

"I'm Jenny, your realtor. This is a beautiful place. Did you want to see the inside?"

"Can we?"

Jenny laughed. "That's what I'm here for."

Mathew grasped her hand and gave it a squeeze. Together they followed the realtor inside the house, and the moment Verity crossed the threshold, she knew it was the one. Large windows allowed bright light inside. Carpet was warm and inviting on the toes. The kitchen was compact, but all the modern pearly cubes were there. They walked into the bedrooms and each was empty but full of possibilities. It was clean, bright, and cozy.

They passed through a patio door and onto a raised back deck. The backyard wasn't large, but big enough for social parties and kids to play. A privacy fence surrounded the property.

"This is the one," Verity said.

"Are you sure? We can take out the carpet, and—"

"I like the carpet," Verity cut in.

"Really?"

"Yeah." Verity tilted her head. "What's wrong with carpet?"

"If you like it, it's great. Jenny, let's put in an offer," Mathew said while his eyes never left Verity's. Affection radiated off him like she was some treasure. He made her feel like the most beautiful, precious thing in the world. She still couldn't believe she was so lucky.

"You haven't seen the bones yet. Water heater, furnace, plumbing…" Jenny insisted.

"It's fine. We can fix anything that needs fixing," Mathew said.

"Great." Jenny clapped her hands together. "I'll get the paperwork started in the kitchen. Come on in when you're ready." Jenny walked back inside with a bounce in her step.

"I have something else for you," Mathew whispered.

"What?" she whispered back like it was some conspiracy.

His hand brought forth a small velvety cube, and he popped it open for her. "I already proposed, but I hadn't bought you a ring first. So, here's the ring to go with my promises. Verity, you make me the happiest guy in the world. Still want to marry me?"

Verity smiled. "Of course."

He slipped the silvery ring with a sparkling clear gem onto

her left-hand digit to show the world she was his. It fit just right. After she admired the ring under the sunlight, Mathew leaned in for a kiss. His eyes were hot and sparkling with lust. Verity wrapped her jeweled hand around his neck and pulled him until their lips crushed together. Mathew explored her mouth like it was the first time. He pressed himself against her and heat flooded her body. Just as her lips tingled with the sensation, he pulled back to adjust himself while she blocked the view of any on-lookers, and his eyelids dropped low.

"Let's go inside and sign for our future." Mathew's husky voice charged her core, but business first. Then they would have the whole house to themselves.

# Chapter Twenty-Six

Two weeks later...

MATHEW CUT THE thread of the last stitch in the kitten, and while Becca brought the kitten to recovery, he cleaned up. Becca returned and collected the instruments for washing and a turn in the autoclave.

A couple weeks, a court appearance, and an ad in the local newspaper later, and Verity Arris became a real girl. Well, she was officially Verity McCall, and he insisted they leave it because in one more month, he would be giving her his name anyway.

Even though Mathew could afford a dream wedding, even after setting aside capital gains taxes for Uncle Sam, a simple courthouse wedding was all Verity wanted, and Mathew was thrilled. He didn't want a big shindig anyway. The leftover cash plus what April had left him, meant there was plenty for what he really wanted Verity to have.

"Thanks for the hand in surgery today, Becca," Mathew said while snapping off his gloves.

"It's no problem. April did the same for me." He remembered April covering surgery for Becca when she was with child.

"Are you doing okay? Is Brad okay?"

"Brad and I are getting divorced. It's for the better since we've drifted apart the last few months and too much keeps reminding him of the loss."

"I'm sorry. Do you need time off? I heard you were planning on moving away."

Becca's head snapped to him while Mathew tossed his gloves in the trash and removed his paper face mask.

"Who told you that?"

"I just overheard, on accident."

"I'm staying now. Brad's moving."

"Don't stay on my account. Verity is quite capable."

"She is great. So different too. Where did you find her?"

Mathew chuckled. He wasn't expecting to answer a question like that. "Let's just say a friend introduced us."

"What about April? She's doing good too?" Becca tugged off her paper mask and tossed her gloves in the trash too.

Mathew inhaled deep. "Yeah. She's great."

They both balled up their paper gowns, stuffed them in the trash, and removed their shoe covers. Mathew dropped into his rolling chair at his desk to report the surgical findings and rubbed Snoopy on the head. Mr. Van Grunden never paid and opted to surrender the dog instead, so now Snoopy was the office mascot who came home with him and Verity every night.

He logged into Quickbooks and downloaded the data. Things were great. The expenses were getting better. Mathew stopped sending payments to April. He wasn't rich by any means, but he could buy Verity a replacement plum cocktail dress without concerning himself with the credit card balance—because there wasn't one.

Mathew stepped out to reception and found Becca had already left. It was unfortunate her marriage failed, and he didn't know the details, but Mathew knew she was in good hands with Kiko.

As for Mathew, he had one surprise left.

"Verity," he said.

"Hmmm." Verity was nose deep in the computer, ever the hard worker.

"I've got something for you. A honeymoon."

"What's that?" Her big green eyes and golden freckles flicked up to him and Mathew's heart skipped a few beats, like a teenager in love for the first time.

"I'm taking you on a trip." He handed her the printed airline tickets. She didn't understand apps yet. "To the Marshall Gold Discovery state park in California. You'll see the 1849 Gold Rush."

"It's still going on?" Her eyes widened in shock.

Mathew laughed. "No. The site is preserved, like a museum. Doc said he doesn't want you flying too far into the pregnancy, so we fly out on Friday. Pack your bags. We're crossing the Rockies."

"No wagons needed?"

"No cannibalism either."

"Well, where's the fun in that?" Verity laughed and placed a maternal hand on her lower belly. It was just starting to show. Mathew's gears fired up at the sight. He loved her belly, and we wanted so many children with her. Heat rushed and his erection woke up, hardening under his dress pants.

Mathew collected Verity into his arms and carried her to his

office. "I love you," he said with a gravelly growl.

"I love you, Matt."

His lips crashed against hers. Their hands caressed each other's bodies, eagerly undressing, while moans blocked the noise from the kenneled animals. Verity and Mathew made good use of his desk for a few hours, even with Snoopy watching from his doggy bed.

# Epilogue

Four weeks earlier…

SHERIFF CLINT NELSON knocked on the Grignon estate's grand entrance again. The garden was unkempt—overgrown dead grass, bushy hedges, and sharp brush narrowed the path more than usual. No birds chirped on this cold December morning. A rustling in the woods turned his head, but it was just a squirrel.

Sheriff knocked again. He opened the creaking door with his hand at the butt of his Colt revolver.

"Jaime, you in here?"

Now, Sheriff had seen a lot in all his years, whether he was minding the law or not, and walking into a palatial estate—the finest in the tri-village area—and finding two dead bodies in the foyer was a new one for him.

Sheriff released the weapon from its holster and gripped it tight. He crouched inside on silent feet. Any enemy would've heard his announcement, but he didn't have to wave a target around for them. Sheriff checked the first body for signs of life as Dr. Frank had taught him, and decided it wasn't worth trying. His throat had been sliced clean through.

The next body, likewise. Most of the blood must've been absorbed by their clothes, because not much puddled beneath them. Did ol' Millie try to clean them up?

These were all Jaime's men.

Sheriff took the stairs and noticed the little birds were silent. With the temperature inside, that wasn't surprising none. He squeezed the revolver's grip and held it up near his chest. The first room at the top of the stairs knocked the breath from him.

"Aw, damn, Millie. What have ya gone and done this time?"

The plump woman was half-bare and leaned over a table in Jaime's punishment room. He checked her throat and there was nothing but an unpleasant stench.

Sheriff checked each room, expecting more bodies, and when he got to Jaime's bedroom, he didn't know if he should chuckle at his accurate prediction or be resigned to more paperwork.

"Well, shit."

Jaime lay on his back with a gash in the center of his chest and...Sheriff inhaled deep and slowly released his breath. "Them's some mighty personal wounds ya got there."

Next to Jaime, Sheriff found Ben Pool. "Now what did you gone and done now, boy?" He checked him for a pulse as well, and at this point, Sheriff was going to assume everyone was dead. Sheriff shook his head and walked out. Down in the kitchen, Sheriff heard a rustling and that wasn't no squirrel.

"Hello? Anyone there?"

The rustling came again, like a doorknob rattling. Sheriff followed his ears and knocked at the locked door.

"You's in there?"

"Let me out!"

Startled, Sheriff jumped back and collected himself. He shouted a warning through the door. "All right, now move aside."

Sheriff wound up for a swift kick and sent the door flying in on its hinges, exposing a small closet.

He smiled.

"Well, well, well, Joe Pool. How's a man like you still alive in all this gruesome glory?"

"Howdy, Clint." Joe Pool's wobbly legs carried him out of the closet. Apparently, the door whacked him a good one.

"When the bandits come armed, sometimes hidin' is smarter than fightin'."

"Looks to me like we have a common enemy. Wanna help me take down the bandits?"

Joe Pool stretched his legs as if stuck in the closet for far too long. "For an arrest or hanging?"

"Whatever happens, happens."

Joe Pool smirked. "Feed me and I'll call it a deal."

Your reviews are very important to me, so if you enjoyed this book, please leave one for Mathew and Verity's story, **Hours to Arrive (Matchmaker Series Book Two)**.

Keep up to date on new releases and receive **Minutes to Live (A Matchmaker Series Prequel)**, the origin story to the Matchmaker series, for free by subscribing to my newsletter here:

Find out the bandits' fates in Jonathan Arris and Becca Wagner's story **Days to Hide (Matchmaker Series Book Three)**:

**Thrust back in time to 1854, she's on a mission to save a good man turned bandit. Falling for him wasn't part of the plan and neither was earning herself a target on her head.**

Veterinary Technician Becca Wagner quits her job when her soon-to-be ex-husband flaunts a new woman and a new puppy at the clinic. Before she can beg for her job back, Becca's asked to participate in a dream study with promises of healing, and she doesn't hesitate. But before drifting off to sleep, she is given a mission and warning: Convince a farmer to accept a crooked sheriff's deal, otherwise he will be killed.

In 1854 Wisconsin, farmer Jonathan Arris turned bandit for his own reasons. The sheriff in town makes him an offer to go

undercover in exchange for immunity from his crimes. Jonathan refuses, knowing the bandits are a bigger threat than the sheriff. But a strange woman inserts herself in his business, and it'll take everything he's got to keep them both alive.

Becca must decide between two futures—the present, where she's jobless but safe, or the past, where she has to risk her life to follow her heart.

**If you love sizzling romance, edge-of-your-seat action, time travel, swoon-worthy heroes, and sassy ladies in a small town setting, you'll love Stephanie Flynn's dramatic historical adventure books. Each is a standalone with guaranteed HEA, but an overarching narrative. Best if read in order.**

# About the Author

Stephanie Flynn has a bachelor's degree in accounting which has nothing to do with her career writing action-packed romance filled with adventure, suspense, danger, and steam. She lives in Michigan, USA, with her husband and kids, and she spends her writing time surrounded by normal cats and a not-so-normal macaw, wishing she liked coffee and knew how to mix a drink. Check out her website for more books: StephanieFlynn.net

SCAN ME

Made in the USA
Monee, IL
20 January 2021

58193610R00184